THE SEA OF THE VANITIES

THE SEA OF THE VANITIES

THE COMPANION NOVELS OF JONAS CELWYN BOOK 1

4 Horsemen
Publications, Inc.

LOU KEMP

Trigger Warnings:
Rape allusions, violence, killing animals.

DEDICATION

Many thanks and love to my daughter, Charmaine, who supported me no matter what, even when I got a third cat. Thank you to friends for their support and feedback: Nikki, Debbie, Peggy, Karen, and Chris P. To authors who have done their best to help me: Anita Dickason, Norm Backstrom, Benjamin X. Wretlind, and Bob Van Laerhoven. Thank you to Lorin Oberweger of Free-Expressions for the original editing of this book and Farm Hall (2023).

TABLE OF CONTENTS

CAST OF CHARACTERS

The Pacific Ocean: The passenger ship the *Passat*

Cassandra Coulter: a passenger. Scandal follows her aboard the ship where she finds murder.

First Mate Jack Browne: a proud, handsome, and superstitious of the area around Cape Horn.

Captain McQuistan: a highly nervous about the sea and his ship. This is his last voyage.

Second Mate Daniel Murphy: an attractive, unscrupulous, and not to be trusted.

Herr Higgins: a businessman who smuggles contraband aboard the *Passat*.

Christian Morse: a psychic aboard the *Passat* for a specific purpose.

Mrs. Pentifax: an elderly, fussy, heavy drinker, aunt to Jessica.

Jessica Byrd: a beautiful niece to the American ambassador to Brazil, traveling with her aunt.

Doctor Rubio: a jolly man who boards the *Passat*, but never makes it to Cape Horn.

<u>John Greely</u>: a hundred years earlier he was the only survivor of the wreck of the *Moira*.

<u>Angelo</u>: a cook and dependable sailor.

The Atlantic Ocean: The pirate ship the *Hussar*

<u>Richard Shaw:</u> a Lloyds of London investigator looking for the pirates.

<u>Captain Peech:</u> the notorious pirate captain of the *Hussar*.

<u>Lt. Borodin:</u> Peech's enforcer and killer of ships.

<u>Lt. Farley:</u> Peech's dealer of death.

<u>The Albino women</u>: Indians attacked by Peech. They do not forget.

LLOYDS NOTICE
VESSELS FOR INQUIRY

The Committee of Lloyds will be
glad of any information regarding
the following vessel–
"THE ABURGINE" four master of
South Hampton, Official No. 197987,
320 tons gross, which was to have
arrived from Gibraltar bound for the
Camans on the 3rd of July 1850.
The vessel was reported by wireless last
on the evening of 14 June, and has
not been heard of since.

Lloyds, London, E. C 18
13th September 1850

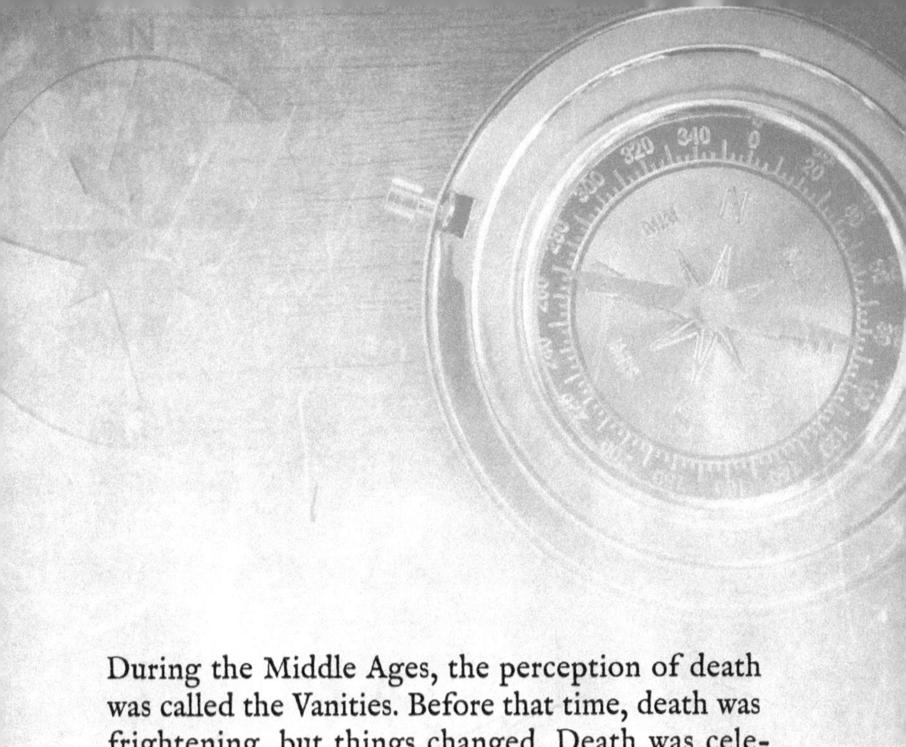

During the Middle Ages, the perception of death was called the Vanities. Before that time, death was frightening, but things changed. Death was celebrated. Gentle cherubs were depicted on the tombs and headstones and in song and prose voices honored death. It was no longer feared.

London

Prologue

In front of Jonas Celwyn, the iron and glass monstrosity, the Crystal Palace, rose into the sky like a huge pyramid, although a lopsided one. From around the world, curiosity seekers, pickpockets, and everyone in between had visited the Great Exhibition of 1851 to see it. The magician gazed at the glass edifice again. More than eight years ago, its architect, Joseph Paxton, had drunkenly described every feature to Celwyn long before it was built. But today? The magician did not remember anything about it except what they'd been drinking.

He had other things to do.

The roar of the four o'clock from Essex disrupted everything from the birds in the trees to a nearby argument between two shopkeepers. It also jiggled the petite tables of the café where Celwyn sat and caused tardy passengers to either hurry to the terminal tracks or make the waiting patrons cough and wheeze as they inhaled the coal-tinged steam surrounding them.

The aroma from a fresh tea service smelled much better. After his waiter departed with the magician's gratitude, the arriving passengers began to disembark. Every one of them would pass by where he sat.

First came a man in a top hat carrying cardboard boxes. No, too old. The next appeared a bit too short to be his quarry. Mr. Richard Shaw should be just over six feet tall and so thin he could have been blown over by the steam from the train. Thirteen more passengers went by before Celwyn stuck out an arm and tapped Shaw's elbow.

"Yes?" the man had the harried appearance befitting his profession—a pinched look and a squint of a much older man.

"Mr. Shaw, please be seated." The magician smiled at him. "May I introduce myself? I am Jonas Celwyn."

Shaw's attention switched to the omnibus that lumbered up the street toward them. The line of passengers waiting for it grew longer as they watched.

"I have some information for you. It will only take a minute." The magician would glue him to his chair if necessary.

Shaw glanced at Celwyn and sat down. When he saw the cup of tea in front of him, he picked it up.

"To confirm, you are the senior investigator for Lloyd's of London, specifically those policies insured on the high seas?"

Shaw sipped and nodded casually, but his eyes had a quickness about them that confirmed his interest.

Without leaving his chair, the magician added roses to the hair of a most becoming woman who walked by them and a donkey tail to the smirking man holding her arm. He turned to Shaw. "I have an appointment soon, and I'll make this quick. If you will take out your notebook, you will hear something useful in your enquiries."

After a long direct look at Celwyn, Shaw slowly brought out his notebook. "What is this about?"

"Pirates." At last, he saw Shaw's unabashed interest; the man couldn't hide his blush of anger and fear. Celwyn said, "Yes. Filthy, nasty pirates."

By the time Shaw departed, he had enough information to chase down a particular set of pirates, especially if they were still in the Caribbean.

Celwyn hoped he would do so soon.

He owed Captain Peech either a grave or a jail cell.

RIO DE JANEIRO

The many men, so beautiful!
And they all dead did lie:
And a thousand thousand slimy things
Lived on; and so did I.

"RIME OF THE ANCIENT MARINER"
-Samuel Taylor Coleridge

Chapter 1

Rio de Janeiro
September 1851

Richard Shaw clicked his pocket watch shut and set off again at a brisker pace. His evening appointment could prove interesting, and if it proved dangerous, so much the better.

As he walked along, smoke from streetlights drifted and curled like sinuous snakes into the blood-red bougainvillea that trailed down walls and festooned trellised windows. The flowers tickled Shaw's nose as he brushed against them, and his walking stick beat a rat-a-tat-tat across the bricks underfoot.

An evening stroll through the business district of Rio was discouraged for most Europeans wearing jewelry and fine haberdashery. Shaw had no worries. He carried nothing of value and had other concerns. Marching along, he was accompanied by the now-familiar feeling of being stalked. It had been going on for weeks, and he assumed a sheep in a pack of faceless and silent wolves would feel the same.

As he neared the water, the lamps appeared less frequently, and the streets shortened and twisted into dead ends. He would have been lost if not for the sound of activity coming from the harbor and the increasing stench of rotting fish.

Rounding a corner at full steam, he collided with a smarmy old man who reeked of something worse than the inside of a barn. Shaw apologized and made to go around, but the man grabbed his arm.

"Yes, err—?" Shaw felt in his pocket for a coin, expecting to contribute to the old man's wine consumption for the evening.

"Mister Shaw?"

Shaw tensed and nodded.

"I'm ye' welcomin' committee." The old man maintained his grip on Shaw's arm and turned toward the docks. "This way, *Sir.*"

Shaw noted the heavy sarcasm that clung to the word "Sir" as he disengaged from the stinking fossil. With another look to the rear, he followed him to the quay.

Dozens of tall ships lay at anchor, resembling drunken ladies gently swaying in the tide as they spread white canvasses like petticoats above the water. Crews worked the night, heaving freight aboard vessels floating in the still water. Nearer the docks, clusters of cargo transport boats and water taxis rode at tether.

The two men stopped beside a dinghy that rivaled the old timer in age and cleanliness. Despite his years, he sprung into it with the agility of a cat.

"All aboard, Mister Shaw!"

"I have an appointment with a Mr. Durazno. Are you taking me to him?"

"That's the idea, gov'ner."

Shaw stepped into the boat, immediately doubting the wisdom of doing so. What if the man just robbed him and dumped him in the water? Yet, he wouldn't sleep knowing he had not tried all avenues. If he must, he'd follow this disgusting creature. It was not that the man hadn't bathed; it was the predatory way he regarded Shaw, like a hunter who'd just shot a deer. Shaw had barely settled in before the old man poked the dock with an oar, and they drifted into the bay.

As his escort rowed, Shaw sat upright. Like a finicky spinster, he couldn't help inspecting the grime coating the plank he sat on and assumed the backside of his suit had been ruined. When the old man began singing in a discordant monotone, Shaw took the opportunity to study what he could see of him under the old-timer's cap. As they passed a gaily lit party boat, lanterns illuminated his face, revealing a devious expression wreathed in amusement.

Hiding a nervous gulp, Shaw held his pocket watch to the light. "My appointment is soon."

"So it is, Mister Shaw."

"Who are you?" He should have asked sooner.

"I told ye," the old man cackled as he rowed. "I'm ye welcomin' committee."

With a shiver of unease, Shaw recalled his conversation yesterday with Commander Florio of the local constabulary. The man hadn't believed him about the missing ships. Shaw wondered if he should have mentioned his encounter with a certain Mr. Celwyn in London. The man maintained the pirates would head south as the summer began in the lower latitudes. Perhaps Florio would have been more interested.

Even before he met with this Celwyn, Shaw's investigation had started. At his desk in London, Shaw had watched Lloyd's underwriters twitch every time they wrote a new policy on a vessel. A junior clerk in Lloyd's south London office had noticed that beginning in October and continuing through December, an extraordinary amount of ships went missing in the lower hemisphere. As a senior agent, Shaw's assignment was to find out why.

Historically, Cape Horn claimed hundreds of ships run under and de-masted as they entered the treacherous waters either from the Pacific, or those who sailed west from the southern Atlantic. The lucky ones succeeded in reaching the Drake Passage and the tiny ports of Chile. But, dead or alive, nearly all the ships were accounted for.

A rumble of bongo drums and a clash of horns from a nearby party boat caused Shaw to lean around the old-timer to see more. The band slid into an Argentine tango as the couples danced and writhed with the beat. A few women lifted handfuls of skirts, exposing a flash of white calf and lacy garters as their partners dipped them low over the deck. Shaw felt his face flush. The crowd on the boat clapped their hands while the music thumped and swayed, the rhythm intoxicating even at this distance. Shaw couldn't help staring. The lights of the party boat stained the water green and gold, shimmering in long fingers across the black water before fading away. He and the old sea dog inched further away from shore.

Shaw's thoughts drifted back to tonight's assignation, and realized he knew nothing about his informant. At the meeting, he might need more than his walking stick. A pistol, possibly.

Then he saw it. Like an enormous bird on the water, a large vessel with its lights darkened floated alone between their rowboat and the open sea. Shaw's unease settled in his stomach and rolled as the swells rose higher, rocking their boat like a toy. He gripped the gritty edges of the seat.

Shaw's nerves jittered. "Enough of this. I wish to return to shore."

"Durazno is on the *Hussar*." The old man cackled. "He's expecting ye with open arms. Do you know what Durazno means in Spanish, boyo?"

No, he didn't, and he wasn't about to ask. While Shaw debated whether to overpower his companion and return to shore or continue in the hopes of finding information, an earsplitting blare of horns tore through the night air. Shaw would have jumped out of the boat, but for the restraining oar, the old man swung out.

A water taxi of at least five times the size of the dinghy bore down on them. Foam swelled from its sides, and the noise from its steam engines increased as it drew closer.

The taxi swerved leeward just before impact, and the passengers on her deck cheered. Shaw's scream died in his throat while the old seaman stood and raised a fist, his curse loud in the empty bay. Shaw only half heard him as the overwash from the taxi caught him in a sudden veil of chilling water. With a crow of delight at Shaw's drenching, the old man resumed rowing.

"You have no lights on this thing!" Shaw shouted. He lifted his wet coat and let it fall again. "They would have seen us!"

"Mebbe." The man rowed on.

Shaw stopped himself. Common sense dictated you did not argue with a criminous barnacle on the fringes of the Atlantic in the dark. A wrong word and the daft bugger would swat him with an oar, and he'd be swimming. Things grew worse. As they drew under the shadow of the ship, the moonlight disappeared as if an evil specter had passed overhead.

The swells of the sea pushed the dinghy into the hull of the vessel with a solid thump. Shaw swallowed his fear, then stood and reached for the *Hussar's* ladder that swung loose above them. If this was to be the scene of his appointment, so be it: he was an investigator and must face danger to succeed.

Under normal conditions, he had no fear of heights, but clambering up a slick rope ladder more than forty feet above the sea seemed a wee bit more threatening than scampering aboard a freighter in Dartmouth Bay at noon. He tried to concentrate on Dartmouth Bay, but in the back of his mind, he knew he was a coward. This terrified him. In the stillness of the night, his only company was the faint music from the party boat. Beyond them, the lights from the harbor winked teasingly through the mist, reminding him of warmth and safety.

Shaw grasped the rail above the deck and heaved himself over.

The running lamps that ringed the deck smoked, lending the scene an otherworldly appearance. In the hazy air, he spied dozens of men in the shadows, their faces and clothing barely distinguished from the darkness. More languished in the rigging. The hair on Shaw's neck tingled as if an icy hand had just wiggled down his back, and he pivoted, inexorably drawn to look, and finding that scores of men stood behind him. Silently.

A foghorn moaned near shore.

"Welcome aboard, Mr. Shaw!"

He whirled.

A heavily muscled man, tattooed like a human painting, stepped from the shadows. He moved with the swaggering, bow-legged walk of all seamen. Small, cruel eyes gleamed under a red bandanna, and his oversized arms and hands hung nearly to his knees. He reminded Shaw of an ape in a black wig. When he spoke, Shaw realized the multitude of sailors stood silent, not out of curiosity, but in a strict form of discipline.

"Thank you, Mr.—"

"Captain Peech."

When Peech smiled, Shaw knew the horror had arrived. The foghorn in the harbor moaned again, bidding him goodbye.

As Peech's smile widened, something slammed into the side of Shaw's head, and the deck of the ship rose to meet him.

CHAPTER 2

Fish. He swam with fish in a black world that shifted, wavering in colors that bounced against his eyes and hurt his head. Shaw fell out of a narrow bunk and onto his face, nearly on top of a stubby candle that flickered in the darkness. It must have been burning for hours to make the puddle it sat in.

A few inches away, wind and sea spray whistled under a door, chilling him. With a groan, he realized that he lay naked on the floor of a ship, not in his too-soft hotel bed in Rio. After a moment, he realized he could touch the door with one hand and use the bunk as leverage to stand. Shaw wobbled and fell sideways onto the straw mattress and lay still.

By timing the bounce of the ship, as she bottomed out after each cresting, Shaw assumed a strong wind propelled the vessel. To where? A set of breeches and a shirt lay in a pile at the foot of the bunk. He rolled over and nudged them with a finger, seeing a jagged rent in the knee above a splotch of dirty brown, presumably blood.

When he bent over to examine the boots beside the bed, he noticed their crusty softness, which suggested many saltwater dunkings. As he dressed, he listened to the waves slapping the hull.

With the ship noises and wind blowing under the door, he must be on the main deck, and the ocean rushed by only a few feet away.

He fingered the tender spot above his right ear. The skin felt hot but unbroken. As he tried to think, his stomach rolled to the left with the ship, then sloshed to the right and down into the next trough. God, he was thirsty.

Shaw tried the handle on the door. It squeaked but didn't give. He tried again, and it wrenched open like a bloated outhouse door.

A full moon swept the sea in veils of silver. It had been years since Shaw sailed this fast at night. Whitecaps, ten feet high, disintegrated into spray, their waves dissolving into the black water. He inhaled the brisk air and looked back. The lights of Rio had disappeared; he felt a chill shudder through him; he'd poked a stick at the lion, and the lion had hooked him, dragging him away.

Heavy feet shuffled on the deck above, followed by a flurry of words he could not understand. The wind carried away an answer from someone that sounded like Captain Peech.

Just to his right, a pair of boots started down a ladder. Shaw backed inside and tried to shove the creaking door shut. It stuck half open. As he leaned into it, a hand snaked around, clutched his shoulder, and pulled him out again to the deck. The momentum nearly hurtled him over the rail.

Two sailors, more than large enough to fill the gangway, loomed over him with eyes as cold as a corpse. After they had stared at him long enough, one gestured to the ladder leading up. When Shaw didn't move quickly, the man threw him against the ladder.

As Shaw swung a leg over the last rung, the sailor behind him shoved him forward until he stood in the center of the bridge.

"Nice of you to join us, Mr. Richard Shaw."

With one hand, Peech spun the helm; with the other, he swilled wine. The ship hit a high swell, and Peech staggered, using the wheel to keep on his feet. A collection of empty bottles rolled into a corner.

"More wine!" Peech barked. He took a swig, and a river ran down his chin. "For my friend, Shaw!" A shirtless sailor leaned over the quarter house rail and came back up with a bottle he shoved into Shaw's hands.

Many men crowded the bridge, some in the shadows, a few much closer. Shaw couldn't hide, but he certainly wanted to. Like dirty peacocks, they dressed in vivid colors, wearing full-sleeved blousons and high-hip boots. A few of them appeared nearly naked. They all comprised the decadent court of Captain Peech.

Flanking Peech, and taller by at least a head, stood a man more noticeable because of the contrast between them. In the moonlight, his skin had the paleness of a man on his sickbed, and his skeletal frame resembled a stark winter tree facing a breeze, especially when he moved his arms. With the patience of a deadly predator, he assessed Shaw like a man memorizes a pretty woman. Shaw flushed and looked at the muscled runt bouncing on the other side of Peech. The runt addressed Shaw, exposing chipped teeth, some of them wood.

"Open it with your teeth, man!" An Irishman, of that Shaw had no doubt, and probably with the worst qualities—hot-tempered, loud, and red hair that shone like a spaniel.

As he worked the cork out and brought the bottle to his lips, Shaw swallowed revulsion. It smelt of pure vinegar. He felt the burn from dozens of eyes upon him until he tipped the bottle. Vile and pungent, the wine burned its way down his throat, bringing tears to his eyes. After he took another swallow, Peech began to sing.

He crooned a few notes, swilled wine, and sang a few more, swinging the helm from side to side hard enough to exaggerate the roll of the ship. With a belch, he flung the empty bottle over the rail, and it shattered like the tinkling of a wind chime. Boots shuffled, and Shaw heard glass scraping against wood.

"So, you *found* us." Peech belched again. "Heh, heh." He lifted a hand, and another bottle appeared from the shadows. "You're aboard *my* ship, you dumb bastard."

Shaw felt like he'd fallen through a trapdoor. During the weeks he'd been asking questions in Rio, someone must have betrayed him.

"To the *Hussar*!" Peech shouted. A cheer went up from his crew. "The scourge of the bloody bastards of bloody Lloyds of bloody London!" Peech laughed, and answering shouts came from the men. "Oh, yes, you *found* us, you did, Mr. Shaw!"

Catcalls, coarse and vulgar, bounced around the bridge. One of the sailors shoved Shaw into the arms of another, who flung him back again. He staggered to a spot in front of the helm.

"Borodin," Peech turned to the skeletal man, "how many of Lloyd's ships have we known?"

The answer came swiftly. "At least twenty, Sir." Shaw had expected a weak tenor, but Borodin's soft and deep voice had an unsettling quality that rivaled Peech's.

"Farley?" Peech turned to the Irishman.

The runt's face lit up. "Closer to thirty. Six alone in the last three months." Farley hopped from one foot to the other. "The bay at Algerras—"

"Ah, they don't count, man." Peech drained his bottle, the rivulets staining his chin. "They was layin' about, no canvasses showing." He grinned at Shaw. "Like shootin' baby chicks in a pen."

Borodin leaned into Peech's ear and rumbled something that sounded like Italian, perhaps Latin. Peech grunted. Borodin and Farley barked orders to the crewmen who hung like colorful monkeys thirty or more feet up in the rigging.

"Coming about, mates!" Peech shouted.

The answering calls from the crew floated from stern to bow. With her running lights aglow and foam billowing from her sides, the *Hussar* moved through the night like a living monster.

Shaw had a good eye for ships, and this one had to be a solid three hundred feet in length. She probably crewed a hundred and fifty sailors or more. His escape would have to be in port or near land; he wouldn't be able to touch any of their small boats before dozens of dirty hands would be on him like the fleas they undoubtedly slept with.

More singsong calls flew between the masts, punctuated with Farley's orders. The *Hussar* settled into a new course. If and when he slept, Shaw hoped the two men flanking Peech would be on the bridge. It wouldn't do to have a drunk spinning the wheel, especially if they ran into something out here in the dark.

Over the creaking timbers and rattle from the empty wine bottles, the wind freshened, and the *Hussar* picked up speed. Shaw stared into the night, alone and bewildered. What was their destination? His plight settled in his stomach. At last angered, he turned on Peech.

"Sir, explain yourself! Why am I on this ship?"

The air went still, and then belly laughs began from the men in the shadows, from Farley, and even a smile appeared on Borodin's taciturn face. Peech shoved Farley to the wheel and advanced on Shaw.

"Explain m'self?"

Shaw held his position, aware of the ring of now-silent sailors behind him.

"You are me prisoner, boy. How much will the stuffed bastards in England pay to see your pecker again?" He pushed Shaw until he stumbled backwards. "How *much*?" His breath reeked of an inner rot worse than fermenting wine.

"Nothing." Shaw bumped into the overhang of the quarter house, and his head throbbed. Peech leaned into him, belly to belly.

"Do you know what I do, boyo?" Peech patted him tenderly on the cheek. "I wreck ships for a livin'." He smiled, and Shaw saw how deep the fire raged in his crazed eyes. "Me fun is watchin' men die!" He slapped Shaw's face with each word, and his belly pushed him backwards over the deck. "Then I fill the hold with the prizes." The laughter from his crew grew. "I sell it all—the rings and gold teeth from fat mouths' a screamin' when I pull 'em out." He looked at Farley. "And what is the best part?"

"The ladies' bloomers!" Farley piped.

"Fine bloomers they are, boyo. All lace and silk—I make curtains for me quarters with 'em." He blew a wave of garlic and onions from Rio into Shaw's face. Peech hugged Shaw, who stiffened with repulsion. "You, me boyo, are a prize." Shaw wiggled free under the catcalls from Peech's crew.

Peech cocked his head, considering. "When bloody Lloyds pays off—and I like them payin', mind you—Mr. Shaw here will feed the sharks. Or not. We'll see."

Shaw tried to sidestep him, but Peech grabbed the front of his shirt and pulled him close again. "Meanwhile, I'll have some fun with ye." Peech staggered, and his eyes grew glassy before he focused again. "Mebbe send bits of your lily-white skin to them bastards until they pay." He released Shaw and lurched back to the helm.

"We sent your fancy coat and Nancy boy skivvies ashore." Farley cackled. "After we rolled your white ass across the deck like a pig." More laughs from the shadows. "They'll be mailed to London before we have our breakfast tomorrow."

As Shaw blindly descended to the main deck, he heard Peech again.

"We'll have an answer, Mr. Shaw. After we round the Horn."

CHAPTER 3

Praise the sea, on shore remain.
-John Florio

"You're daft, man!"

Shaw sat up and rubbed his eyes. The shouting had come from right outside his cabin. *Bugger it all;* he couldn't even sleep without Farley's noise. Shaw pulled on his boots and stepped onto the deck. Like a thin smile, a sliver of moon hung high above the ship, signaling a very late hour.

A few feet away, Farley and two pirates leaned over the rail, smoking and arguing.

"I say you're mad—" the runt shouted; the rest of his words were lost in the roar of the wind as the *Hussar* bounced across the waves. It had only been a few days since they left Rio, and each night seemed endless. Shaw wondered why he had ever deserted his bed and bath above a London greengrocer.

The ship jerked as if the wind had been sucked down under the sea, and he stumbled against the rail. The pirates and Farley ignored him, but they had felt it too and turned their attention leeward. Farley stopped talking.

At first, Shaw saw nothing, only that they sailed into black water under a thickening mist. The ship slowed, and her speed faltered as she entered a dense fog. Shaw felt a shiver of fear as an opaque world swallowed the *Hussar*, and a strong pervading smell of decayed meat engulfed them. What in the world could be causing it? Rotting fish, he could understand. He drew a hand in front of his mouth, fighting an urge to vomit.

More pirates joined Farley, making noises of disgust. When dozens more arrived on deck, their cries of revulsion and unease blended into the mist.

Shaw realized the *Hussar* had come to a complete stop and rested on a high swell that slapped her hull with a lazy hand.

"I don't like this," Farley said, backing away from the rail. "Don't like it a'tall."

Peech leaned out of the bridge and yelled his opinion.

"*Fog*?" Peech glared down at the group beside Shaw. "There's no fog here this time of year!" With a curse, he turned and bellowed out the other side of the bridge. "Light the rest of them running lamps!" A barrage of invectives blasted the pirates as they ran to obey the order.

Farley had backed up until he stood at Shaw's side. More telling, the Irishman had lost color and stared fixedly into a thick shroud off the stern. The idea that this sadistic bastard could be frightened both amused and sobered Shaw at the same time. He noticed the other pirates huddled under the mainsail, nervously glancing to the sea and jabbering again. Superstition is a sailor's middle name.

The smell grew worse as the fog settled around them in a heavy pall.

"Light them lamps!" Peech clambered down the rail. Farley didn't acknowledge him but stared into the fog.

"Quiet for once, Mr. Farley?" Peech eyed the swirling mist and swigged more wine. "Smells pukey out there. Something's dead."

Shaw agreed. But what? The fog swallowed the lights from the *Hussar*. He couldn't see more than half the ship's length reflected in the water. As he stared into it, he could understand why sailors reported frightening apparitions in fog. Every one of them watched the insidious vapors mixing into the shadows and the wisps of air wrapping tendrils around the ship.

The fog had crept over the decks, cloaking the crew as they clustered at the rails like brightly dressed ghosts. They murmured in hushed whispers, and Shaw would have enjoyed their discomfort except for the certainty that he would share it.

They waited.

The fog turned bluish, thicker, and the smell more intense. When the pirates noticed the change, their mutterings grew. Shaw, like a few others, leaned over the rail to study the oily water.

"Don't like this," Farley grumbled. "Not at all."

The hair on Shaw's neck prickled and stood on end. When he turned, a lone pirate stood dead center of the deck, scratching his crotch, and rubbing the sleep from his eyes.

From beside him, Farley made a gurgling sound and vomited over himself. The unease in Shaw's stomach tightened when he saw what caused it.

A pallid shadow emerged from the sea, slithered over the rail behind the lone pirate, and as it pooled on the boards, it became a glowing green mass that solidified and grew. Shaw couldn't move or speak as it took shape. The stench overwhelmed them, replacing the air they breathed. Shaw couldn't help it—he grabbed Farley's arm, pointing wordlessly towards the mass behind the lone pirate. Farley's eyes widened, and he staggered back into the rail.

What they saw reminded Shaw of one of the old sea legends that he'd never quite accepted, but he believed it now.

Nearly as tall as the pirate, she stood in beauty, both ancient and decadent, with long black hair waving to her knees. Even through the fog and gloom, her eyes glittered like emeralds, and her lips were blood red. Thighs perfectly formed, muscled yet soft, made him think of the paintings of goddesses. Her breasts were full and high.

The pirate half-turned. Startled, he stepped back, and most telling, he leaned toward her.

When she smiled, even from across the deck, Shaw felt his being reach toward her like the pirate had done. When she raised an arm to the pirate, the urge to touch her overwhelmed Shaw, and he stepped forward. Farley whispered, "No," and pulled him back. "Let her have him; maybe she'll leave the rest of us."

Shaw didn't understand, but as Farley spoke, the pirate took one step forward, then two steps more. She seemed to glow with pleasure as she shook her mane of hair, drawing it around her shoulders.

When the pirate touched her, she embraced him, and her hair writhed, becoming snakes that slithered over his face and arms and down his back. The pirate screamed once. The creature's arms became claws, ripping off the pirate's ear and then his arm. It licked him, peeling off his face. Worst of all, Shaw could hear the teeth tearing as it ate, shredding bits of flesh and muscle.

Shaw smelled burning wood and pivoted. At the aft end of the ship, Borodin lit torches and handed them to a waiting group of pirates. Peech joined them, brandishing a torch in each hand.

The torches made a movable bonfire that quietly approached the creature. In the silence, Shaw could only hear the crunching of the bones of the unlucky pirate. The stench still filled the air, but now it smelled like burning flesh as the army of flaming torches drew closer. Behind Borodin, more torches flared and advanced.

One boot with a bloody calf lay where the pirate had embraced death. Nearby, the snakes writhed on the deck and across the boot, coiling and uncoiling with glittering green eyes. The apparition hovered over the pirate's remains, looking like nothing more than an ugly mass of blood, bone, and hair.

"Now!" Borodin flung his torch on the creature. A dozen torches followed. Under shuffling feet, more torches flew onto the blazing pyre.

A long screech split the night, and the fire seemed to dance. Within the flames, the thing writhed, turning again into a beautiful woman, melting to liquid and then mass, before backing toward the rail. Under an acrid cloud, it dissolved to a pale green vapor, once more slithering over the rail and back into the sea.

CELIZE, CHILE

Fishes live in the sea, as men do a-land;
the great ones eat up the little ones.

-William Shakespeare

CHAPTER 4

October 1851

The view from atop the final pass in the mountains felt like a turning point, the beginning of my return. Many thoughts troubled me, yet the panoramic scene could not be ignored.

"Alto."

"Si, Senorita Coulter." The driver reined in the horses.

The heat washed over the carriage in shimmering waves, and I fanned myself with enough vigor to lift the curls that threatened to stick to my forehead. The horses stamped their feet, expressing their fatigue and impatience as the setting sun began its descent toward the west, where it hung between the clouds and the horizon. I smiled; for as far as I could see, below the bleeding sky awaited the blue and mysterious Pacific.

The port of Celize rested in a bowl of lush vegetation, squeezed into a few feet of sand before the bay. Red-tiled roofs dotted the town, crowding an ornate hotel, and further away from the water, the locals lived in huts with the jungle nipping at their doors.

At least two dozen tall ships lay at anchor in the bay. Most would sail west to where the Māori lived. As various smaller craft performed loading and transporting duty to the larger vessels, I squinted into the sun and spied a majestic square rigger. She seemed to be the center of activity, posing like a queen in the middle of the bay. With certainty, I knew the ship must be the *Passat*.

Once we arrived at the wharf, the driver unloaded my luggage, except for my overnight bag. I stood to one side and inhaled the pungent scent of horses, fish, and unwashed bodies. Heavy cooking smells wafted from across the street, riding the ruckus of the cantina.

Few women ventured upon the quay. To do so unescorted invited an offer to exchange flesh for money with lust-starved sailors of questionable hygiene, not to mention the attentions of the Spanish authorities. With this in mind, I had donned a conservative traveling costume. The prudish collar made the tropical heat worse. And it itched.

Even so, I stood out. Pale skin, unruly red hair, and a figure men have called voluptuous cannot be disguised. I gripped a sturdy, sharp-tipped parasol. While waiting for my luggage to be unloaded, I'd used it twice.

"Miss Coulter?"

I flinched and turned, wishing for a mustache and glue.

A tall Englishman, also overdressed for a steamy afternoon, regarded me with deep eyes I found disturbing under their intense scrutiny. He looked too prosperous to be a reporter, but I wondered.

"I am Christian Morse. We will be sailing together."

"I'm pleased to meet you, Mr. Morse."

"Perhaps we can find a place to sit and enjoy some refreshment?"

I had planned on doing so. Now, it seemed a good idea to find out how Mr. Morse had come to recognize me in a small village at the edge of the Chilean jungle.

"Thank you. I believe I will join you, Mr. Morse."

From under one of the trees that shaded the outdoor café, we enjoyed a view of the harbor while I silently compared the bay of Celize to Boston harbor. Over many summers, my Bostonian uncle had made a practice of teaching me about ships that I remembered as a most magical time of sea lore and wonder. Of the several boats berthed here, some were cargo vessels, others barkentines crossing royals above double top-gallant sails. I spotted a few single masts with jib booms and more slender lines that would sail faster but carry less cargo.

The *Passat* caught and held my attention once again. Painted a pristine blue and topped by a white band, she made the other ships look like a herd of poor stepsisters who hadn't done their laundry. With four masts and better than three hundred feet in length, she was a proud and beautiful ship. She appeared seaworthy, too, so much so I did not feel anxious about our voyage. Even so, her seaworthiness could be put to the test; her itinerary listed a daring passage south around the Horn, and onward to Rio de Janeiro, then the Caribbean. All of this would occur before a long trans-Atlantic voyage to London and cities on the Continent.

The outfitting of the *Passat* continued. Bronzed and shirtless sailors in colorful breeches loaded scores of barrels, nets of bananas and limes, and cases of brandy. This would be a merry voyage indeed.

A transport boat bobbed like a child's toy below the *Passat's* massive hull, maneuvering to keep steady in the swell. From her deck, crewmen pulled upward on the lines, lifting a hog swathed in ropes high in the air and over the top as it squealed. Next came a pen of chickens with the sense to huddle together and play dead. Omelets.

On the other side of the ship, more sailors heaved aboard bag after bag of what must be nitrate. There was a nitrate mine located inland from here, and I assumed nothing else of that quantity and weight would be exported from the Chilean jungle. The bags would fetch a handsome price in Bavaria so that the making of steel could continue.

As the last bag of ore swung slowly upward, one of the crew leapt over the side, sitting astride it like a horse. He waved the ship's flag as cheers from the crew rang out across the water.

I glanced to my left. Mr. Morse sipped juice and watched the proceedings with a mild air of boredom until he narrowed his eyes to track a smaller transport boat that approached the *Passat*. The vessel floated low in the water, laden with a mountain of luggage, trunks, and a wire cage, probably containing birds, on top of the pile. From this distance, they could have been colorful mice.

Minutes dragged by peacefully. I drank warm orange juice, expecting a question or three from my still-silent companion. Sundown had fled, leaving us sitting in the early gloom of evening as the *Passat's* running lamps came alive, one by one, each light a step closer to departure.

I shivered and turned to Christian Morse.

"How did you know my name?"

His smile held a measure of satisfaction. "I recognized you from your concert posters."

Perhaps. But, many of those posters did not bear a likeness to me. It would be prudent to know more about Morse ... his profile seemed familiar. From this angle, his blond hair appeared a shade too long to be fashionable, and his clothes, though dated, looked expensive. Theatrical. Not a reporter.

"What is it you do for a living, Mr. Morse?"
"I'm a psychic, Miss Coulter."
Well, well. This should be a most interesting voyage.

Long after midnight, sleep still eluded me. I blamed the heat. As unease flirted with my excited nerves, I flapped the thin sheet over my body, creating a breeze that did little but billow the mosquito netting. With a refined, and acceptable, ladylike curse, I retrieved a letter from my purse. It wasn't the heat causing my agitation.

From the bay, shouts from inebriated sailors carried across the water as I stepped onto the balcony. This late, the view presented a grand sight, with most of the tall ships decorated with lights around their hulls, bridges, and masts. The *Passat* hummed with last-minute activity. A tiny thrill rode a wisp of wind from the bay and flew up my nightgown, tickling my bare legs. I clutched the letter, able to read it with my eyes closed.

My dearest Cassandra.

I crumpled the letter into a ball.

My dearest Cassandra.

I'd fled New York by ship and train to the west. Running far. Pain improved my performances.

Through my agents in Caracas, I have determined your whereabouts.

I'd canceled my remaining singing engagements and moved out of Shepherd's Hotel, traveling further south.

And I am satisfied of your well-being. Please be informed I will marry this Christmas Day. A social match.

I thought, do so, by all means.

I wish to rekindle our relationship and have made arrangements with the hope you will return to New York. Your apartments will be—

"Damn you," I whispered.

All my love, Charles.

"In your ear, Charles," I said as loud as I dared.

From the bay, a ship's bell rang three times. An answering blast resounded from the *Passat*. Three more bells sounded. Again, the ship replied. The ringing echoed into the night as each ship wished the *Passat* a safe voyage.

Oh, that it was.

CHAPTER 5

THE PASSAT

The interior of my cabin exhibited the attributes of a fine hotel, as well as the influences of a brothel and church.

It only took a few steps to tour the small room. For months I would have to live with the red velvet wallpaper—which appeared as expensive as it was tawdry. When I bounced on the bunk a few times, it seemed to be of excellent quality. The large stained-glass window above an oversized Bible gave the room an interesting atmosphere.

A door slammed from the direction of the stern; I opened my door a crack and heard Mrs. Pentifax emerge from her cabin with loud comments about harlots and the Inquisition. With a laugh, I hustled outside to observe the whirlwind of activity before our departure.

Sailors ran across the deck and clambered up masts and yards. Every one of them seemed relieved to be underway at last. From their midst, the first mate shouted terse directions. It was good to see that Mr. Browne spared no time getting the ship's bow up and running under a strong wind.

The breeze freshened, and I leaned over the rail, hatless and exhilarated, as the tugboat piloted the ship out of the harbor and the *Passat* made sail with her canvasses snapping in the off-shore winds.

Four bells rang from the bridge, announcing the late afternoon.

We'd gathered in the salon, the passenger's social center for the next few months. It had the attraction of an expensive womb; dark, cosseted, plush, and faintly fishy. Small leaded windows allowed air and light to filter inside, and brocaded sofas lined the walls along with a handsome bar that promised good cheer. The warm glow of a dozen oil lamps bathed the room, and we had positioned our chairs in front of the fireplace as far as possible from the door. It would seem like any social gathering on land, except for the constant swaying of the ship and occasional bottoming out that left one's stomach behind.

"Will the Captain join us?" Doctor Rubio asked as he took a sip of brandy. The sea air had already tugged at his mustaches until they drooped on the sides of his big-bellied glass like strings of black seaweed.

"Perhaps," Herr Higgins replied.

Higgins had been the only one of the passengers Christian Morse couldn't identify. Although short and stout and with the constipated appearance of a crabbed-handed banker, Higgins's rich baritone had been a surprise. Even from ten feet away, his slicked back hair smelled strongly of Macassar's hair oil. According to the comments I'd overheard, Higgins traded goods internationally, and the shrewdness in his eyes said he did it well.

"What is your destination, Mr. Morse?" Herr Higgins asked as he deposited himself in a chair beside the fire.

Morse shrugged. "I'll change ships in Rio and then proceed to London."

"Ah. From where did you depart?"

"Mexico City."

"But isn't that a roundabout way of going to London?" Higgins asked with a polite frown, as if he was trying to understand something illogical. "Wouldn't overland trains or a series of stagecoaches to Panama have been preferable and easier?"

Morse treated us to another elaborate shrug. "I haven't seen Rio yet, Mr. Higgins. It is one of the few places I haven't visited."

I happened to be looking directly at Morse as he replied, and for some reason, his explanation seemed evasive. Why, I couldn't have said. It might have been the tone of his voice, or his seemingly rehearsed reply, but I knew he lied.

"Well. It will be quite an exciting voyage just to see a new city." Doctor Rubio wagged his bald head with disapproval and refilled his glass. "I had business on the coast here, or I would not have undertaken this journey."

"So did I." Although my reasons were not as straightforward. My purpose was to keep moving further from the scandal in Washington and from anywhere else the reporters could find me. Before anyone could ask more, I turned to the young woman, Jessica, sitting beside me. "What about you?"

"We were in Paraguay. And we heard the reports of banditry in the mountains." Jessica glanced at the only other female aboard—her aunt. "So, we decided on this voyage instead of an overland trip."

Auntie had arisen a few moments before and now confronted the doctor as he attempted to return to his seat. "Have you rounded Cape Horn before, Doctor?" Mrs. Pentifax cornered the man, her overlarge bosom protruding like a shelf between them. Doctor Rubio could have sat his drink there while he lit a cigar.

"Yes." In one word, the good humor left the man, replaced by a reverential somberness. "It is a bad place." The doctor crossed himself and drained his glass.

"But it is the only passage between the Pacific and the Atlantic," Christian Morse said, as he left the bar to join the others by the fire.

"It is the only way. But our fair passengers are in for an ordeal." Doctor Rubio smiled at Mrs. Pentifax. "Perhaps traveling north by train and then boarding a boat would have been wiser."

"It would not have been practical." Jessica shook her blonde ringlets like a pedigreed dog after a bath. "We must meet my father in Rio."

A crown would have looked about right on the girl; she displayed a certain kind of queenly disregard for those beneath her.

"Then, God help you, my dear." Doctor Rubio excused himself to replenish his glass again; either the man held his liquor well, or he did not want to talk about this.

"Cheery sort, isn't he?" Higgins leaned back and lit a cigar.

I coughed and crossed to open one of the windows, struggling with the latch until a bronzed hand interceded. He must have come into the salon as I crossed the room. I inhaled the cool, salty air and turned to gaze into the deceptively soft eyes of Mr. Browne. Close up, he looked dangerous, but not criminal, and somehow, I no longer felt like a sack of flour like I had when he handed me onto the ship—more like bread to be kneaded.

"Miss Cassandra Coulter." I extended my hand.

He kissed my fingers and murmured, "Jack Browne, First Officer."

What he would have done next, I didn't know because we were called back to the sofas by Mrs. Pentifax's wave.

"Mr. Browne, we have so many questions."

Mrs. Pentifax did not speak; she chirped, adding to her over-sized-pigeon appearance. She had drunk more sherry than I would have been able to, and her words slurred together to keep from falling apart. With a coquettish leer, she leaned into the first mate as he joined the group.

Jessica raised her chin to regard him. "Please tell us about the Cape, Mr. Browne. Doctor Rubio says it is quite dangerous."

The ship's officer studied everyone from Higgins to Morse and then me. I may have been wrong, but in each instance, he not only formulated what he should tell us but sized up each of the passengers for seaworthiness as if they were a new crewman reporting for duty. Who would need to be pampered and lied to? Who could be counted on to brave whatever happened?

"I'm sure the Captain will answer all of your questions," Mr. Browne said.

"Are you sure it is that dangerous?" Mrs. Pentifax persisted as if she'd heard a nasty rumor and would disembark if so.

The first mate hesitated. "Every seaman has respect for the Horn, Ma'am."

"Why?" I asked. I'd always found hints disquieting.

Browne's eyes met mine, and his attempt at propriety vanished. "There isn't a more dangerous spot upon Earth for a ship. Not one." He eyed the others. They had abandoned their poses and personalities to listen. "Sailors call the Horn the 'Sea of Darkness.'"

"It sounds romantic," Jessica Byrd said.

Oh, my. I well-remembered that wistful look she wore; when you are young, any excitement is romantic, no matter the nature of it, providing it meant a look at the world. At twenty-six, I didn't consider myself ancient, but I had formed a revised definition of the word "romantic."

The first mate's serious expression brought a frown to his face, and I wondered about a phenomenon that could inspire such respect in a commanding man such as Mr. Browne.

"How many leagues is it to the Horn?" Morse asked.

Mrs. Pentifax asked, "Yes, how many days until we get there?"

"The time varies," Browne said. "Let me show you something."

He strode aft to the far wall of the salon to the map that had been pinned there at eye level. We made an eccentric group crowding in front of the chart, some of us pretending we knew what we saw. It had been drawn in black ink and painted in bright colors. Intricate details of each country of the world caught the eye, along with delicately drawn skulls that floated in the waves of the North Sea, Cape Horn, and the Cape of Good Hope. A morbid homage to past wrecks, perhaps?

"There." Browne tapped a finger on a narrow straight between the tip of South America and the beginning of the South Sandwich Islands that heralded Antarctica.

"Why can't we pass through here?" Mr. Higgins pointed a pudgy finger at the Straits of Magellan. The distance appeared not as far south, nor as wide across.

Mr. Browne smiled, but his expression contained little mirth. "The mortality of ships is even greater there, sir. The winds fiercer, our chances, less."

"When will we reach the Horn?" Christian Morse inquired as if this were a normal voyage and only a matter of time until they arrived after a wonderful sea holiday.

"Depending on the winds, one to three weeks." The first mate seemed to forget us, talking more to himself. "I'd feel better if we got by before the end of the month."

"That is nearly four weeks." Higgins eyed the map.

"True. We may sail right on through. Or," Browne paused to down the contents of his stein in a gulp. "We may never get through."

He had forgotten the passenger's land-lubbing sensibilities.

With a cry, Mrs. Pentifax swooned, beaching herself across Doctor Rubio as he backed up and landed on the sofa. Having seen a few ladies overcome before, it looked like a real faint. As Jessica rushed over with a glass of water, Doctor Rubio struggled to shimmy out from under.

Mr. Higgins confronted him. "Sir! How can you frighten us so?"

"I believe in telling the truth. Cape Horn is dangerous." Browne gestured outside to the sea, where the waves ran high. "Ships have been dashed on the rocks. Torn in two. De-masted and left to drift until all aboard starved." He raised his voice. "It may take months to get through this time of year!"

The first mate regarded Mrs. Pentifax and Jessica. He took his time assessing me. "If we encounter serious storms, you could be confined to quarters for days—even weeks, at a time."

I thought, In a pig's eye, Mr. Browne.

"And the cyclones," Doctor Rubio whispered, his eyes saying he'd seen one or two. Higgins sent him a quick look and managed to set his drink on a table.

"Or we may sail on through," Christian Morse murmured with a sardonic twist on his handsome lips.

CHAPTER 6

Latitude 50° 46' S, Longitude 75° 46' W

I dressed for dinner, in red.

While surrounded by the harlot-inspired wallpaper and posing in front of the mirror, I decided that crimson certainly set the tone. Scented and powdered, I left my cabin just as a wave hit us. The boom creaked, swinging around high in the yardarms and signaling a wind change. Spray misted my hair and skin. In the distance, the blackness stretched forever under the twinkle of the stars. A good grip on the rail helped until I reached the entrance of the salon and stepped inside.

Just as we sat down to dinner, the door opened again, and Captain McQuistan joined us. An imposing and stately man, he wore a pristine uniform and his dignity. He reminded me of my grandfather, except the Captain's speech rang with more Irish than English, and he seemed far too serious.

From across the silver, fine china plates, and crystal, Mr. Morse spied it, too.

"Captain, a beautiful table and excellent dinner," he lowered his voice, "But you appear to be preoccupied."

Although Morse had spoken softly, the other passengers stopped talking.

"We seem to be riding a little low, the cargo a mite heavy."

The nervous way the Captain played with his mustache indicated that it wasn't just the cargo. But, perhaps I was being fanciful, reading more into the atmosphere.

"What will you do?" Doctor Rubio asked.

"We may have to heave some of it over. Maybe, maybe not." Captain McQuistan resumed eating, a signal he had dismissed the subject. "The weather is unpredictable."

"Mr. Browne said it was important to reach the Atlantic before November." I hated to ask, but we had a right to know. "Is that just because of the weather?"

The Captain's right eye twitched. He raised his brows in irritation and shrugged. Before he could reply, Mrs. Pentifax asked, "Where *is* Mr. Browne?"

She had consumed all her roast beef and had begun an attack on mine. I put out a hand with a fork upraised.

"The First Mate is coming off watch. He'll join us after dinner," the Captain replied.

"Why by November, Captain?" I asked. Christian Morse and Mr. Higgins seemed just as interested to know.

"Mr. Browne told us many ships have been lost trying to round Cape Horn," Jessica said.

Captain McQuistan nodded. "Many have. The most famous is the *Moira*."

If he'd been hoping to distract his audience, the Captain succeeded. Mrs. Pentifax stopped picking at the dish of vegetables to stare, which was remarkable. Jessica's eyes widened in curiosity, and Morse knocked over his wine.

"I understand they never recovered the ship." Morse mopped the spreading stain. His voice seemed concentrated. I couldn't think of a better description; he had become rigid and bristled with an inner control.

"They didn't. At the time, every salvage boat in the world, and every treasure hunter with a set of oars, tried to find her." The Captain leaned back in his chair and pursed his lips, his dinner forgotten.

"I remember the stories. More men died trying to find her than died on her." Doctor Rubio patted Jessica's hand. "This was nearly a hundred years before you were born, my dear."

"Why did so many people look for this one ship?" I asked. "Merchant ships would have a certain amount of treasure on them, wouldn't they? But would one ship have that much more than the other?"

To my surprise, Morse answered.

"The treasure lost that night equaled the cargo of several Spanish galleons. The *Moira* was even larger than this ship. And they carried a multitude of priceless artifacts from the jungles." He added, "Some were religious icons so rare; it is said only drawings exist now. The lot of it was worth more to the Incas than the Torah to the Jews."

"You seem to know a great deal about it," I said.

Morse hesitated and then sent me a queer smile. "Not really."

"Did anyone survive the wreck?" Higgins asked. Instead of checking for the Captain's answer, he inspected Morse as he asked the question.

The Captain said, "There was a passenger, John Greely. A whaler picked him up on one of the islands beyond the Cape." After a discernible hesitation, he added, "That seemed strange, too."

"How so?" Doctor Rubio asked.

"The storm was terrible." Captain McQuistan spoke quietly, and I could almost feel the old seaman's suspicious nature intensify. "The wreck of the *Moira* was witnessed by another ship. Mind you, the other ship was none too sure of its own position, but they were damned sure they weren't floundering on the rocks more than a hundred miles away from where Greely was found!"

"Surely, there is some explanation," Morse said.

"The water would have been at near freezing. No one could have swum that far and survived," Captain McQuistan countered.

Morse shrugged. "Perhaps he clung to some debris."

"Aye. Mebbe. But there were stories."

"Such as what, Captain?" Jessica asked.

He stopped himself, interpreting her youth and innocence as a signal that the details did not constitute dinner table talk.

"I heard he'd jumped off the whaler in port and was never seen again." Doctor Rubio's eyes bounced from Morse to the Captain and back again.

"Well, I heard that he survived and made his way to Europe, where he disappeared," Higgins said.

"Then the secret of the ship's location died with him." I cocked my head at the Captain. "He would be long since dead by now, if it has been over a hundred years since the wreck."

Doctor Rubio mused, "Or, he returned and died trying to recover the treasure like the others."

"Perhaps." Higgins stared at his plate without looking up.

Curious. Out of so few passengers, so many of them knew a great deal about the century-old wreck of the *Moira*. I brought the subject back to the original topic. "Captain, why do you want to be around the Cape before November?"

"Superstition." Captain McQuistan smiled around the table, but the smile didn't warm his eyes. "Just an old sea dog's bogy."

"Your First Mate seems to have caught it, too," I said.

The Captain sighed. "I suppose he has. Can't blame him." He moved bits of his dinner around his plate, talking so low we leaned closer to hear him. "All sailors treat the Horn with awe, Miss Coulter. There are hundreds of ships who never make it by."

His voice grew hoarse. "Thousands of men have died. Their ships run under."

Tears glistened in the Captain's eyes as he pushed away from the table, stood, and began to pace. Mrs. Pentifax opened her mouth to interrupt him. I glared at her.

"Every voyage around the Horn brings out our fears." The Captain opened the salon door and gazed out, letting the creaking of the ship and salt air blow in. "I'm a silly old man," he said more to the sea than to the room. "But I prefer to be through the Horn before October 31st, All Hallows Eve." He faced us. "In Ireland, we fear evil. And respect it." Even bathed in the warm light of the room, the Captain looked drawn. "The veil betwixt the living and the dead is at its thinnest just before midnight on the Eve. We must be through before then. We must."

CHAPTER 7

O il lamps glowed, casting the room into shadows and streaks of gold.

With dinner over, Captain McQuistan retired, and Angelo, the ship's cook, distributed bottles of port and cognac. I stood at the leaded windows, my back to the others, enjoying the solitude of being alone at sea, yet able to touch the warmth of a hearth fire and hear the normalcy of conversation.

I glanced over my shoulder. Mrs. Pentifax had trapped Doctor Rubio by the sofas. It didn't take long to interpret the few words I could hear and the elaborate gestures of the matronly passenger. With hints and girlish blushes, she expected a medical diagnosis of some ailment. She also wanted an opinion with a disclaimer that she was too young to be worried about it. Encouraged by the doctor's reply, Mrs. Pentifax clung to his sleeve when he would have escaped.

Across the room, the lee side salon door opened to admit First Officer Browne.

The second mate arrived with him. It took a moment until I understood and grinned. Wily Mr. Browne. While he introduced Daniel Murphy to Miss Jessica Byrd, I made sure he caught my smile. I even saluted Browne. When he saw me, he tightened his lips. Mr. Browne, older than Jessica by quite a few years, had noticed her attentions, although proper and oblique. Tonight, he presented the young and handsome Murphy with a flourish, transferring her curiosity.

A while later, I strolled the perimeter of the salon, passing the bar where Herr Higgins conversed with Mr. Browne, whose eyes kept track of my movements about the room. I noticed his dress whites fit him well, but I did so in a more circumspect way by peeking through my fingers as I patted a yawn. When their talk turned to trade in western Europe, I stepped out the door.

The smell of the sea at night was bolder, denying the cloak of blackness that would mute everything. The sea filled my senses with the scent of fish, brine, and mystery. Little sounds were amplified. I closed my eyes and felt the waves skimming the ship, letting the breeze lift my hair and drop it again.

While I counted the seconds until the ship rose to a crest, descended, and ascended again, my thoughts drifted ... Philadelphia ... a year lost. Betrayal and scandal. Then Taos, Mexico City, Panama, and Lima. "I will wed at Christmas time." *Good for you, Charles*, I thought. The silvery water glimmered through my tears.

Damn him. They weren't for Charles. I'd cried for him in too many places; on riverboats, in hotels, and trains loaded with chickens and bandits while I sat beside sweet-faced women who could smile and hold nothing in their hands.

I had acclaim. More money than I needed. I clenched my fists and relived the thunderous applause of full houses where they shouted my name. What did I want?

A soft handkerchief appeared under my nose. Sniffling into it, I wiped my eyes. I hated weakness. Most of all, in myself. If he'd said a word, I would have chucked him over the side.

Another minute passed, and Browne steered me inside.

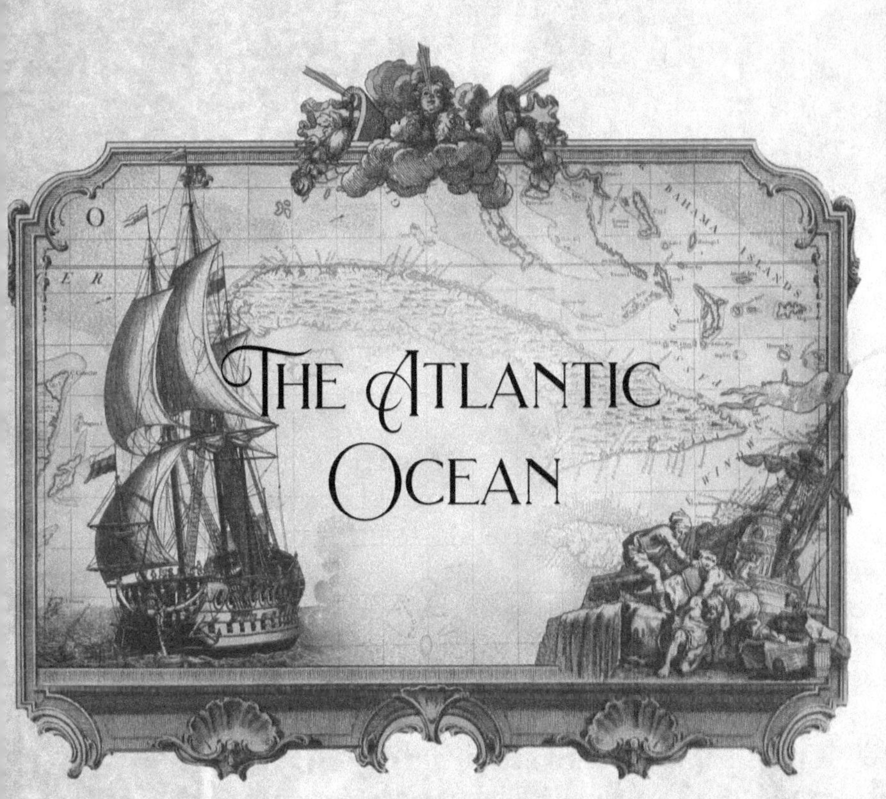
THE ATLANTIC
OCEAN

CHAPTER 8

Latitude 29°35' S, Longitude 48°05' W

Uncertainty, fear, and the motion of the ship kept Shaw awake long into the night. For hours, he had no trouble hearing Peech's drunken singing on the bridge above him. The sailors' grumblings and raucous laughter provided a menacing undercurrent to the ghastly circus on the *Hussar*.

His bunk had no sheets, no blanket, and he shivered in the clothes they'd left him. Once, he thought he heard a woman's outcry coming from beneath the ship. In his fancy, Shaw wondered if a mermaid screamed from under fathoms of water. Curious, he had stood in his doorway, drenched in sea spray, but heard nothing other than a brawl between two drunks careening down the deck.

Desolation cloaked him, and he finally slept.

Shaw awoke to find the sun had traveled a few hours upward, burning through fluffy clouds before spilling through his tiny porthole. After a cool night, the morning held a promise of tropic heat. He tried not to think of how far from land they had traveled. From the sun's angle, and the direction they traveled, the closer to the Pole they traveled, the warm air would turn to rain and ice.

His stomach rumbled, intruding into his troubled thoughts. If he sat still long enough, would they come get him? He decided it wouldn't matter. After pulling on his boots, Shaw went on deck.

"Here." Farley appeared beside him, fairly dancing in anticipation. He handed over a biscuit and tin cup. "Eat up. The Cap'n wants me to show you the ship and your duties."

Shaw bit into the biscuit. Peech displayed his contempt for Shaw's ability to escape by "showing" him the *Hussar*. Duties? Shaw swallowed the flavorless bread and sipped tea. He could taste the grease, but he drank it all. Water—always rationed on ships— could not be refused.

Farley nattered like a gossiping fishwife as they walked the decks. Despite the filth, the ship felt solid; she sailed fast, jumping the waves like a steeplechaser. Shaw made note of each gangway, portal, and storage locker, knowing a chance to flee would come. Did his captors know of his knowledge of ships, or did they assume that he only counted Lloyds' money? Meanwhile, Farley—unlike Borodin—couldn't keep his mouth shut.

Shaw half-listened. The runt's freckles, fertilized by the sun, covered his wide face with a rosy glow and a wholesomeness that contradicted the cruelty in his eyes.

They traveled across the leeward deck, stepping over boxes and coiled rigging until they came to a mass of tangled lines. Farley stopped and waited. Shaw let his face go blank.

"All right. Watch me, you bastard." Farley bent to show him how to undo, properly knot, and coil the ropes.

For the next few hours, Shaw worked his hands raw, feeling the strain in the muscles of his back and legs. In the middle of the south Atlantic, his captors could do worse than force him to work. He labored, not willing to discover what refusal would bring. Farley sat on a barrel next to the rigging and talked the entire time.

"You aren't the first pansy ass we've kidnapped. No, sir." Farley spat beside Shaw's foot and the spittle blended into the grime of the deck. "We grabbed a priest up in Grande last year."

Shaw wiped sweat from his eyes and resumed knotting ropes, remembering the reports.

A Portuguese priest, Father Elias, had been ambushed while traveling in a canoe upriver, along with local Indians, to the port of Grande. Under a volley of shots, the Indians had died, and the priest fled into the jungle. Later reports maintained that Father Elias hid a cache of gold bars from the jungle mines before his capture.

"What happened to him?" Shaw sounded hoarse; he hadn't spoken since the previous night.

"He wouldn't tell us where the gold was." Farley pointed to more rigging, and Shaw moved to it. "Stubborn bastard. We sent word to the church in Grande that we had him." The runt shook his head. "The mayor of the town tried to barter. Ha. But the Cap'n, he figured the priest had the gold."

"And?" Shaw asked as he took off his shirt and gazed into the blazing sun.

Farley jumped off the barrel and danced a jig to the rail and back. "We pulled out the priest's toenails. The whole time, he don't say nothin'." Shaw swallowed his revulsion and went on working. Best to not let them know his thoughts; either they'd use them against him, or their atrocities would get worse.

Beside him, Farley bent over to coil lines, anything to keep moving. "We cut off his toes. He don't talk, just keeps a-prayin'. We got tired of his moanin' and pitiful looks." Farley guffawed. "So, we dumped him upriver where the little fish with the big teeth are."

"Piranha."

Farley hopped from one foot to the other, clearly enjoying the memory. "Yessir. Just threw him in, finally a-screamin'. He's still prayin' with his feet all bloody." Farley bounced up and sat on the barrel again. "When they ate him, the water got all lathered up like a pink bubble bath! Ha, ha!"

Midday passed, and Shaw became a working part of the crew, yet separate. None of the sailors came near him. After a while, their curious looks changed to glances of indifference. Shaw thought bitterly that he could only entertain them when he rolled around the deck with his naked bum in the air.

All day long, Farley flitted close by him like a red-haired gnat, or Borodin observed him with the solemnity of a cat. His quarters remained separate, too, near the galley, not below deck like the rest of the crew or beside Peech's. His status evident; he represented the live prize from which the crew would profit.

Lunch consisted of a piece of salted beef and another biscuit. Shaw sat on a pile of rigging and ate his food. By that time, he was too hungry to savor or disparage the taste. He'd just picked up his tea when a commotion broke out on the stern. Men scrambled up from the crew's quarters and across the decks shoving and yelling. When Captain Peech's bark rang out, they cheered. Deceitful and murderous, these men from many lands all obeyed one man—Peech.

More shouting. Shaw began to trot and rounded the corner of the forecastle. The men stood three and four deep, but he was able to see over them.

Stripped to the waist and lashed between two poles, a crewman—really little more than a boy—hung a few feet off the ground. The boy's hair, dirtied a dull brown, covered his shoulders, and without a shirt, he had the naked chest of a young girl. His face held no expression, save the fear dancing in his eyes.

Pacing in front of him and spouting a torrent of the language they all spoke, Peech held court with an obvious hangover, growling obscenities and kicking everything out of his path. After a few minutes, like a cup of good American coffee, the ranting seemed to revive him. His words spewed forth full of venom and were as lively as if he was calling an auction. While Peech waved his arms and harangued his men, they listened, absorbing every word.

Most were in their twenties and thirties, but a few had the gray hair of old men. Some could be the hapless boy who dangled in front of them. Even though they were little more than children, they seemed as cold as the sea; their greenness had already turned black.

Peech's eyes radiated power. He had them chanting "*El Hussar*" and raising their fists like a dirty army devoted to a religious madman. Borodin stood to the side, face impassive, taking in the crew's reaction. Shaw hated to, but he moved close enough to ask sotto voice, "What is he saying?"

"There must be discipline." Borodin shrugged. "The *Hussar's* safety comes first."

"What did the boy do?" Behind him, Peech roared like a bull; Shaw had to strain to hear the scarecrow.

"Slept on watch."

Shaw felt Borodin's gaze rake the side of his head. Like Farley, the man was curious whether Shaw knew the significance of the offense.

He made his question bland. "Is that so bad?"

Borodin hesitated, then answered. "On watch, you hold the safety of the ship in your hands. Anything could have happened."

"But it didn't."

"He must receive punishment. We kept him in irons until the Captain was ready."

Until he woke from his drunken stupor, Shaw supposed.

The bells for the afternoon watch sounded. Peech's harangue came to an end, celebrated with more cheers and shouts from his men.

"What language do they speak?"

"Ours." Borodin's reply sounded enigmatic.

Farley pushed his way forward, elbowing the others to take his place by Peech. In his arms, he cradled a large, coiled rope studded with bits of metal that caught flashes of the sun. The crowd tensed, reminding Shaw of bloodthirsty, hungry dogs as a ripple of tension arced through them. A few of them mirrored the horror in the boy's eyes.

"What is he holding?"

Borodin didn't answer.

With increasing dread, Shaw studied what Farley held so tenderly until, with a last torrent of curses, Peech slung his arm around the unlucky lad and squeezed him tenderly. Then laughed. Farley grinned broadly and stepped behind the boy, whispering something in his ear. As the runt uncoiled what lay in his arms, the boy winced.

Shaw turned away, but Borodin gripped his arm.

"Part of life, part of death, Mr. Shaw."

Shaw had recognized the cat 'o' nine tails. Depending on who used it, the cat was the traditional instrument of either punishment or torture. Only fifty years ago, the Queen's Royal Navy regularly dealt discipline with it; too many seamen declared missing or dead died by the cat's tail.

The thing looked horrible. Eight feet long, rough, and knotted with spikes of razors and embedded jagged metal, the cat was stained in dried blood and old offenses. Like a tassel on top a knitted hat, a cluster of razors decorated the tip of it.

Farley whipped the rope high into an arc above the boy, snapping it, the sound and action intended to terrorize.

Into the hushed air, the first lash descended lazy and slow. The boy flinched as a long curve of blood from his shoulder to buttocks rose like a red snake. His knuckles turned white, and he held the scream back. Shaw read the derision on the faces of the crew.

Farley talked as he worked, circling his victim while whispering words of torment that contorted the boy's stoic face. Shaw felt sick—both fascinated and repulsed by the savagery. He flicked a glance at Borodin and saw no reaction at all.

"On with it!" Peech yelled from the rail of the bridge. He held a fresh bottle of wine in each hand. "Wind's comin' up."

Farley nodded. His almost toothless grin was like a grinning death head. "Aye, Sir."

Faster than Shaw's could blink, the cat 'o' nine tails laid open the boy's back. Before blood spurted, Farley raised it high again. Shaw jerked forward, but Borodin pulled him back as the third lash took off the boy's ear. A plume of blood squirted wide, causing the jeering crowd to step back.

"God—" Bile rose in Shaw's throat. He lunged for Farley. Again, Borodin yanked him back, throwing him toward the back of the ship. Shaw swung a fist. Borodin blocked it.

"Move!" Borodin threw him into a bulkhead. Shaw bounced off and charged Borodin. Another shove, and Shaw went sprawling into a stack of barrels. Borodin kicked him down as a long scream cut the air and then stopped. Shaw wiped blood from his nose and started up again.

"Sit, Mr. Shaw," Borodin spoke softly and planted a foot on Shaw's chest. "We have to keep you in one piece. Challenge the crew, and they'll tear you up."

The Pacific Ocean

CHAPTER 9

THE PACIFIC
NEAR ISLA WELLINGTON

To me, the next day meant exploration and an opportunity to live what can only be imagined through the stories told by sailors—the beauty of a ship at full sail, flying, skimming over the waves, and romanticism of the sea. The romance didn't feel as tangible as sweet music or even as lovely as a carpet of flowers, and yet, oceans held a certain mystery and secrets I couldn't begin to fathom. As I was soon to find out, the ship did also.

After a few hours of hanging over the rail with the wind in my face, a diversion became necessary. I wouldn't want to overdo the romanticism.

Under normal circumstances, I wasn't as bold as to snoop into the nooks and crannies of a hotel or railroad car. But over the next few months, I would be reading every scrap of paper and book on this ship, talking until I couldn't talk anymore, and probably still be bored to the gills. Therefore, I explored storage bins, cupboards, and opened unlocked doors with circumspection. Being a lady, there was a limit to my nosiness; I considered occupied state-rooms private ... once I knew I'd happened upon one.

My investigation continued to the lee side on the main deck, where I threw open the first cabin door after the salon and then shut it just as quickly. Flat on his back, Doctor Rubio snored like a train stuck in a snowstorm. I closed the door with care. Having learned a bit of discretion, I twisted the handle of the next door more slowly and quietly.

"Oh! I'm sorry." I blushed and started to back out again.

Herr Higgins turned from the bureau, dropping the object he'd been holding. If it hadn't been for *his* blush, I would have shut the door and not looked further. Instead, I saw the tailored jackets with the flared lapels that Mr. Morse wore in an open trunk, and the length of the trousers on the bed suggested a man much taller than Higgins.

He'd followed my inspection and then the deduction in my eyes.

"Excuse me." Higgins brushed by and on out the door, saying, "Apparently, *you* have an appointment here."

It took a second, and then I understood. The man had just insulted me—insinuating I had an amorous assignation with Morse.

"I'm sure I would not," I said aloud. *It wouldn't be with Morse, either.*

Why was Higgins in here, I wondered? The donkey's ass. I crossed to the bureau and picked up what he'd dropped. It appeared to be a scrapbook of sorts, and the album had fallen open to a picture of a vessel, the *Moira*, the missing treasure ship from last night's conversation. *Really? The same ship that Morse claimed not to know much about.*

Interesting. Curiosity won. I glanced at the door, knowing I risked discovery, but there must be a moment to see what Higgins had wanted, and Morse had lied about.

Turning pages rapidly, I listened for footsteps while scanning the photographs and newspaper articles that had been pasted to the pages. The journal appeared to be a gallery of shipwrecks going back to the middle of the last century.

Mr. Morse had certainly pretended ignorance last night. Perhaps Higgins suspected as much and decided to verify his hunch.

The photography of the *Moira* appeared grainy and faded, but despite the poor quality of the picture, I gazed at what was unquestionably a large ship. At the bottom of the page, a series of smaller portraits caught my eye. One of the captions read, "John Greely." As I studied it ... the picture reminded me of Morse himself. Especially the icy eyes. But he would have been nearly a hundred years older, so it could not be. Possibly his great-grandson?

Steps thumped along the deck outside the door and stopped. I ditched the album and stood. The steps continued along. Not needing another hint, I tidied up and departed in a swirl of skirts.

At the end of our second night together, the inevitable happened, but not before the post-dinner conversation colored the voyage with a promise of something of more interest.

After a fine dinner of roast quail, young peas, mashed potatoes, and talk of the good weather of the day, Captain McQuistan again excused himself as soon as he finished his brandy, leaving Browne to chaperone the passengers. The first mate made a tour with the bottle, filling glasses, and dispensing charm. The brandy tasted good. With my chin in the air and gaze averted, I didn't speculate on anything more.

When the rest of the passengers crossed to the corner by the pianoforte, more out of boredom than of curiosity, I tagged along. Mrs. Pentifax navigated to one of the couches and squeezed herself between Jessica and Morse as Browne approached the sofas.

Morse's next words brought me back into the conversation, and the boredom evaporated.

"... yes, I am a medium, Doctor Rubio."

"Ooh! How thrilling—" Mrs. Pentifax clapped her hands.

"Tell us more, Mr. Morse," Jessica said.

Of course! I should have made the connection back in Celize. The infamous Parisian parties of 1846. The Queen's very own Prince Albert had not been the only well-known name to frequent the soirees that Morse instigated; they had been as popular in the diplomatic circles as in the theatre world. While not in the same league as Abigail Adams or Descantier, Christian Morse enjoyed a reputation applauded by an audience who believed in his powers.

"... a common occurrence is the movement of objects across rooms," Morse said.

"Is it trickery?" Mrs. Pentifax asked.

Morse feigned judiciousness by pursing his lips. "Well, in some cases, there have been frauds exposed. But my sittings have been free of any taint and are true psychic occurrences."

"How do people cheat during a *séance*?" Doctor Rubio asked. "I thought the sessions took place with locked doors and windows."

"That is a normal precaution." Morse straightened his shoulders. "However, my standards are of the highest order."

I bet his fees were also.

"Then there are spirits? And ghosts?" Jessica's eyes widened, full of interest.

"If they are properly summoned, they appear."

"It's a parlor game. Nothing more." Browne's contribution stopped short of a challenge.

Morse bristled. "I assure you it is not, sir."

Browne just raised his brows. I had seen many a first mate, and had to admit, he was the handsomest. It could have been his strong features, his eyes, or something else, but I wouldn't feed his vanity by telling him so, no matter the circumstances.

As I listened to them, I thought about the scrapbook in Morse's stateroom. Why did the man pretend ignorance about the *Moira* last evening? More to the point, why was Herr Higgins so interested in Mr. Morse's room? They didn't appear to know each other before the journey. Meanwhile, something most annoying brewed only a few feet away.

"You don't appear convinced, Mr. Browne." Morse sent me a shrewd look. "Perhaps you prefer a more direct form of entertainment."

A flush warmed my neck and face as, one-by-one, they turned to stare. Only Jessica and Mrs. Pentifax appeared confused.

Christian Morse stood, bowing toward me like a concert hall promoter. "I give you the world-famous chanteuse, The Red Rose."

The first mate's expression was as bland as if he'd been asleep in the sun. Browne tilted his head back and used the opportunity to study me, but he'd been doing that since we'd boarded. The others had audible reactions.

Jessica's eyebrows drew together. "You are a *singer*?" She said the word with a mixture of high-class distaste and curiosity. "I do not recognize your name."

"Oh, Miss Coulter!" Doctor Rubio gushed. "From a distance, I was privileged to hear one of your concerts. When I visited Lisbon, I could not get a ticket for your performance."

I smiled in acknowledgment, but my attention stayed on Mrs. Pentifax as she gazed down her nose at me in precisely the same way as Charles' mother had done. In fact, she looked like her.

"You!" Her finger wavered as she struggled off the sofa and waddled forward. "You seduced the President's son—" The digit wiggled right under my nose.

The urge to bite her finger was too strong to ignore. As I opened my mouth, Browne pulled me, not gently, to the bar. The roaring in my ears drowned the exclamations from behind. The room blurred. I'd thought I'd left the ignorance behind—and the paragons of virtue. No, I hadn't possessed the blue-blooded pedigree required to marry the president's son. And his mother had shown no reluctance to explain it to me publicly. Talent and fame couldn't replace lineage.

Browne pushed a glass into my hand. I shoved it back and turned toward the door.

"Coward."

I had the words ready as I turned back, but meeting his gaze, I decided not to play.

"Good night, Mr. Browne."

CHAPTER 10

The next day the ship experienced gorgeous weather, a moderate breeze, Mrs. Pentifax accidentally locked in the lady's loo for over an hour, and a particularly fine dinner. By sundown, I decided it had been a good day all around.

The salon's lamps warmed the room, along with our good spirits. From my position at the dining table, I studied Browne over my cup of tea. He stood just inside the door, and his glance flicked from one to another of us. I returned his regard, knowing he was about to be greeted by news sure to make him raise a disbelieving brow. Mrs. Pentifax's wave caught his eye.

"Oh, Mr. Browne! We're having a *séance*! I'm sure we'll see something from beyond. Or behind us..." Her speech showed the effects of many dips in the port bottle. "Oh, it doesn't matter. We'll have a splendid time." She plopped down on a chair with a decided thump and picked up her glass again.

"Mr. Morse has agreed to lead us." Doctor Rubio pushed chairs up to the dining table that doubled as the salon's gaming table. Higgins helped, seeming as interested as his conservative countenance would allow. To me, we sailed through a pitch-black night just as we faced the psychic world—blindly.

The psychic in question appeared properly otherworldly from his position of a languid drape across the bar. His expression looked remote and detached as he nodded at something Jessica murmured.

From across the table, Mrs. Pentifax raised her voice to get my attention, "Miss Coulter." Avoiding eye contact, she said, "We had tickets for your show in Richmond two years ago. We couldn't attend. The critics said it was a rare performance."

An apology of sorts. Maybe I wouldn't put a fish head in her bed.

"Perhaps you will perform for us one of these evenings." Stated it like she had just asked the maid to iron a blouse.

Mrs. P would need to change her bedding.

"Some other time." I rose. "Do we need to turn down the lamps?"

It took a bit of time to set everything up, but eventually, Doctor Rubio locked the last window and returned to the table where Mrs. Pentifax gripped the doctor's hand and Browne's. Then came Jessica on Higgins's left. On his right was my courageous self and then the psychic.

The velvet drapes and the wood paneling of the salon cosseted us in near darkness. As the sea rocked the *Passat* with a gentle hand, a curious atmosphere descended upon our little group. Nervousness prevailed, and quick, excited glances bounced around the table. A droning organ played slowly would have been perfect; Morse couldn't have stage-managed the scene more theatrically if he'd tried.

Yet, no matter the mood, I couldn't help but take this seriously. In my travels, I'd witnessed participants before and after a *séance* and saw the look in their eyes afterwards. Some people never appeared normal again, as if they'd been disconnected from whatever centered them.

Not caring to remember the incidents in detail, I focused back on what was happening in the room, and our eyes adjusted to the solitary light from a thick candle burning in front of us. Lingering cigar smoke from Messrs. Rubio and Higgins clouded the air, giving the room an even eerier character. I pinched my nose to head off a sneeze. A fine cigar is a pleasure to inhale from a second-hand point of view; I hadn't smelled one recently.

"Please join hands." Morse's monotone sounded far away.

Minutes passed as waves rhythmically slapped the side of the ship. While the table quieted, Herr Higgins wiggled in his seat, and sweat beaded above Doctor Rubio's mustaches. I gripped his hand harder than I intended to, enough to make him glance at me in surprise.

Morse bothered me, but if pressed, I wouldn't have been able to say why. Contact couldn't be avoided any longer, and as I grasped his hand, a fire-like jolt seared through me, tingled, and then faded. The psychic's fixed gaze didn't waver from the candle. On his other side, Higgins appeared blandly attentive; nothing had electrified his countenance.

Was I that fanciful? I shivered—more evidence of why this gathering wasn't a good idea.

"Please do not speak until I reach a certain point, if I do. Then talk only when invited to do so." Morse's voice had lost the lazy, condescending tone, sounding more professional.

The room grew colder. I wondered about the strength in Mr. Browne's hands ... which led to other feelings and sensations I hadn't felt for a long time. In the candlelight, his face seemed craggier, harder, and although he tried to hide it, his eyes looked worried still. What had Browne seen in Cape Horn?

Cold. A draft danced in the air, caressing my skin, then leaving to return again. Jessica bit her lip and looked pale.

"Close your eyes." Christian Morse's voice sounded further away.

Browne's gaze sought mine, the dare was implicit—*you first*. I smiled and waited him out.

"Please close your eyes."

Browne shrugged. His eyes shut, and I felt my courage slip just a bit.

The candle flickered violently. Probably an omen of something nasty about to happen. I took a deep breath and closed my eyes.

Nervous feet shifted. Minutes passed. From outside the salon door, a sailor called out before his heavy steps trod by us. We heard the ship's bell signal the hour, and from behind the bar, the mantle clock chimed in concert. Doctor Rubio's palm grew wetter, and I increased my grip. In contrast, Morse's hand felt perfectly dry, like contact with the dead.

Over the next several minutes, faint sounds from the crew filtered through, along with the normal ship noises. Another set of heavy steps walked by outside and receded just as a large wave slammed the *Passat*, crested high, and quieted.

Morse began to quiver, sending spider feet tiptoeing across my skin. I tried to jerk my hand away, but he held on.

Something cold brushed my cheek. The cold came again, sliding down my neck and encircling it; the sensation felt like nothing I could describe and nothing I wanted to see. I cut off a yelp.

This was *not* a parlor game. I shut my eyes tighter.

Morse's voice rumbled deep and imploring, asking a question I couldn't hear. Yet, I felt his connection—right down to my fingertips.

The ring of cold began to squeeze.

My eyes popped open. Everything appeared as before, and I closed them again. Trying to shake off the cold didn't work—it gripped my will along with my neck. I couldn't move. Nor talk. There was an advantage to living in the real world and having the sense to leave the unknown alone. Oh, to be in Boston again, in front of a safe, logical fire with a lazy dog snoring at my feet.

Morse continued speaking in a low and indistinct murmur. Could anyone else hear him? Beside me, Doctor Rubio's hand dripped sweat, and he shuffled his feet as the medium's voice rose, the pitch plaintive, growing louder until it suddenly stopped.

This time, the silence had quality. A presence. An atmosphere of waiting enveloped us, the tension sharp, the ache-like pleasure denied.

It began.

Faint but growing stronger, an army bursting into a black void, a thousand voices flooded the air around us, all speaking at once, blurring together in many languages, their words tumbled. Men talked, argued, and sang until everything changed. The air shuddered, and their cries became prayers in a fractured prism.

Chattering.

A loud explosion shook a multitude of windows, mingling with the howling and shrieking from the unseen men as more and more voices arrived in an unstoppable chorus. The blast reverberated like reports from dozens of guns, followed by echoes of other explosions. The chattering rose in pitch and fever.

"When?" Morse demanded, trembling so violently I could barely hang on.

The grinding of heavy chains against wood joined with the cacophony of voices and explosions ... then came hundreds of boots running frantically ... timbers breaking apart, repeating over and over as the voices rose higher.

Chattering.

A sudden eruption of rushing water felt so close I thought I would drown. The scene fused into a concert of terror, bleeding the long screams from the dying and entwined with the rending of wood. The plaintive praying to gods of many lands became guttural praying that begged for mercy. Their desperation turned into cries of panic as the crunching of bones and gasps from drowning men competed with the screaming. The noise redoubled as a massive rush of hissing water arrived, bringing an avalanche of roaring sea-water that smothered the growing crescendo of garbled screams.

The chattering rose.

Christian Morse was on his feet, dragging me with him. The cold squeezed; I couldn't breathe.

Chattering.

Could-not-breathe—

Chattering.

The noise imploded.

—*I saw it* without opening my eyes—I saw them. For the smallest second—*something too horrible*.

The cold squeezed. And the world faded to black.

CHAPTER 11

It could have been minutes or hours later that I awoke, aware of a sense of weightlessness and being wrapped in a gray cocoon my mind hid in and never wanted to leave.

Footsteps stopped, and a door creaked open. Cold air replaced warm arms as I was laid onto something flat. When a hand smoothed my brow, I pushed it away and snuggled into the darkness.

Cold water splashed my face. I cursed and swung my fist. A larger one caught it.

From a few inches away, his eyes, unguarded and concerned, met mine. He slowly released my hand. I pushed him back and tried to sit up. Being the intelligent rogue he was, Browne held me down and backed off the bunk. Beyond his shoulder, I could see Mrs. Pentifax hovering in the doorway like a grumpy fairy.

"You shouldn't be in here, Mr. Browne," she sniped.

"I am the ship's medical officer, Ma'am," Browne said as he loomed over the bed.

"It still isn't proper."

She made my head hurt. "Go stuff yourself, Mrs. P."

"Oh!"

The door slammed.

The first mate swept clothes off a chair, pulled it close to the bed, sat, and stared. I returned the regard, not liking the worry that flooded his face. He withdrew a pocket watch and reached for my wrist. In the next few seconds, the frown disappeared, replaced by a different kind of tension. Well, well. His hand felt warm and very real. For days, I had speculated on what a close encounter with him would be like. Now, I wished he would leave.

Callused fingers explored my hand, traveling to my elbow. Shivers of pleasure ran up my arms.

"Does this hurt?" He moved my arm out and then inward again.

I shook my head without looking at him.

My breath caught as he undid my boots, unwinding the laces slowly and sliding the boots off to cup each heel, his touch gentle.

"Does this bother you?" He flexed my foot.

I shook my head. Oh, no … *Not at all*. A tell-tale pulse beat in his neck, keeping time with my heartbeat. It seemed we both had the same level of tension.

He moved to my ankle, running rough hands up my calf.

"Does this hurt? Anything feel broken?"

"No."

He held my knee and experimentally moved my leg up and down a few inches. I shuddered and bit my lip. Days of wondering had only primed my curiosity. His closeness now perturbed me; his touch plainly an intimacy I wasn't ready to face.

I squirmed and sat up to face him.

Browne cleared his throat, his expression impassive as he re-checked my eyes, and then he grunted, and his touch moved to my neck. When his thumb pressed against my throat, it hurt. I pushed him away.

"Explain."

It could have been a coincidence, but the air grew chilly. I spoke in a raspy whisper, "Someone choked me. In the *séance*."

"Ridiculous. Everyone held hands. No one else was in the room."

"And the shots we heard? The other noises?"

"Perhaps the *séance* was a bit too much for you—"

Like a pool of rainwater in the sun, I could almost see the sensuality dissipate in the room. I pointed to the door.

"Get out."

Browne didn't move.

"Didn't faint." It came out hoarse.

"No?" He raised his brows.

"Get out—" I tried to get up and help him out, but he was up and moving.

"I'll send a cabin boy with some tea for your throat."

"Fine." I lay back, exhausted. There would be no confidences between the first mate and myself. I wouldn't bother.

Twice during the night, my cabin door opened. Maybe more. My dreams were many and vivid. One dream that repeated itself a dreadful amount of times concerned a downhill train ride with colorful ghouls chasing me while they waved body parts and sang songs from Rigoletto in discordant falsetto.

At times, I drifted awake. The porthole emitted a dim light that seemed like a slow-moving fog with sinewy, ghostlike arms that reached into the cabin. I couldn't tell who had entered the room. Nor could I lift the blanket of lethargy that lay across me. Before dawn, I held a stuffy head and vowed that I wouldn't sleep again without locking the door. And I wouldn't drink any drugged tea from the first mate.

It hurt to move. It hurt to think. Bending over to discover where each article of clothing lay proved to be a highly complex mission. I rarely indulged in liquor to excess. Surely, the narcotic stupor I swam in could rival one of Faust's more devastating mornings after. Finally, with my ablutions complete, I ventured on deck.

The cool morning air lifted the layer of miasma shrouding my senses, but whatever Browne had dosed me with made my stomach roll with the heavy swells under the ship. I do *not* get seasick. Damn him. Lady-like or not, when I found Mr. Browne, I might show him what doctored tea looked like all over his boots.

The sun sat on the horizon, combating a bank of heavy clouds as it rose, fighting to light the dawn. Overhead, sailors climbed like monkeys in the rigging, swinging from spar to yardarm and shouting good-naturedly. The *Passat* hummed with readiness for the day.

When I approached the rail of the leeward deck, I spied someone I knew.

"Good morning."

"Miss." Daniel Murphy nodded as he leaned against the midship's bulkhead, sipping from a steaming tin cup and calling out orders. In the quarter house, the helmsmen conferred with two crewmen while other seamen sauntered about in the bowlegged swagger peculiar to sailors and cowboys. Beyond them, the waves shimmered from black to silver gray, transforming into a mushy green as the sun burned higher. With it came more activity as hands rolled barrels across the decks and unfurled canvasses. The smell of bacon cooking floated by.

That did it.

Afterwards, I leaned over the side, letting the spray mist my face, breathing deep, glad to be empty. Retching had scraped my throat raw. It also removed all traces of Browne's remedy for whatever he thought I had caught from the *séance*.

"Seasick, Miss Coulter?"

Browne had approached to stand a few feet away, almost hiding the smirk on his face. But not quite. A lucky man, our Mr. Browne; if only he'd arrived a little sooner. I turned on him and he backed up a step.

"What did you put in the tea?"

"Laudanum." His eyes twinkled with manly self-satisfaction. "Good for hysterics and a known sleeping aid."

"*Hysterics?*" I tried to yell. "I do *not* have hysterics!" I stamped my foot.

"All women do. Why did you faint last night?"

"Someone—something squeezed my throat until I passed out."

"We held hands in an empty room." He looked as smug as a canary. A big one.

"And what we heard?" I asked.

"A fake parlor game."

"I'm referring to the gunshots."

The playfulness faded, and he averted his gaze to the helm. "They weren't gunshots."

"No?" I asked. Why did Browne look suddenly evasive and somber?

"They were—"

A long scream pierced the morning, followed by two shorter shrieks, as if the screamer didn't have enough air.

Mr. Browne, being a gentleman, pushed me out of the way and bounded aft.

"Damn you Browne, wait for me!" I lifted my skirts and ran after him.

The door to the last cabin on the starboard side stood open, and a small crowd had already gathered in front of it. I leaned around Browne's rear and looked inside.

Blood on the floor and above the bed, flowered in a wide spray up the wall.

Like a butchered walrus, Doctor Rubio lay on his side, his luxuriant mustaches drooping into his blood. Poor man. Crimson covered the bed, clothes, and the corpse, which had fallen to the floor. With each roll of the ship, blood coursed out the door and trickled across the deck. The rivulet neared one of Mrs. Pentifax's slippers as she stood there in her frilly dressing gown, providing more screams. It may sound morbid, but the entire scene reminded me of a play with action, drama, and terrified accompaniment from a soloist.

Jessica arrived much more quietly and peered over my shoulder. When a strangled gasp escaped her, I steered her to her aunt, and as we passed by the galley with its cooking smells, I persevered.

Mrs. Pentifax appeared deflated and pitiful. She wrung her hands and frantically looked from the corpse to the crew and back again.

"It would help if you would take her to the salon. Get out the brandy," I suggested to Jessica.

"But she won't drink this early," she objected.

"Of course, she will." I recalled Auntie's familiarity with the port bottle on several occasions. But for myself, the thought of spirits made my stomach sing ascending and descending circus music.

While we talked, doors banged open further along the deck, and the two remaining passengers came running in various stages of undress. Shouts dropped from the rigging, followed by sailors, and still others ran up from below decks, squinting into the emerging dawn. Browne barked at them until they retreated again.

As he buttoned his shirt, Captain McQuistan arrived in front of the cabin door. One look and his thundered expletive drew the rest of the sailors from the front of the ship. A glimpse inside the room caused Morse to grope for the rail and lean over the side. With a gulp, I turned away, afraid my empathy might become a physical sensation. When I looked again, Browne grabbed Morse's shoulder and propelled him toward the salon.

Moments later, a pair of sailors flanked a grim-faced Daniel Murphy as they entered the cabin with a stretcher.

The salon door lay only fifteen feet away from the doctor's cabin, and although I tried hard, I couldn't overhear Browne and the Captain as they conferred in front of it. Browne spied me, turned around, and lowered his voice. I directed a curse about fleas and his underwear at him. Assuming he wore any. As the odor of hot vinegar floated into the salon, I slammed the door.

"What is that *smell*?" Jessica asked.

"Blood is most easily removed with heated vinegar." I recited another tidbit courtesy of my non-sea-faring uncle. In this case, he'd seen crews cleaning the carnage off the decks of the whalers in port. My thoughts remained on what Browne and the Captain discussed. I'd give my brand-new sable and ostrich feather hat to be able to hear them.

"How do you know that?" Jessica said.

I began, "From—"

"It had to be one of the crew." Mrs. Pentifax's beady eyes bounced toward me. "They're lower class. Killing is easy for them." Auntie seemed recovered. From the set of her jaw, she appeared ready to engage in any skirmish she could find.

I ignored her. Between the gore and my stomach, it wasn't worth stuffing the old lady on the sofa and sitting on her.

"Why would anyone murder that man?" Jessica asked. Mrs. Pentifax patted her hand and managed to look down her nose at the others in the room.

No one had an answer. Higgins swigged the brandy bottle and kept his glassy stare glued to the back of Morse's head. The medium sat on the sofa like he would in church, straight-backed without moving or speaking. He didn't even turn around when the salon door swung open, allowing a grim-faced captain and first mate to enter.

"When did Doctor Rubio die?" Higgins blurted.

Morse regarded them with unfocused eyes.

Captain McQuistan pulled at his cap in irritation and asked, "Why do you need to know?"

Higgins glanced at his shoes and then longingly at the fresh bottle of brandy on the bar before saying, "I heard a noise ... just before dawn." He took care with each word, perhaps because of the shocking nature of what he saw or because he concealed something. "As you know, my cabin is near Doctor Rubio's." He stuttered, "W-was near it."

The Captain hitched his trousers and sat on the couch a proper distance from Mrs. Pentifax. Browne did the same before he began writing in a small writing tablet and avoided my eye. Only good breeding kept me from walking over there to see what Browne wrote.

"Captain?" Mr. Higgins asked.

"Doctor Rubio died within an hour or two of dawn. It will be in my report. Which begins with an interview with each of you." He nodded to his first mate.

"Why with us?" Mrs. Pentifax shrilled. "It was one of your crew!"

"That may be," Browne said. "But without a motive, it's hard to believe."

"You are insinuating that *we* have a motive?" Mrs. P's lips compressed until a baby mouse couldn't have squeezed through.

Browne assessed the room like he had the first night, only this time, the question wasn't whether we could swim. He wrote a long note as everyone watched and waited and listened to the ticking of the clock over the bar.

"How did he die?" Jessica asked.

"It was a knife. The killer probably tossed it over the side," the Captain said.

Morse asked, "Could a woman have performed the deed?" He wouldn't look at the others. Jessica's lips snapped shut, and she glared at him.

"Yes," Browne replied, still scribbling on his tablet.

"Hell," the Captain cut in. "We'll check everyone. And we'll begin by asking all of you where you were. Your pencil, Mr. Browne." He set his jaw and ground out, "I still have a set of irons in the hold ready for the scoundrel who did this!"

CHAPTER 12

J ust yesterday, I'd been anticipating a boring voyage. Dead wrong. If the Fates had offered me a choice, I would have gladly taken up knitting rather than see gentle Doctor Rubio murdered so cruelly.

After another half-hour, Browne and the Captain finished their inquiries and departed. Their questions hadn't been unexpected, just where we had been for the last few hours, and did we see or hear anything. The answers had all been highly uninformative except for Herr Higgins's initial statements to the Captain.

Of those of us remaining in the salon, a suspicious atmosphere still clouded every word and wary glance exchanged.

Mrs. Pentifax arranged herself on a brocade chair with a view of the others and the port bottle on a stand beside her; she knew her priorities. Meanwhile, I walked the room, avoiding Morse, who did the same. We resembled well-dressed inhabitants in an ornate zoo: pacing, turning, and pacing again. I'd never thought of the salon as small, but it certainly had become so. Higgins peered out the lee side windows, probably wishing he'd stayed home counting his money.

Soon, we'd be allowed out onto deck again. Until then, the conversation lagged, then spurted like blood.

"None of us can prove we didn't do it," Morse said.

"Especially none of us blood-thirsty women, Mr. Morse?" Jessica inquired sweetly from her seat by the fireplace.

Higgins crossed to the bar and rubbed a finger on the brandy bottle but didn't pour. "If I understood the Captain correctly, we are all suspects." The trader had developed a furtive look coupled with an insulting way of eyeing his fellow passengers. His favorite was Morse.

"I killed him for something to do." I waved my fan at him coquettishly.

"Really!" Mrs. P sputtered.

"Death isn't anything to be frivolous about, Miss Coulter," Higgins said.

"No, it isn't." I leaned forward. "But you act like you expect one of us to brandish a bloody knife. I find that rude."

"My father will be horrified this happened." Now that her initial shock had worn off, Jessica didn't look worried; instead, her dreamy expression seemed to romanticize the excitement and the unusual.

"The Captain will *have* to post a guard for our safety," Mrs. Pentifax said. "One of those filthy sailors could kill us in our sleep. Some of them do not speak English. And they have no morals. None."

"Oh, Auntie," Jessica complained. "You shouldn't say that." I had a feeling the girl objected on behalf of one of the crew in particular. Our conversation yesterday afternoon hinted as much.

It had happened a few hours before cocktails. From her deck chair, Mrs. Pentifax had announced she would retire for a nap before dinner. What kept her in her seat long after that was the prospect of leaving her innocent niece leaning over the rail of the *Passat* beside an influence such as Cass Coulter.

I remembered being eighteen, too. Jessica's wings fluttered against the door of the golden cage, just as mine had. The world awaited her while her aunt pretended nothing existed besides the port bottle and blue-blood pedigrees. I believed in reality without secrets, which eliminated lust for the forbidden.

Under the late afternoon sun, the *Passat* had climbed waves with ease, spraying Jessica's face and hair with mist. Mrs. Pentifax had finally bustled off, still casting suspicious glances over her shoulder.

"Your aunt has a … a strong personality," I ventured.

"Almost as much as my mother," Jessica agreed with a roll of her eyes.

"Your destination is Rio?"

"Yes. My parents are there." She adjusted the bodice of her dress. A few inches of ivory skin had turned pinkish with the afternoon heat. "My aunt is escorting me back from San Francisco."

"It's a long journey." It might be very long if the weather turned bad.

Jessica nodded. "My father is the American ambassador to Brazil."

"High society."

"I suppose." Jessica frowned. "Most of it is so boring. And I can never go out alone or go to parties."

Translated: I can't meet any boys.

"But with a chaperone, you're allowed out."

Jessica shook her head, white-gold curls reflecting the setting sun. "Not often. And my aunt can… ah…"

"Have a strong personality?"

Jessica smiled. She might have said more, but one of the more handsome sailors strode by, shirtless, and his bronzed muscles straining under a load of cut planks. He nodded to each of us and offered a polite "Ladies." Jessica blushed under his twinkling regard.

Just then, I caught sight of Mr. Browne overhead in the quarter house. He ducked back in, his ears practically wiggling.

"That," I said loud enough to be heard on the bridge, "is a fine-looking man who just walked by." I nudged Jessica, and she giggled.

"He certainly is. Don't let my aunt hear you."

All I had wanted was a self-satisfied first mate to hear.

What connected that pleasant interlude to our present situation, post-murder, was the same well-built sailor that Jessica had noticed and defended against her aunt's uncharitable remark. This time, his duty did not appear as pleasant as he and another sailor stripped down and washed-out Doctor Rubio's cabin. The preparations for more hot vinegar sent me to the other side of the ship.

Perched on a fairly clean container bin, I fed bits of hardtack to the screeching gulls that flapped their wings against the wind, hovering a few feet off the side. As I threw more bread, they made quite a din, swooping and cawing, catching the crumbs before they bounced into the sea. One bird landed on the rail a few feet aft, waiting for the next bit to be broken and thrown. His black eyes seemed honest in their quest for food. I threw him the piece of bread. Unlike the devious coldness of humans, if Nature was angry, she killed quickly in an open fight of beaks and claws. Not with a knife in a darkened room.

A few feet away, Christian Morse lounged in the shade with his long nose purposely buried in a book. Plainly, he didn't want to talk. The title of the book looked French—as sardonic and unreadable as the medium himself.

For a while, I thought about every word and gesture made to Doctor Rubio. He appeared to be such an innocuous man. Who would profit from his death? I could not imagine anyone being afraid of him, or that he aroused any passionate jealousy or blinding hatred. He just seemed ordinary. Also, Higgins had been snooping in Morse's room, not the doctor's.

I looked up. Since our departure, the canvases had lost their freshly laundered look, becoming dirtied and sporting streaks of gull guano in blacks, grays, and pale yellow as if part of an artist's canvas. It seemed unusually quiet on deck. One sailor sat in the crow's nest with his attention on the horizon, and two more straddled the mizzenmast repairing a sail.

After several more yawns, I became aware of a curious sight.

Since the ship's bell had sounded the hour, Herr Higgins passed by once, then twice, his demeanor like a kid bent on no good. With his stout legs, protruding belly, fancy vest, and shiny shoes, he could have been part of an animated window display from a men's shop. Added to his unnatural level of activity, he seemed twitchy. On his third pass by, I followed him; life on a ship, despite a murder, could be tedious. Even without Doctor Rubio's misfortune, I would have trailed him.

Herr Higgins rounded a bulkhead and neared the open area midship, walking slower. I hung back and then slipped to the side of the bulkhead.

With most of the deck hands out of sight, what was the trader up to? I kept my steps light and continued forward. Ahead of him, center of the ship, Daniel Murphy conferred with the Captain and the chief steward, Mr. Thomas. They huddled at the mouth of the hold and their words drifted by in broken bits, too faint to overhear.

Being much closer, Higgins could listen to them without any problem; he'd crawled under an overhang and crouched there, eavesdropping. I about-faced and circled around the deck as fast I could in my skirt, feeling my face flush with exertion. As I passed Morse, he put his book down to watch me hustling by.

The voices from men by the hold grew louder as I came around the last corner and slowed.

"...too heavy ... under the nitrate."

"Can't see it," Mr. Thomas muttered. He looked surprised as I arrived, doing my best not to puff like a racehorse who ran too hard.

"Good afternoon, Miss Coulter." Browne bowed. "I'd be remiss if I didn't inquire if you felt better?"

Damn it. He must have arrived while I was on my way around the deck.

"Yes, I do, thank you. How deep is the hold?" I peered into the hole, finding a yawning blackness above the gray outlines of the cargo. Browne's hand automatically started for my arm. I jerked my arm back, thinking that this little female would not faint and fall in. Given some encouragement, he'd probably dose me with laudanum again.

"Thirty-five feet, Miss," Daniel Murphy answered.

"Thank you. Are we overloaded, Captain?" I asked, remembering his earlier worry that the ship sat too heavy in the water.

"Yes," he clipped it.

"And you can't get to whatever is causing the problem without moving thousands of pounds of the nitrate?"

Browne's eyes narrowed as he assessed me. Then his polite mask settled in place again.

From under my eyelashes, I observed the second mate with surprise; Daniel Murphy looked like he wanted to help me into the hold headfirst—if his lowered brows and dark look in my direction could be believed.

"Bright as you are pretty, Miss," the Captain said as he knelt beside the hold. "We're overloaded, and it's slowing us down. Mr. Thomas has verified the bags of nitrate. The poundage had already been accounted for." Captain McQuistan stood up again to his full height. "It is perplexing."

"And dangerous if we hit a bad storm?" I persisted.

"I'll heave the lot over before I let anything happen to this ship."

As I wandered back to my cabin, I mused about the connection between a greedy trader eavesdropping in his fancy clothes, a murder, and the heavy contraband the *Passat* possibly carried. From the resentful look in the second mate's eyes, I could guess who had smuggled it aboard. But did that mean he had murdered the doctor?

After a cool sponge bath, I lay on my bunk and watched the sun prism through the stained-glass windows. Thoughts of New York and the cherry blossoms bordering the Potomac swam through my head, which led to thinking about Charles. Such a supremely prudish ass.

His letters resided in my trunk below a reserve of undergarments. Could I have been that romantic and silly? I grimaced, remembering I'd saved every one of them. Now, they embarrassed me. Clothes flew with stockings and shoes as I unearthed the bundles. Arms full, I went on deck thinking that for a rear-end of a donkey, Charles spent an inordinate amount of time writing.

As the first bundle sailed over the rail, I blinked away an unwanted tear of remembrance, but as each successive one pirouetted before plunking into the waves, the feeling changed; freedom from the past felt good. When the gulls arrived, they cawed their hunger, only to turn away in disappointment.

As the packets flew, I began to enjoy myself, going for distance. Just as I finished my task, a noise came from the stern. Another bundle, shrouded, sewn shut, and made heavy by weights—judging from the exertion of the sailors under it—was lifted to the rail.

At a signal from the first mate, the maritime pall bearers launched Doctor Rubio's remains into the sea. As the waves swallowed the offering, I met Browne's unreadable and unsmiling gaze. He didn't turn away. I did.

The sun sank slowly in the late afternoon, moving as if descending a celestial chain into the sea. This was the romanticism of the sea. The view appeared so changeable, and the water reflected a deep azure under the brilliant light. In any direction, the *Passat* appeared to be the only ship upon the waves. With each mile that passed, the morning's horror fell further behind, and to everyone's relief, the crew planned some sport.

They had rigged up a long tether and large hook that looked the more appalling for the size of a mouth that could swallow it. I appreciated being upwind of the hunk of souring beef the crew impaled on it. After a crewman flung it off the stern, we didn't sail five minutes more before a general cry went up, and the crew crowded to the stern.

A white shark, nearly as big as Browne and fatter than Mrs. Pentifax, thrashed on deck. Under dares from their mates, the liveliest of the sailors took turns trying to catch and subdue the powerful tail of the monster. Seconds more, and the hair on my arms tingled; Browne joined me, leaning against the rail. After minutes of his silent scrutiny, I said, "I hid the knife under my bunk."

"Maybe we should go look for it." His eyes twinkled, and he leaned a bit closer. "You know, most ladies talk about the weather or other such subjects." He stood up, blocking the sun.

"Maybe you shouldn't treat me so familiarly." I wished to hell he didn't look so good.

"How should I treat you? Like a murder suspect?"

"Why not?" I patted a yawn with my fan and showed him my back.

The shark flipped over and slid into the opposite rail with a loud thump. Razor-like teeth gleamed, and it flipped again, slapping the deck with eyes full of hate. A young crewman leapt over it, laughing.

"They're having trouble taming the shark."

"They're careful. If he catches a man just right, he'll break a leg or arm." Browne studied the tussle with a critical eye.

In another minute, a cheer went up, and the men swarmed over the shark. With a flash from a knife, blood spilled. I turned away. Blood had visited the ship this morning. Beside me, Browne's voice sounded as hard and impersonal as a stranger's. "Bloodsport is the same for the shark as it is for man." He waited until I faced him. "He'd have no mercy if you met, Miss Coulter." Over the top of my head, he watched his men and the shark. "It's what's in his gut that interests me."

"Why?" I could only see white entrails and blood oozing between the boots of the sailors.

"We find bottles, things half-eaten. Old shoes."

Or a bit of Doctor Rubio, I thought.

"Perhaps Doctor Rubio and the shark have something in common."

Minutes went by. We observed the disemboweling of the shark in silence, and I was beginning to think he would say no more when he said, "Did you know the doctor well, Miss Coulter?"

"No, he—"

"Then don't grieve too long. People die." He turned away.

A good exit line, but it was wasted. I had just remembered what I'd wanted to ask before Mrs. Pentifax's screams had stained the morning red.

"Mr. Browne."

"Yes." He pressed his lips together, but he couldn't hide his curiosity or his attraction. I felt it distinctly, recognizing his formality

as a caricature of intimacy. Cold would never describe him, but his
practical view of life had no soft edges.

"I've talked to the others. They don't remember anything about
the *séance*, and Mr. Morse won't discuss it."

"What do you want to know?" He sounded wary and tried to
hide it by not looking at me.

"What did you see last night?"

"Nothing." His lips barely moved.

"What do you mean, 'nothing'?"

"Just that. I saw nothing until you fainted."

I felt my face flush, a sure sign I wanted to smack him. "I didn't
faint. Did you hear anything?"

"Some."

I ground my teeth; I could swim to Brazil before this jackass
cooperated. "If that explosion, which you admitted hearing, wasn't
gunshots—what was it?"

Browne gazed toward the south, beyond the bow of the *Passat*.

"Have you ever seen ice, Miss Coulter? Fields of ice, larger than
ships? Bigger than islands? Sometimes they're submerged. There
are bergs that measure as long as trains." His voice lowered. "In a
strong current, they can race through the sea faster than a ship, and
you are dead before you ever see them." He'd been serious before,
but now he looked like he'd never smile again. "When ice breaks
apart, the sound is like the crack of gunshots."

"I've never heard this before."

He stared at the horizon and the scene he'd painted, not the
bright sundown of pinks and golds flooding the sky above the daz-
zling sea. "The sound can be heard for miles."

Chapter 13

Death is a comingling with time;
in the death of a good man,
eternity is seen looking through time
-Johann Wolfgang von Goethe

Near the Argentine Sea
Latitude 30°39' S, Longitude 48°05' W

Shaw worked. His thoughts remained dark as he coiled rigging, hauled buckets, and stacked and rolled canvasses. It had been a deliberate murder. Certain they hadn't washed all the boy's blood away from this morning's spectacle, he avoided the stern end of the ship. Above him, the skull and crossbones fluttered proudly above the crow's nest.

As he worked, he considered Peech and the crew of the *Hussar*. The details fit everything he knew of the missing ships in his investigation and what he had heard from that man Celwyn in London. Before that encounter, he had studied Lloyds' archives listing the stories and drawings of the pirate ships. The number of reports and the unexplained losses pointed to a singular form of malevolence.

One of the pirates pushed another one into him with a curse. God knows, Shaw saw the wickedness around him now—piracy was a scourge romanticized by folklore until seven score years ago, and it had flourished for centuries long before Christ. For a moment, he pictured himself as a bearded, sandal-wearing 13th-century detective sniffing out clues in Beirut's harbor.

Hours had passed since the punishment of the boy. Shaw didn't know if the lad had lived or died but assumed the latter. Every time he thought about it, Shaw relived his anger and helplessness. Was life worth so little? So fleeting? He tried to shake off his guilt for not stopping Farley and concentrated on what he could control.

Meanwhile, Peech had disappeared, probably to drink out of the blistering sun. The men on the afternoon watch went about their work, seemingly subdued. Long past three bells, the sun began to descend, a signal the horrid day would end soon. Or so Shaw thought.

A call echoed from high up the mizzenmast. On the mainmast, one of the sailors answered and signaled to the lookout. The effect was immediate; men ran across the decks and pounded up the stairs from their quarters below. Someone must have roused Peech from the salon. He stepped outside, slapped a crewman on the back, and squinted like a muscled rat just exposed to the day. Shaw winced as Peech swept by, calling, "Come along, Mr. Shaw—the game is afoot!"

Shaw hesitated, deciding where to hide. Borodin grabbed his arm and shoved him up the ladder behind Peech.

The view from the bridge encompassed the whole sea. This was the first time Shaw had seen the panorama in daylight. On the starboard side, the sea appeared flat, glimmering, and empty. Many leagues away rode a ship seeming like little more than a black speck upon the water. Shaw willed it to run as if the devil sailed behind her.

The mainmast creaked as the *Hussar* turned toward the other ship. On orders from Peech, Borodin and Farley competed with the flapping chains and the canvasses snapping in the wind. As the crew scurried and ran, Shaw gazed upward into the glare of the sun.

Down came the skull and crossbones. Up went the white and gold insignia on the flag of Portugal.

"Comin' about!" Peech yelled.

He backhanded a sailor out of his way, barking more orders down the deck. Shaw realized he watched the efficiency of the ship as something other than an instrument of plunder; she was an oiled and complex machine of destruction. As he spent more time on the *Hussar*, would he change? Would he lust for blood like them? The corruption of the ship nipped at his morality, and he didn't like it.

The *Hussar* gained on the other ship, cutting through high waves and rolling swells. Her speed came easy. She'd only been cruising before, and now she stalked her prey, running in hard.

Borodin appeared at Shaw's side and raised a spyglass. The other ship, also within range of a glass, had seen them. She started to turn tail, much too late.

Shaw squinted. Peech's quarry was a three-masted barkentine, her sails fresh and white even at a distance. Borodin thrust the glass into Shaw's arms and joined Peech at the helm. *Really?* Shaw stared at Borodin's back, trying to understand. One minute, they ridiculed him; the next, they included him in the *Hussar's* bloody business. He wondered at the complexity of his treatment from prisoner and valued property, to an experiment in moral corruption.

Aboard the fleeing ship, men scrambled up masts like frenzied ants, others swarmed the deck in seeming confusion. She only had two cannons near her bow, far fewer than she would need against the *Hussar*. Shaw brought the glass higher, scanning above her canvasses, to find her flag and painted insignia. On her stern, he spied her name, the *Ascencion*. The other ship made an about-face, heading due south. To his disgust, Shaw felt his blood heat with the chase. When he brought the glass down, Borodin's gaze penetrated his. Shaw looked away.

"Open it," Peech commanded. Borodin motioned to men who hovered near the bow to take up positions next to the winches. From under the *Hussar*, a grinding noise began, vibrating the entire ship. Shaw wondered what they were doing but was more concerned with what the other ship would do now.

With the spyglass, Shaw could make out the faces of the sailors and even the brass buttons of the uniformed officers on the *Ascencion's* bridge.

"Watch us, boyo!" Peech cried with a nasty kind of glee. Shaw jumped. From right beside him, Peech winked and slung an arm over Shaw's shoulders.

"There she is, Mr. Shaw, waiting for us."

"Did you know," Shaw ducked free of Peech, "she was out here?"

"You'd like to know, Mr. Bloody Lloyds of London." Peech laughed.

"Why—"

"I don't tell me secrets," Peech said and returned to the helm.

Shaw glanced back to the other ship. When they were still a league away, the *Ascencion* slowed and stopped. Hundreds of sailors clustered on her deck, and the ship's officers conferred on her bridge; they probably assumed they could reason with whoever pursued them. Poor bastards.

The runt and Borodin stood together at the *Hussar's* wheel, each of them representing Peech's tools of death. Farley killed men; Borodin killed ships.

When their prey lay dead in the water, Peech nodded to Borodin, who had the wheel. They moved forward; the ship's course corrected slightly north. Before, she had sailed to cut off the other ship; now, she headed directly toward them. Shaw assumed the *Ascencion* would be boarded, her hold looted of whatever Peech wanted, and her men taken prisoner.

The *Hussar* gathered speed. With a frown, Shaw glanced at Borodin and back to the scene. They were sailing too fast when they should have been slowing before the other ship. Shaw felt the blood drain from his face.

They were going to ram her.

He took a step toward the ladder leading down. Peech collared him and flung him against the wall of the bridge.

"Leaving already? I think not." Peech rested his belly over the bridge rail and winked at him as he swilled wine.

Orders rang out overhead. With his legs spread, Borodin gripped the helm, eyes on the other ship.

"Why?" Shaw yelled above the din. Across the waves, they faintly heard a cry that went up on the *Ascencion*.

Peech took a deep drag of wine and belched. The *Ascencion* grew larger as they closed in on her. The *Hussar* couldn't stop now.

Shaw braced himself on the rail. 'Why?" he repeated.

"She's empty." Peech shrugged.

"Then leave her be!"

"She's practice, boyo." Peech laughed. "Practice."

In the next few seconds, Shaw knew the faces of the fated sailors, young or old; he would remember them like this. He wanted to hide from it but couldn't tear his eyes away. Most of the men huddled on the bow, wide-eyed and terrified. Some kneeled, praying. They looked like his father, his brothers. *God.* Two men jumped over the side.

"Hold on, Mr. Shaw." As the tension on the *Hussar* climbed, Peech braced himself and threw his bottle over the rail. Shaw could only stare at the doomed men.

At the moment of impact, Borodin swung the helm hard to starboard, and the *Hussar* lifted her bow like a shark, turning teeth up for the kill. The impact was a thundering blow to the stern of the *Ascencion*, in turn shaking the pirate ship and jarring her mid-air until she hit the water again.

A flurry of orders rebounded across the decks as she came about, slowed, and turned for another pass. Shaw could see that it wouldn't be necessary.

With his fist raised high, Peech shouted, "Got her!"

The *Hussar* had ripped a gaping hole in the side of the *Ascencion*, and she gulped seawater.

The men aboard the other ship roared in disbelief and rage at the *Hussar*. Some couldn't move until they all began to at the same time. In less than a minute, the rending of the timbers from the other ship reached them, and she pointed her nose to the sky and started to go down. The men on her decks scrambled in all directions, holding on to anything they could find. On her hull, a ring of paler wood exposed above the water line gleamed like the white thighs of a woman.

The doomed sailors jumped and fell into the water, leaving behind the captain of the *Ascencion* as he stood alone on the bridge, somber and at attention, his uniform pristine in the sun. He faced the *Hussar*. To Shaw, it seemed like he stared at Peech, unerringly knowing his nemesis.

A belated chill covered Shaw, and he whispered to the captain of the *Ascension*, "Do something. Don't bloody well just stand there."

With a rolling, sucking noise heard loudly across the waves, the sea displaced the air in the other ship's hold. The vessel jerked downward, and, like a wooden doll, flung the captain of the dying ship off the bridge and into the sea. Over the screams of hundreds of men, the ship sank under the waves in the afternoon sun.

Peech leaned close. Shaw smelled the musty scent of sexual release. Repulsed, he backed away.

Farley stood on a short spar above the *Hussar's* bow, waving a triumphant arm, dancing, and swooping like Neptune's elf of destruction. Borodin remained beside the helm and scanned the surface between the ships. The shadows on the bridge kept Shaw from reading much of Borodin's face—no regret or triumph, and he didn't want to come close enough to see his eyes.

In less than three minutes, the *Ascencion* had disappeared, all hands lost. Sated, the *Hussar* resumed course due south. As they passed the wreckage, Shaw descended to the main deck and leaned over the rail, searching for pale faces floating in the debris, but seeing nothing but blue water.

He shivered, feeling much colder than the sea and more helpless than the crew of the *Ascension* had been. He should have known what Peech would do.

He should have done something.

CHAPTER 14

Boiled potatoes, a piece of gristly meat, and a not quite stale biscuit—again. Shaw stared at it for minutes, knowing he couldn't eat. He held onto the cup of tea and dumped the rest over the side, aware, as always, that his movements were watched. As he walked to the stern, he thought of the afternoon's carnage and again wallowed in his guilt and cowardice.

Even though he couldn't have prevented it, surely, he could have rendered some damage. A shove over the side would have done for some of the pirates. Even better if he could have maneuvered Farley, Peech, or Borodin out of sight for a second until it was done.

Richard Shaw, a murderer? Yes. He relived the faces of the doomed sailors before the impact and the tearing of the *Ascencion's* hull. There was moral justice in murder. Murder to prevent murder. He should have acted.

A few feet away from the stern, the red tip of Borodin's cigar glowed in the dark. Of the three, Borodin fascinated and repulsed him the most. Shaw also feared him the most. The skeleton man smoked quietly, half turned toward the sea. Thousands of stars and a full moon decorated a clear sky, reflecting silver light across a glassy surface. Shaw stood by the rail a few feet from Borodin, inhaling the clean scent of brine in the still air. The wind had deserted them, and the *Hussar* lay stagnant and drifting idly, a sleeping monster ready to gobble the unwary.

His thoughts turned melancholy. What if they never made it through Cape Horn? He sighed. Even if they did, security would be strong if the pirates cruised into port or dropped anchor in any bay. They'd lock him up. Unless, of course, Peech planned something particularly foul and wanted him to watch while he fed on his abhorrence like a hungry ghoul.

Shaw sighed. It could be months before an opportunity came. Very little happened on the southern coast of Brazil this time of year. As far as he knew, there were no American settlements or any from the other seafaring nations. Few of the islands boasted inhabitants, and the pirates could dally in these waters to give Lloyds in London time to answer the ransom, probably entertaining themselves by picking off other ships while they waited. Then the *Hussar* would cross over to the Pacific. She'd sail up the coast of Chile before Shaw had a chance of escape.

At that point, he wondered if he would die. Lloyds had experienced extortion attempts before. Shaw didn't know if they had paid them. Even if they did, the pirates had no obligation to let him go.

In the water a few feet from the hull, moonlight reflected on a school of silvery fish. They swam in groups, clustered in a cloud, and exploded in different directions. Shaw leaned over the rail in time to see the last of them swim downward. When the deeper water agitated, they rushed to the surface again. Something down there appeared to be hungry.

Borodin, as motionless as Farley was twitchy, slid over to stand beside him. The smell of his cigar dissolved into the salt air, and after a minute, he spoke.

"Life ends, begins, and ends again." He puffed a few times before tossing the butt in an arc to sizzle in the water.

"Is that your excuse for what happened today?" Shaw asked.

"If you like." Borodin shrugged.

The more Shaw thought about it, the angrier he became. To Borodin, the men of the *Ascencion* were like the silver fish, swimming from death. "You cannot justify what this ship did." He heard his voice quivering. "You cannot!"

Borodin's chuckle sounded soft and menacing. "But we can." His words sent a cold shiver through Shaw. "And we *are* death, Mr. Shaw. Do not mistake that."

"You are bloody murderers."

"If you like." Borodin sounded bored, focusing again on the water.

Like a hand drew a glittering wand through the depths, long swirls of phosphorescence passed under the *Hussar*. Darker shadows, ominous in size and indistinct in shape, passed through it. The shadows ranged from the size of a table to half the length of the ship. As they watched, the disturbance gathered into a mass and moved a few hundred feet east, where it solidified and brightened, shimmering violently. It became a sparkling storm under the water.

"Squid," Borodin said.

The school of squid must be enormous to produce so much iridescence, Shaw thought. The underwater light fractured into a myriad of pearlized colors that moved swiftly upward through the black water. The sea churned. Currents didn't react that way; life and death battled just below the waterline. Shaw assumed more entertainment for Borodin.

More death, too.

The agitation increased, and the sea rocked with high swells and indistinct shadows. The iridescence blossomed and exploded in spray as a sperm whale, jaws locked onto a giant squid, broke the surface, and rose out of the water. The whale curved into a halfmoon, coming down on top of the squid with a tremendous splash.

Like lovers, they flipped over, and the squid wrapped itself around its enemy in a ferocious embrace. With suckers bigger around than a barrel, the squid clung to the hide of the whale as the monsters thrashed on the surface.

Under the moonlight, the foot-long teeth of the whale gleamed as the creature sunk them into the squid's body, securing its hold. With the light from the *Hussar's* lanterns, Shaw could see details; the black saucer-like eye of the squid reflected intelligence and a distinct malevolence.

"Squid's more than twenty years to be that big." Borodin lit another cigar, his eyes alive and keen, fixed on the combatants. Shaw half turned. In the last few minutes, most of the pirates had crowded the deck to watch. He shivered and gazed at the sea again.

The monsters still thrashed in the water, and the squid's splinter-like mouth bothered Shaw in its simplicity and ugliness. The whale held on, massive jaws squeezing the squid as the monsters began to sink under the surface, locked in a death struggle, causing the churning water to roll into the *Hussar*. With a last violent splash, they descended to the infinite depths, still trailing luminescence.

Shaw walked the deck, exhilarated by the aquatic battle yet troubled by his fascination with it. It seemed easy to make moral connections between the pirates and the violence of the sea, which led to wondering how he would die. Would he drown? Worse fates floated through his head, keeping him from his dank cabin and sleep. He paused beside the salon.

Through the open door, he spied Captain Peech holding forth under a cluster of smoking lanterns and surrounded by sycophantic drunks. At the other end of the table, Farley and half a dozen pirates poured wine onto themselves and the others while they sang and caroused. Shaw moved on.

When he reached the prow, he stopped in front of the bowsprit to lean over the side. If he jumped in, would the promise of the ransom be worth the trouble to fish him out again? He started to turn away and then stopped.

A few feet below the waterline extended a wide-ribbed wooden horn plated with iron. It measured three dozen feet long and resembled the curved horn of an enormous metallic bull. The horn and the area around it were plated in heavy steel. It took a second, then Shaw understood. He gazed at Peech's method of punching a fatal hole in a ship; it must be especially frightening if the *Hussar* had her nose in the air as she bore down upon her prey. She'd look like a demon from hell.

Shaw sighed. He remembered some of Farley's babbling. If his boasting rang true, the reported lost ships could be accounted for. Peech collected the flags of each ship he plundered—his "trophies." The ones he didn't board, like the *Ascencion*, were "practice."

Shaw strolled to stand under the forecastle, the raucous sounds of gambling and tinkling of broken bottles raining down from curtainless windows. Shaw's boots crunched on glass as he passed the entrance to the crew's quarters below deck. In the dismal mood he swam in, he didn't know what to do. Killing himself was an option he'd only just begun to toy with.

A faint cry came, so very foreign to the ship. It made Shaw's heart hesitate. He recalled the screams he'd dreamt the first night on board.

Again, the scream came, longer, drawn out in pure pain.

It was a woman's scream.

Shaw grabbed the hand rope and swung down steep stairs, stopping at the mouth of a dark passage. Something small with sharp nails scrabbled across the wooden boards, butted his ankle, and ran on. As his eyes adjusted, another scream provided an audible beacon, sending him to the corridor on the right. The stench of feces, urine, and decaying vermin curdled the air.

Like creeping into a cave, he groped his way down the companionway, led by voices and the shadows that moved in front of the light spilling into the corridor ahead. The coarse laughter grew louder, then a series of thuds and whoops of excitement.

Shaw hesitated outside the open door, at first unnoticed by anyone. Pirates stood and squatted everywhere. Some slept. Others leaned against walls smoking and cuddling wine bottles. Shaw stepped over the legs of a snoring pirate and into the room. To his left, tiers of hammocks lined the walls, piled with bottles, clothes, and more pirates. A cloud of musty sex pervaded the room, and a single lantern smoked, swaying with the rocking of the ship. The light fell on the woman chained to the wall.

An iron-like hand gripped Shaw's arm, and another hand gripped his neck, propelling him out of the room and stumbling along the dank companionway. When Shaw pulled free, Borodin pinned him against the wall to whisper, "You can't help her now, any more than you could have a week ago." He shoved Shaw forward again. "Move!" The pirates nearby scrambled out of the way as Borodin herded Shaw back toward the stairs.

"You can't kidnap a woman and—"

"But we can, you pansy ass," from the corridor just ahead came Peech's snarl, startling Shaw.

As Borodin propelled Shaw to the stairs, Peech walked with them. "Mr. Shaw, no heroics. The men would carve you up in little pieces before they'd let you take away their toy. And boyo," Peech laughed, "there's always a line down there for the entertainment."

Shaw didn't wonder at what Peech had just said. Not at all. It was enough that he again displayed so little regard for human suffering. For life. They followed him up the stairs, where Peech motioned at a pair of pirates to stand guard in front of the passageway.

"Just so you don't get to thinking like a hero, Mr. Shaw," Peech said as he swaggered away. The echo of the woman's last scream trailed after him, turning into a torrent in a language Shaw couldn't decipher. He wasn't sure, but he thought Borodin had flinched at her words.

Shaw asked, "What did she say?"

Borodin swung Shaw against the rail.

"She cursed us, Mr. Shaw. She cursed us to Hell."

Unlike Peech, it appeared Borodin took curses seriously.

CHAPTER 15

BEFORE THE DRAKE PASSAGE
Latitude 58°07' S, Longitude 68°25' W

Becalmed.

In my imagination, and for all appearances, the *Passat* floated like a lonely bubble in a vast bathtub.

For two days, we'd waited. All hands watched the sea, a glassy turquoise plain that stretched as far as anyone could see. Clouds squatted on the eastern horizon, and to the south, they clustered thickly, without their white fluffiness and their dense masses unbroken.

In the last twenty-odd hours, all the ship's brass had been polished, the sails mended, the decks sanded and cleaned. Since there was nothing else to do, the crew resorted to fishing. I rather wished I could do the same, but alas, being dressed in a corset, bloomers, blue silk dress, bustle, three petticoats, blue suede and ostrich feathered hat, stockings, and other accessories—such as ribbons and powder—I knew it for a lost campaign.

I did learn something. The larger fish that swam in the upper regions disliked salted pork as bait. The crew lamented this fact loudly, but the chief steward would spare nothing else until we'd entered the Atlantic. Mrs. Pentifax had already started complaining about the food. I suspected that she would be complaining more before we sailed into Rio.

The fishing activity took place near the stern. With the disbelieving looks I'd received from the Bosun when I suggested I could participate fresh in mind, I had left them to it and hustled off to the bow. Upon arrival, I found Christian Morse leaning over the rail and, as usual, closed-mouthed. Since the night of the *séance*, he stared at and through me and declined to carry on a lengthy conversation. Could he suspect me of murdering Doctor Rubio? I wondered. Or did he dislike me? Either way, he made it plain he would not talk of the parlor game that we had all participated in.

Not to be stymied, I had sought the opinion of the others. After dinner the previous night, I'd asked Jessica what she remembered of the *séance*; her response wasn't enlightening. Today her reply was, "Nothing but a great deal of noise." Less helpful was her aunt's insistence she had seen the actress Eliza Logan holding a monkey in a gold dress. She also said she thought there were supernatural forces telling her of danger on the ship. A little more port and Mrs. Pentifax would be seeing sea monsters.

Today, under a strong sun and the windless panorama, none of my suspicions about the murder and the other passengers made much sense. I turned my gaze across the water to where the sky met the sea. "Nice weather," I said.

"Yes, it is," Morse replied.

That social chore done, I draped myself over the bow.

The current moved sluggishly by the ship, and the light color of the sea indicated we floated in shallow water. An iron chain, with links bigger than my hand, looped off one of the unused gunwales. It dipped into the water and returned like an aquatic garland to the next gunwale.

"Aren't those interesting?" I pointed to the tiny silver-sided fish that swam in and out of the links of the chain.

Morse shrugged and said, "Look over there." With a finger, he indicated the area about twenty feet off the starboard side. A small flotilla of tiny sea creatures advanced toward us. I raised my brows at Morse.

"Argonauts." They sported miniature sails, the effect like an army of fairy-like ships. "A type of mollusk." He explained, "They float their shells and extend a foot up to catch breezes too small for us to notice."

"How do you know this?"

Morse's superior expression bloomed. "Biology studies at university. And a few years ago, I glimpsed some off the Fiji Islands." He nodded toward the mollusks. "The argonauts signal many more days without wind."

With that encouraging remark, I left him, retreating to the coolness of my cabin. With the absence of a breeze during the day, the temperature had gone up again, and the sun made me sleepy. I drew the curtains, dimming the room to shadows and muted colors. After placing my dress over a chair and removing my boots, I lay on the bunk and closed my eyes.

In my dream, Captain McQuistan changed into a young and vibrant man. Gone was his querulous voice. Windows rattled when he spoke. He towered over the sailors who'd shrunk to the size of mice, and his hair grew longer until it billowed upward in the wind and wrapped around the masts. The tiny crewmen jabbered back...

With a shudder, I awakened, certain another piece of the puzzle had fallen into place. But I could no longer remember it. My watch said that only twenty minutes had elapsed, more than enough time to frighten myself.

I dressed quickly and went back on deck, unwilling to be alone.

Hours later, after arranging my hair as artfully as I could for dinner, I admired my silhouette in the looking glass, turning this way and that. My costume appeared elegant but subdued. Sometimes, clothes represent a controlled glimpse of the wearer's personality, showing the world exactly what you want them to know, and no more.

I stepped inside the salon and let the door close behind me with a bang. For the most part, the passengers were pie-eyed. They seemed to be having a wonderful time laughing and smiling as if nothing had happened to one of us. Dwelling on the tragedy wouldn't bring the doctor back. I knew that. But what about decorum and respect?

Mrs. Pentifax was inebriated enough to ignore the cook's swarthy features and working clothes as she tried to engage him in a waltz. Angelo smiled nervously and sidestepped her while he attempted to set the dinner table. The old woman giggled, then wiggled, and every time he turned around, she tried to entice him with a full drink and a view of her cleavage.

The music inspiring Mrs. Pentifax came from the diminutive pianoforte beside the bar. Higgins would play a few notes, take a gulp from his brandy, and pluck at the melody again until he would stop altogether mid-stanza and use both hands to light a cigar.

The second mate, Daniel Murphy, had cleaned up handsomely, and he smirked as he danced with Jessica, holding her closely. From her pained expression, I didn't think she appreciated his familiarity, or perhaps she did not want to cause a fuss by objecting. Later, I'd berate myself for not seeing the situation for what it was.

Meanwhile, Christian Morse had accosted Browne, and he pointed to the spots on the world map that we'd discussed the first night out. When Browne tried to move away, Morse talked faster, jabbing his finger at something in the lower hemisphere. Browne shrugged. That shrug could infuriate a nun, but it didn't stop me from wondering what Morse talked about. The medium downed the rest of his drink in one swallow and glared at Browne's profile beside him.

I hadn't yet invented a good enough reason to join them when Captain McQuistan entered the salon. The passengers disengaged from the crew, and dinner got underway. As the Captain pushed my chair in, I caught his brooding glance and understood his thoughts—*you don't celebrate murder.*

When the soup arrived, Murphy left us to man the evening watch. Browne sat across from me between Mrs. Pentifax and Higgins. The first officer appeared freshly shaven and smelled of lemons. I noted a dimple, usually hidden in a day's beard, now visible when he smiled. Inwardly, I sighed. This would be a long voyage.

The dinner conversation, over grilled halibut and probably the last green vegetables, turned to travel. I noticed everyone carefully avoided the subject of Doctor Rubio. Each person, except Browne, seemed anxious to keep the conversation from lagging. They could have simply acknowledged the event and faced the fact that someone malevolent traveled with the *Passat.* Perchance, the killer sat with us at the table.

With that pleasant thought, the dinner conversation continued.

"The gambling ships of the Orient are renowned for their tables and fantastic stakes. I have made the trip twice." Morse buttered a roll and went on, "The last time, we stopped in the Philippines. Some of the islands are quite uncivilized."

"Why?" Mrs. Pentifax asked, and she backhanded her water glass. Jessica righted it and sopped up the water.

"The natives remember too much of the Spanish occupation, and they can be a bit hostile." Morse shuddered delicately.

"Did they attack you?" Jessica's eyes widened.

"Err... no. However, a volcano erupted."

"Please tell us about it, Mr. Morse," Browne continued to eat, eyes on his plate. I spied the amusement he thought he'd hidden.

"It was nothing. Really," Morse murmured.

Then why talk about it? I wasn't in the mood for social games. Murder put me in a temper. If I had brought a book to read, I could have taken meals in my cabin and read about torrid encounters or my favorite—ghost stories.

At the urging of Jessica, Morse acquiesced. "We had stopped for a short layover while the ship was refit from the crossing. As you know, a volcanic eruption is a fascinating spectacle. One night the ground shook so hard I fell out of my hammock and found myself tangled in the mosquito netting." He smiled around the table. "I looked like one of those Egyptian mummies."

I couldn't help a glance at Browne, thinking of what I could do to him if he was tied up like a mummy. He grinned right back at me. I flushed. Damned if he couldn't read my mind. I turned away and shifted my chair to face Morse.

"In California, *we* experienced an earthquake," Mrs. Pentifax announced. "More than one."

Morse upped the pace of his story. He was used to the social stage and had no intention of sharing it. "The eruption we experienced was followed by the cries and shouts from the villagers. I ran outside and could *not* believe what I saw."

"And what was that?" Browne asked dryly.

Morse squared his shoulders. "Red rivers of lava oozing from the top of the mountain against a starless night. Smoke from the burning jungle." His voice rose theatrically as he relived his adventure. "Screeching monkeys. The villagers running. Lions roaring." He eyed Mrs. Pentifax, challenging her to top his account.

"I didn't think there were lions on those islands." As I spoke, Morse shot me an annoyed glance.

"What did you do?" Jessica asked.

Morse colored a bit. "We helped all we could."

"What did you do?" Browne pounced.

"We, ah ... decamped for the ship."

I suppressed a chuckle. He probably scampered for the ship with his bum hanging out the back of his nightshirt.

"Excuse me." Higgins cleared his throat. "I have a question for the Captain."

I had forgotten the Captain, and from the way Jessica and Morse turned to look at him at the head of the table, they also had. He hadn't said anything since sitting down, just gesturing to have his glass steadily refilled and listening to the conversation.

"Yes, Mr. Higgins?" The Captain leaned back, his plate cleaner than the rest, except for Mrs. Pentifax's.

"Have you finished questioning the crew?"

"Yes, I have," Captain McQuistan replied.

"And do you, ah, have a suspect?" Higgins blinked rapidly as he spoke, and his index finger beat a tattoo on the tablecloth.

"No, Sir." The Captain's eyes met each of the passengers as he scanned the table. "The murderer of Doctor Rubio still walks among us."

After dinner, I strolled the deck. The wind had finally picked up at sundown, and we ran at full sail, trying to catch what gusts we could before darkness completely smothered us. Even in my warmest cape, I shivered; each successive night would be colder as the ship neared Antarctica.

Despite the gaiety and intimacy of dinner, the atmosphere aboard the *Passat* seemed out of balance. Along with the murder, a vague sense of an awaiting catastrophe hung like a singular black cloud above the masts; I felt it wherever I went on the ship. The Horn would be a challenge. It would be nice if the ship met it at top form, with all the spirits on her at rest and the hands aboard her empty of knives.

Again, I pondered every word spoken, any act or hint of malevolence that might account for what happened, and couldn't think of a thing. The victim could have engraved his epitaph, "A Jolly Man Whom No One Noticed." I groaned aloud. Why hadn't I taken smaller boats up the coast to Panama and crossed to the Atlantic by land?

From the forecastle came the conversations of the crew while they played cards. Maritime law decreed that sailors did not use crude words and that their pastimes remained innocent enough for church. Those working on the *Passat* lived up to this code and seemed like a wonderful group of men. I ventured further along the boards until I stood under the bridge where the helmsman and another crewman moved about in the quarter house, both silhouetted against a full moon.

As the bite of the wind increased, I huddled in the shadows between the main bulkheads, isolated from the rest of the ship. Beyond our running lights, the blackness of the night and sea spread far, broken only by the bits of foam riding the waves. Old sailors called them the Captain's daughters. I wondered how many more days it would be until we sighted Cape Horn.

My uncle maintained that navigation was a chancy business because of too many inaccurate maps and questionable instruments. Even correct measurements of stars and navigation points sometimes did not help. Tonight, the stars winked benignly from a clear sky. Tomorrow? The ship could be off course by hundreds of miles.

"No!"

Jessica.

"NO—" The cut-off cry came from near the bow. I stumbled over a coil of rope and ran forward. At first, I couldn't see anything, then heard panting and sounds of a skirmish, followed by a thud. Out of the gloom, Jessica's pale face hovered like a small moon surrounded by a dark form large enough to pick her up and throw her over the side.

"Stop!" I yelled as I looked for a weapon.

The shadowy figure pushed Jessica to the deck and turned to run. He took two steps before an even bigger shadow flung him against the rail.

I flinched as Browne backhanded him, using one hand then the other, hounding him down the length of the ship. There was enough light to see Daniel Murphy's hungry eyes and the long scratch that zigzagged down his cheek.

Jessica sobbed. I helped her up.

"Come, we'll go clean you up." I urged her toward the cabins. There was no need to ask what had happened.

"I don't—"

"Yes, you do," I insisted as I hustled her along. "Your aunt's a snob, but after this morning, she needs none of this." I eyed the smudges on Jessica's face, the torn dress, and tears. "We'll say nothing to her. Agreed?"

Once inside my cabin, I pinned her hair into place as the younger woman began to cry.

"He asked me ... he wanted to kiss me." She wept. "I'm eighteen years old. I've never," Jessica sniffed, "been kissed. I thought it was time." She ended her admission with a wail loud enough to wake her aunt. "He tried to t-t-take advantage of me."

Feeling much older than my twenty-six years, I could have told her that perhaps it is *never* time.

CHAPTER 16

You never enjoy the world aright,
till the sea itself floeth in your veins,
till you are clothed with the heavens
and crowned with the stars.
-Thomas Traherne

"You are missing something, Ladies."

Captain McQuistan spoke quietly from his position near the bow. He and several of the crew had gathered along the starboard rail.

I removed the hat covering my face and sat up. Judging from the angle of the sun, it was nearly noon. Jessica yawned and rose from the deck chair to my left. On the next chair over, Mrs. Pentifax continued to snore. Thank God she didn't sleep in my cabin. Nothing had been said to her aunt about last night, and Jessica wanted to keep it that way. She also promised to not wander the deck alone at night.

We joined the Captain at the rail. Below us, four of the crew had gotten into a skiff as it was lowered into the water. Without much wind, the skiff landed smoothly, and the sailors began to row.

The sea resembled a lake, and the setting sun split the glass-like surface with a wide, golden band. At first, I didn't see anything. But, by following the Captain's directions, I spied something about an eighth of a league to the west. It floated in the middle of the shimmering sunlight and appeared to be a gray lump, perhaps a rock. I squinted but couldn't tell exactly. There are those who'd say I needed spectacles, but I did not plan to wear them.

"It looks like a turtle," Jessica remarked. "A very large turtle."

The *Passat* drifted closer, and I studied the gray shape until I could discern its head and make out the splayed feet. It moved up and down in gentle rhythm with the current as the skiff edged toward it. The sailors rowed with vigor but dipped their oars quietly. In the next minute, I felt the hair on my neck rise. Sure enough, Browne stood behind me and spoke over the top of my head. "Turtles dive if they're spooked. This one looks a good five hundred pounds. Be a shame if they lose it; we could use the meat for the ship's larder."

"Why didn't you row out there with them?" I asked.

"I've done it a dozen times. Let someone else have a turn."

As we watched, the skiff drifted to a stop less than half a ship's length from the turtle. Two of the sailors began swinging a loop of rope above their heads, mimicking the vaqueros in Texas.

One of them let fly the lasso. It landed in front of the turtle, and he yanked on it until the rope encircled the turtle's head and front flipper. The second loop fell short of the turtle by several feet. The third lasso hit its mark, surrounding the turtle's left rear foot. To the cheers of everyone crowding the deck, the sailor pulled it taut. The turtle thrashed and pulled, and the sailors held steady. The turtle flipped over on its back.

"Yes!" The Captain shouted. "Good work, men!"

The crew secured the lines to the boat and began rowing back to the ship.

Browne left us to supervise the landing of the turtle. If we hadn't needed the meat to feed us all, I'd have been more upset to see such a majestic beast of the sea captured. In this instance, there was a point to the hunt. After it had been hauled aboard, Jessica and I remained at the rail under the shade of her parasol. A few minutes more, and she sighed. "The longer we're out here, the happier I am. Maybe it's the sound of the waves or being alone. It soothes me."

I smiled. "But it doesn't offer many social opportunities, and I thought you were anxious to reach Rio?" If she chose not to talk more about last night's incident, I would respect that. In fact, her next statement showed remarkable resiliency.

"Oh." Jessica's eyes twinkled. She confided, "I'll have plenty of time for that if I can escape my chaperones." She glanced at Mrs. Pentifax, who continued to snore like a stevedore. "But I do feel happy out here. It's hard to explain."

"I'll just be delighted when we arrive in Rio," I said. Though the romance of the sea could not be denied. Just as peach pie is good the first few times, after that, a trifle with fresh raspberries would be nice. And a hot bath. To conserve fuel, we were limited to one hot bath a week, and the rest of our toilet had to make do with cold seawater. I scratched my side just thinking about it.

"Yes." Jessica held her bottom lip between her teeth. "I can't help but think of this as an adventure. The other times I've sailed— it has been."

"How so?"

She leaned over the side, staring into the fathomless water. "The first time, I was swimming off a yacht on the Maine coast. I swam further than I should have. And then I almost drowned." She glanced at me, and her voice turned earnest. "But it didn't frighten me, and it should have. There were beautiful fish everywhere ... I was not afraid."

"What happened?"

"The other swimmers pulled me up to the surface." Jessica gazed to where the water met the haze on the horizon. After a moment, she confessed more to herself than me, "It was almost like I didn't want to come back. Perhaps it had something to do with my dreams."

"What dreams?" I glanced at her aunt, wondering what she'd think of Jessica's notions.

She shrugged, and a faint blush tinted her cheeks. "I sometimes wonder if I wouldn't be happier down there." She nodded at the water, and her blush deepened. "Don't mind me."

"Hmmn." I couldn't think of anything to say. It was a strange confession from an apparently balanced young woman.

"Of course, I'm glad they found me," Jessica added with a sheepish smile. Somehow, I didn't quite believe that she welcomed the rescue, but considering it was a past event and not likely to be repeated, I didn't dwell on it.

"I am, too. What about the other time you sailed?"

The hesitation was longer this time, and the silence broken by the regular snorts and noises coming from Mrs. Pentifax's lounge chair.

"You appear to be remembering more," I prompted her.

"Yes. A friend I grew up with, a man that I had hoped to marry, was killed at sea."

"I am so sorry!" It wasn't hard to spot the tears brimming in her eyes.

Jessica tried to shrug away the emotion. "James was near Barbados when their yacht was attacked by pirates. A survivor described the horrific incident." She paused, probably replaying the scene in her thoughts to keep from crying.

I decided to change the subject. "What about the other time you sailed?"

Jessica brushed her hair back, and another moment went by before she spoke. "The second time, I fell off a boat. Thankfully, it was anchored. A stiff breeze caught me at a low rail, and over I went."

"These skirts are like kites in a wind." I lifted a handful of skirts and petticoats.

"Yes, they are." Jessica again stared into the sea, the color deepening in the afternoon shadow from the *Passat*. "This time, the water felt *right*. Welcoming. I can't explain it," she said quietly. "I didn't want to come back. I *belonged* down there." She shot me a look. "It is unlikely I'll ever find a man to marry who understands this. Most people want to breathe air, not water." She tried to smile. "They say I fought the crewmen who rescued me." She shivered and glanced over her shoulder. "Please don't tell my aunt."

I kept a sympathetic look on my face. Strange longings meant nothing new. Nor vivid imaginations running amok like a fairy tale in overly romantic natures. I had no intention of repeating this to Auntie.

"Of course not," I assured her and patted her arm. "Just make sure you don't fall in now. I'm going to take a nap before dinner."

Just as I passed Mrs. Pentifax, the old woman turned on her side, leaving her face partially exposed to the rays. Baby whales looked about the same as they sunned themselves. It took a moment to adjust the umbrella attached to the back of her chair until the old woman snored in the shade again.

As I went along the deck, I deduced this must be free time for the crew since few of them appeared to be on deck. Overhead, Browne moved around on the bridge, and beside him, the white locks of the Captain's hair cut into the gloom of the shadows. Forty feet up, the crew in the canvasses shouted back and forth at each other as I arrived at my cabin and yanked the door open.

"What?!"

Herr Higgins whirled. He'd been bent double with both hands in my traveling trunk.

I stood between him and the open door. For a stout man, he could move fast. He shoved me sideways onto the bed and stopped in the doorway.

"It's your word against mine, Miss Coulter. You see, I *wasn't* here."

"Excuse me, you *are* here!" I got to my feet.

"I'll deny it!"

"What were you looking for?" I saw he'd mixed my intimate clothes with my shoes and toilet articles. A perfume bottle lay on its side atop the bureau.

"If you must know, a bloody knife!" Higgins hissed and slammed the door behind him.

I collapsed on the bed. I didn't believe him. The periodicals I'd brought along lay opened and scattered in the mess. He was looking for something else. But what? I picked up one of my petticoats from the floor and saw he'd trampled it and torn the lace. Damn the man!

Worse, he was right. It would be his word against mine.

In contrast to the previous evening, dinner that night regained some sanity, and the gaiety remained civilized and subdued.

The Captain and Browne arrived early, either to observe murder suspects or because they desired our company. Mrs. P, with her puffy eyes and general air of being exposed to bad weather, sported a doozy of a hangover, having spent the latter part of the afternoon cradling a port bottle. Aware of the old lady's tendency to become overly familiar, Angelo kept his distance on his trips to and from the galley. Meanwhile, I didn't restrain myself from directing malevolent looks in Higgins's direction.

Tonight, Browne had been seated to my left, Christian Morse to my right. It would be impossible to ignore Browne, and I felt his presence as distinctly as if he brushed fingertips from my shoulder to wrist. It seemed my attraction to him worsened with each passing day. I sighed; *damn it*. He probably trolled for women in the exotic ports he visited, dress whites enhancing his tanned skin. I imagined him kissing other women. Despite that unpleasant thought, I could just imagine the look in his eyes if I allowed him to take me in his arms.

Then I realized I'd been leaning toward the first mate and hastily turned toward the head of the table.

"Attention, please." The Captain tapped his water glass with a spoon, and for the moment, some of the worry dissipated from his eyes.

"Ladies and Gentlemen." He winked at Angelo as he wheeled in the serving cart with a broad smile. "It is said that green turtles are part fish, part fowl, part flesh." The Captain waved a goblet of port, its vivid color rivaling the rose of his cheeks. "Green turtle soup, à la Sir Angelo."

Clouds of spicy aroma blended into the swirls of steam. One sip and I agreed with the others. Angelo should be knighted.

After dinner, Angelo began clearing the table for the passengers' nightly game of bridge and socializing as the Captain retired.

"Count me out." Higgins waved his cigar like he shooed flies. He had remembered to light the cigar before settling near me on the couch. Without making too much of a show of it, I moved away. The man repulsed me.

Again, I wondered what he had stashed in the hold of the ship and what he thought he could pilfer from my room. Until this afternoon, his antics had been none of my business. Just a tidbit for my curiosity. For that matter, I also wondered about the picture of John Greely in Morse's room that I wasn't supposed to know about.

"I want to write a letter. To California." Jessica arose and kissed her aunt on the cheek. Courier service in the lower Americas had a reputation for haphazardness. Once posted in Rio, it would be months—if ever—before the letter arrived, but perhaps Jessica did not know it. "Good night." Jessica excused herself and accepted her wrap from Browne. I eyed her critically, perhaps maternally. If the girl harbored any nervousness from the event last night, she did not show it.

"I'll walk you to your cabin." Morse prepared to rise out of politeness; I doubted he knew of last night's incident.

"No, thank you." Jessica refused, tilting her chin a little higher than normal. She intended to brave it out.

Browne, under the premise of needing air, made a point of watching her walk the deck to her door. I caught a nod from him, ascertaining she was safely inside. We had talked little of last night, mostly agreeing to keep an eye on Jessica. Browne had grimly assured me the second mate would not dare to repeat his offense.

I wasn't so sure. There's a look of appreciation, or lust, if you will, in a man's eye. In Browne's expression, his perusal of me smoldered—but with moralistic restraint. From what I'd seen of Daniel Murphy's countenance each time he beheld Jessica, he was a wolf eyeing a particularly tasty sheep.

Jessica may have decided on a quiet evening, but her aunt seemed revived by dinner. She'd eaten enough to revive several people.

Her small piggy eyes settled on the psychic. "You'll be my bridge partner, Mr. Morse." Her tone left no room for argument. No visible signs of a hangover remained, and she was as pushy as ever. As she shuffled the cards, I realized I was beginning to like the old lady.

I raised a brow at Browne. His shrug said he supposed he could put up with me to win a card game.

As play went along, I could not fault him. He finessed, as I already knew he could. He also played cards well. Early in the game, we could see Mrs. Pentifax wouldn't benefit from Morse's psychic talent. Either he didn't care or hadn't turned it on. She accepted defeat by tipping the sherry bottle steadily. When we reached the last game, she listed to the side, her head on the first mate's shoulder. I would have suspected her of looking at his cards, but when she did sit up, she'd blurt, "Three hearts..." every time and sag again.

A little before midnight, I arranged pillows on the sofa while Browne and Morse transported Mrs. Pentifax to it, shuffling under the load. "Three hearts and sweet dreams, Mrs. P," I told her and tucked a shawl around her shoulders. We'd collectively decided against transporting such a load all the way to her cabin.

As I reached for my wrap, I found the-never-too-far-away Mr. Browne by my side.

"I would be honored to escort you about the deck, Miss Coulter."

"Thank you," I replied. I could walk myself, but I had questions to ask him, and this made an opportunity for privacy.

His hands lingered a bit too long as he draped my cloak across my shoulders. I stepped back and gave him a look, aware of the speculative eyes of Higgins and Morse from their positions across the room.

A three-quarter moon worshipped by clusters of tiny stars hung high in the heavens. Moonlight silvered the water, the deck, and Browne's face as we stood at the lee side rail. Without the miasma of sexuality that enveloped him, I could have mistaken his impassive profile for that of a statue.

"Your throat appears to have healed."

Browne's deep baritone affected me favorably when I allowed it to do so.

"I'm fine, thank you," I said.

"Yes, you are."

Inches away, he leaned backward on the rail, his gaze roving across the bulkheads and beyond the masts to the waves on the starboard side. A blanket of mist lay across the sea in a sparkling veil.

"Is that your medical opinion?" I touched my throat, remembering the gentleness of his "examination" the night of the *séance*.

"Maybe." He turned around and rested his elbows on the rail as he studied me. My pulse quickened, and I refused to meet his direct gaze, staring at the sky instead. "It's a beautiful night." I never tired of counting the stars or imagining why they twinkled and winked.

"There isn't enough wind."

I faced him and smiled. "You're not a romantic, Mr. Browne."

His eyes glittered. "If you mean, do I believe in speaking as strangers on moonlit nights," he pulled me into an embrace, "I do not."

I felt his lips brush mine, tentative and questioning.

"I believe in doing what I've wanted to do since you rode down to the quay in Celize." His kiss deepened.

A blush warmed my cheeks. I took a step back, remembering another first kiss that had turned out so wrong.

Browne spoke again, his hand cupping my chin. "Before Celize, I'd seen your picture on the marquees in cities where we docked."

"You didn't recognize me."

"No. You are much more beautiful." His thumb moved to my ear, then dipped lower to explore the tell-tale pulse in my neck.

I sighed, wondering if I kissed him again, would I regret it later?

"Is it true you were mistress to the President's son?"

A bucket of cold seawater couldn't have separated us faster. I found myself several feet away, shaking with rage. All the heat he'd generated went to my head. Damn him!

"How *dare* you!" I whispered.

"Princess, the world knows—"

Interrupting, I shook him off. "They know nothing!"

I whirled and started off. Tears blinded me as I ran toward my room. I rounded the corner and heard a muffled groan from Jessica's cabin. Then a thumping noise. Another groan and the sound of a blow.

"Help!" I cried.

I wrenched open the door, flooding the cabin in moonlight. Jessica's dress was pushed up under her arms, and one of her stockings had been stuffed into her mouth. Murphy held her hands above her bruised and tear-stained face.

He leapt off her and fumbled with his trousers. I grabbed a water jug and raised it high. Jessica whimpered as Murphy moved toward me.

Browne shouldered me into the corner and with a long arm, yanked Murphy onto the deck. I scrambled to the door in time to see Browne's first blow send Murphy halfway down the ship. As crewmen came running, I slammed the door, shaking with anger.

Jessica whimpered again.

I felt like screaming; no, it is never *time*.

CHAPTER 17

Calmly the wearied seamen rest
Beneath their own blue sea.
The ocean solitudes are blest,
For there is purity.
The earth has guilt, the earth has care,
Unquiet are its graves;
But peaceful sleep is ever there,
Beneath the dark blue waves.

-Nathanial Hawthorne

The next morning, the sensation of the *Passat* falling into a deep trough awakened me, then she creaked and strained to climb again. A peek out my window showed the ship moved under a strong gale, riding fierce winds that had arisen during the night.

What had actually awoken me was bumping my nose against one of my traveling trunks. I'd rolled across the floor after the ship dropped into the trough. For most of the night, I'd sat on the floor next to Jessica, holding her hand and murmuring words of comfort through the long hours.

No one had argued when I moved her into my cabin last night. A faint pink had touched the eastern sky, signaling the coming dawn when Jessica's whimpers finally diminished, and she slept. I struggled to get up without waking her.

When I looked at Jessica, the stark morning rays revealed a deep bruise that discolored an entire side of her face. Just as telling of the violence, her split lip had scabbed over. The wet compress I had held to her eye lay under the bunk. While I watched her sleep, she thrashed from side to side and clenched her hands.

Last night it had taken the Captain to quiet Mrs. Pentifax when she heard the tidings. And it all seemed so fruitless; the Captain, Browne, nor anyone else could put Jessica's peace of mind back together again. In a fierce whisper that ended in an unladylike threat, I had stopped the flow of Mrs. Pentifax's recriminations and obtained her help moving Jessica to my cabin next door.

It had been a long night. Quietly, I gathered a change of clothing and went to exchange places with Mrs. Pentifax.

Mrs. P answered my knock on her door promptly. I noted the older woman had the decency to look a bit ashamed when she bustled out the door to take her place sitting with Jessica.

As I dressed, the *Passat* bounced like she raced an invisible ship, skimming across the waves. I had to hold on to the dresser or fall, and when I emerged onto deck, the wind blew my hair loose and whipped my skirts. High above, the canvasses were pulled taunt, ready to fly free of the lanyards. To save me guaranteed aggravation, I had ditched my hat and settled on a scarf knotted under my chin.

After a preliminary glance around, I stopped to reconnoiter; I needed a word with the first mate, but he didn't appear to be on deck. Walking to the bow, I drew more than the usual curious glances from a few crewmen who had been on duty last night. Some met my gaze. Others did not. I knew they were not like Murphy, yet it seemed they felt the tension by proxy.

On top of the turmoil from last evening, with the weather change, the ship seemed positively alive. After so many days of calm weather, the men were invigorated as they shouted back and forth and scampered up and down the masts. I sidestepped two sailors loaded with bales of rigging as they scuttled across the deck. Right behind them came a crewman who appeared too young to be away from home. He duck-walked by me to midships, carrying a bucket on a rope and wearing a silly smile.

"Ma'am." He tipped his cap and tossed his bucket over the side. I blinked. He disappeared over the rail after it.

I blinked again, disbelieving. "Help!" I screamed. The tragedies seemed to be piling one on top of the other.

"HELP!" I rushed to where he'd stood and pointed at the sea.

"Man overboard! Man overboard!" echoed behind me.

In the waves, I saw a quick flash of the boy's arm before it was swallowed in the hissing foam.

"Lay aback!" came a command from the bridge. It sounded like Browne. Then a flurry of orders resounded over the deck as the sails were reversed, slowing the ship until she reared and almost stood on her nose. Crates and barrels rolled as the ship keeled over dangerously and then righted again.

A skiff swung over the side, the chains holding it slamming against the hull. The deck swarmed with all hands, and every crewman moved in a rehearsed drill. Twin life buoys, thrown at the alarm, bobbed in the ship's wake a great distance behind.

Browne swung hand over hand down ropes and into the skiff before it reached the waterline, joining three others. The skiff bounced high as it landed, threatening to turn over as the men started to row, even as the last restraining rope came flying loose in the wind. I scanned the cresting waves in the distance again, seeing nothing. He'd been nothing but a boy!

In a mounting sense of futility, I clung to the rail and watched the drama unfold. Muscles straining, Browne and the other crewmen made slow progress against the wind and tall swells. It seemed an interminably long wait as they inched ahead, and time slowed as they rowed to the top of each wave, teetered on the crest, and descended again. From on high, the mate in the crow's nest shouted fierce directions relayed from crewman to crewman, across the deck to the bow, and out to the skiff.

A wave swamped them, swallowing the boat, then coughing it up again. I frantically counted the men, searching for Browne, realizing I *had* to find him. I cursed, using every passionate word I knew until I saw him and the others again, red-faced and rowing toward an empty sea.

An hour later, a grim-voiced Angelo answered questions as he served breakfast. One of the boy's duties had been to retrieve the seawater everyone on the ship bathed in and used for everything except drinking.

"What exactly happened?" Higgins asked.

"If a man is careless, he will toss the bucket over unsecured." Angelo refilled my coffee cup, but without his usual good humor. "A strong wave will pull him over. He will die."

We finished eating in subdued silence.

The wind blew my skirts as I climbed the ladder of the poop deck. It was the first time I had been on the bridge and saw the fine wood and the instruments sitting on the tables built into the quarter house wall. The wheel lay dead center, and to my right, maps fluttered, tacked to the walls.

Browne stood at the lee side rail with a glass to his eye, scanning the sea. Charts and stacks of calculations had been pinned under a paperweight behind him. The helmsman sent me a shocked look. Browne didn't seem surprised when he lowered the glass. He was annoyed.

"It's unlucky to have a woman on the bridge, Miss Coulter."

"I need to talk to you." I wouldn't say the first mate had avoided me since the previous night. I am much more fair-minded than that.

"Talk," Browne commanded, as gruff and distant as if we'd never met.

"About last night..."

"Mrs. Pentifax says her niece will remain secluded and that she'll attend to her," Browne growled. He raised the spyglass again, rudely hinting that I should leave.

"And Mr. Murphy?"

The glass came down. "The proper reports were written up."

"I want to know..."

"I'm responsible for the man's actions." Browne's eyes blazed. "You do not need to remind me of my duty!"

I swept an arm across the table, sending maps and paperweights flying. "Don't yell at me, Browne!"

"I'll damn well throw you off the bridge!"

I circled, putting the chart table between us. Out of the corner of my eye, I spied the helmsman grinning as I feinted to the left. Browne lurched that way and slipped on the fallen maps. I ran for the aft-end ladder. He caught my sleeve, then my waist.

"Force, Browne?" I struggled. "You don't know what I wanted," I shouted, pushing against his chest. "But you get your back up and act like that animal!"

He turned white and dropped his arms.

"I wanted to know what you did with the man. That's all." I brushed the tears from my eyes.

Browne's fingers dug painfully into my shoulders. "You thought I—"

"No-I-did-not-think. I'm asking." I pulled free. "The hell with you!" I turned and started down the ladder.

Browne heaved himself over and landed flat-footed on the deck as I reached it.

"He's in irons below." His voice was controlled. "When we reach port, he'll be charged."

"Thank you."

Browne said quietly, "We needn't argue, Miss Coulter."

"That is all we seem to do." I looked at him, searching for something, but I didn't know what. For the moment, we were alone by the rail. Either that or the rest of the crew thought better of interrupting us.

"No, it isn't." His eyes softened.

For a second, I forgot why we stood there, only seeing myself reflected in his eyes. The wind blew spray between us. Surprisingly, worry crept into his expression.

"There's something wrong, isn't there?" I asked.

He hesitated and then walked a few feet closer to the bow, pointing in the direction the *Passat* sailed. Masses of opal-colored clouds filled the upper regions of the sky. "Do you see the haziness in the distance?"

I nodded.

"For where we are, it isn't natural. And the barometer is unsteady."

The haziness spread as far as I could see under the opalescent clouds.

"What does it mean?"

"A cyclone," Browne replied, his mouth set in a grim line. "It's big and coming toward us."

I felt the first prickle of fear slide down my back as I watched the horizon.

"We could sit still, and it would overtake us, even without the wind driving us into it," he murmured more to himself than to me.

"We can't outrun it?"

"No." He shook his head. "The barometer is fluctuating like a drunk's eyes. When the storm breaks," his voice hardened, "I'll have to bring Murphy on deck—we'll need all hands."

He expected a fight about Murphy being free. "I understand about Murphy." His hand felt rough and warm as I brushed my fingertips across it. "I asked about him because I didn't know, don't know your temper."

"And what did you think I did to him?" He snatched his hand away.

"I saw your face. And heard the blows." I felt him staring at the top of my head. "I didn't know."

"Perhaps by the time we dock in Rio, you'll know, Miss Coulter." His voice was tight with anger.

"Perhaps." He couldn't blame me for doubting him. When he calmed down, I hoped he'd agree.

Pointing toward the gathering storm, I asked, "How far are we from the Horn?" The clouds reminded me of an immense wall spanning the sea to the heavens and separating us from the south.

Concern displaced his anger. "Sixty leagues. The storm will blow us into it or beyond into the icefields."

Shoulder to shoulder, we watched the towering clouds in the distance. "You need calm among the passengers." An uneasiness grew in my stomach like an army raged a full battle inside.

"Yes."

"I'll talk to Mrs. Pentifax and the others and do what I can."

"Thank you." Browne's gaze was on the horizon. "Have you seen a cyclone before, Miss Coulter?"

"No, but I've seen ships limping into ports in North Carolina after one. There wasn't much left."

"This could be worse."

CHAPTER 18

At luncheon, the Captain paid a brief call to the salon. His usual air of worry had grown tenfold along with the gusts of wind that whipped the sea.

He stood at the head of the table with his hair blown awry and gripped the back of the chair. It took a moment until I understood; he was summoning the nerve to speak because his long-held premonitions had dried up in his throat. Mr. Higgins continued to eat and regarded the Captain with a sharp eye while Morse put down his fork and didn't bother to hide his amusement. I glared at him. Why did the man find our predicament amusing? The others hadn't when I reported events to them.

When the Captain spoke, the tenseness in his voice choked his words, "...we anticipate large waves and a fierce wind. This is a good ship, and she'll make it through. That's all I have to say." He concluded his speech with something I'd expected but didn't agree with. "By this evening, you'll be confined to quarters."

A dead silence accompanied him to the door. As it closed, Morse remarked, "So we die before the Cape, eh?"

A half-hour later, a grinding noise floated into the salon from an open porthole, and I excused myself to find out what it could be. At the mouth of the hold, crewmen operated a hand winch, and even putting their backs to it, they gained only a few feet of chain per minute. At last, a bag of nitrate cleared the opening.

Two sailors disengaged the chains and ropes and lowered the tackle again. More of the crew wrestled the nitrate to the side and pushed the bag up to straddle the bulwarks, then over the side. When the bag hit the water, it sank in seconds. Morbidly, it seemed to sink faster than the remains of Doctor Rubio.

The door to the salon slammed, and Higgins marched by me to stand at the lip of the hold. Sweat glistened on his brow. He swiveled and called up to the bridge.

"Captain!"

Browne swung down the ladder and motioned for a fresh set of hands to take over at the winch. "The Captain is busy, Mr. Higgins." Browne squatted by the opening. I moved closer and saw that a few of the crew moved like ghostly shadows amid the mountains of boxes and crates a long way down.

"How can you throw over your cargo?" Herr Higgins sounded peevish, pacing to the rail and back again in a quick step.

Browne took a turn at the winch, each rotation bringing the grind of metal on metal. "We're too heavy, Mr. Higgins."

"But your investors!"

"Our investors are on land, counting their gold." Browne's voice became as hard as any ore, and he reddened under the strain of cranking that much weight. With his eyes on the chains disappearing into the hold, he said, "We want to live through the storm, Sir. The more weight we carry, the likelihood we'll turn topside in the winds." He relinquished the winch handle to the next crewman and stretched his back before facing the trader.

"But you'll be losing—"

Browne tapped him on his perfect silk four-in-hand. Higgins flinched.

"Better than losing the *Passat*."

Higgins wasn't about to give up that easily. He started to argue with Browne about wind currents and false storm warnings. What better time to investigate the investigator, I thought. It would also be nice to know if murder ran with greed. As the trader debated with Browne, I slipped away toward the cabins.

When I arrived in front of Higgins's cabin, I leaned over the rail, appearing to enjoy the watery sun and the extraordinary waves until no one, I hoped, noticed me. I backed up to the door and wiggled the handle.

"Humph." When I stepped inside, I couldn't believe it. And they say women have large amounts of traveling costumes and toiletries.

Good grief. Higgins possessed enough shirts with starched collars to last until well after the new year. I counted fourteen pairs of shoes. Someone of this much wealth would usually travel with a valet or servants. Why didn't he? As evidence mounted of deadly shenanigans aboard the *Passat*, the trader proved to be highly suspect.

From the other side of the door, a loud crash came, followed by a muffled expletive and laughter from the crew. The interruption reminded me that I couldn't linger. It took another five minutes before I found something interesting; a Buenos Aires newspaper and the date on it was just prior to our departure. The back page carried the same picture of the *Moira* and another article like what I'd last seen in Morse's room—what a liar Herr Higgins had proven to be.

This time I read the article through and whispered a few choice words as I did so; no wonder so many newspapers reported the story. In a few days, it would be the one hundredth anniversary of the disaster. It was sobering to read the details of the wreck of the *Moira*; men lost forever, widows made, and orphans, too. Each bounce of the *Passat* was a reminder of any ship's frailty against a ferocious storm on the seas.

There had been only one survivor, just as the Captain had said: John Greely, the mysterious sailor we'd discussed the first night out. I read on. He had subsequently jumped ship in Liverpool, according to an unverified report and was next sighted in Lisbon. This time, the report was confirmed. But there, the trail ended.

As I replaced the stolen article into the thief's hiding place—which happened to be his shaving kit—I found something I hadn't seen before under a towel and a noxious-looking bottle of hair oil. Another article had been cut out precisely along the edges.

JUNE 14, 1762, PARIS:

JOHN GREELY, THE ONLY SURVIVOR OF THE WRECK OF THE MOIRA, CONTINUES TO BE NEWS. ACCORDING TO DON CAPARILLI, THE CELEBRATED MEDIUM TO HIGH SOCIETY IN ROME AND PARIS, JOHN GREELY IS ALIVE, SO TO SPEAK. HERE IS HIS STATEMENT.

"LATELY, DURING MY SESSIONS, I HAVE SEEN JOHN GREELY ON ANOTHER SPIRITUAL LEVEL. NOT THE ONE THAT ALL WE NORMALLY INHABIT. HE IS INSANE. THERE! I HAVE SAID IT. I WOULD ADVISE ANYONE WHO ENCOUNTERS HIM TO BE CIRCUMSPECT. HE BELIEVES HE IS IMMORTAL, AND I BELIEVE IT, ALSO. THIS TRANSFORMATION MAY HAVE OCCURRED DURING THE WRECKING OF THE MOIRA. PERHAPS HE EXCHANGED HIS SOUL FOR THIS. I DO NOT

KNOW. BUT HE HAS SPOKEN OF HIS DESIRE TO RETRIEVE THE TREASURE, AND HE HAS ADOPTED A NORMAL PHYSIQUE AND A NORMAL LIFE.

BEWARE! IT HAS BEEN NEARLY A CENTURY SINCE GREELY ESCAPED DEATH, BUT IN APPEARANCE, HE LOOKS AS IF IT WAS YESTERDAY. MON DIEU! HE IS STRONG AND DANGEROUS."

EDITOR'S NOTE: IT MAY BE ONLY COINCIDENCE, BUT THREE DAYS AFTER THIS INTERVIEW, DON CAPARILLI WAS FOUND STABBED TO DEATH IN HIS BATHTUB. PARIS POLICE HAVE THE MATTER UNDER INVESTIGATION.

I slid off the bed and replaced the article faster than you could say, "amen." A distinct shiver slid up my spine and down again. Could John Greely be onboard the *Passat*? Was he masquerading as Morse, Higgins, the Captain, or one of the crew? It was *not* Browne. I set my jaw. It was not.

"Just a moment. I'll get my coat."

Bejeebers! Higgins! From just outside the cabin!

I squeezed behind the door as it opened, gathering my skirts close so they wouldn't protrude beyond the frame. Higgins pushed the door open, and I sucked in my stomach and scrunched my shoulders. He took two steps inside and snatched a coat off a chair just to my right. Then he backed out once more, slamming the door behind him.

I breathed again and eased the door open to assume a position at the rail outside Higgins's cabin. After what I'd read, my thoughts didn't dwell upon the play of the sunlight on the waves or the brisk scent of the wind; my mind flirted with the possibility of real danger, and when that proved distressful, I shook myself like a dog with fleas.

One of the crew, Ensign Fredricks, passed by with a "Ma'am" and a smile, but it was fleeting as his attention went beyond me to the storm which threatened us. In the last few hours, the haziness on the horizon had become more distinct. Even with the cyclone, we still had to get through Cape Horn, and there was Jessica to consider, too.

I knocked on her cabin door. Before my blazing discussion with Browne this morning, we'd moved Jessica back to her rooms. As I stepped inside, Mrs. Pentifax hustled out to get some air and looked like she needed a glass of spirits. Jessica sat by the window like a beautiful prisoner. Her gaze remained fixed on the waves as they flew by outside.

Even in the dim light, the ring of black bruises around her neck contrasted with the stark white of her arms. A plate of food sat untouched beside the bed. But with each visit, I noted her eyes had grown harder, her chin firmer; she was angry, and I was glad. Better to actively fight what life has wrought than to wallow in misery.

Jessica confirmed the observation by asking, "What will they do to the bastard?"

I did not comment on her swearing but answered her question. "He'll be charged when we reach Rio."

"That isn't good enough."

"I agree."

She turned from the window, her clenched fists tight with fury. "I won't let him get away with this!"

"We have to get through the storm first and let your wounds heal." Close up, her bruises were developing new ideas about color. "He isn't going anywhere," I added.

"You're damn right; he isn't!"

I could hear the hesitation in my voice as I asked, "Perhaps you should rest?"

"Yes, perhaps I should." A queer look stole over her features. For some reason, I was reminded of her confession of happiness when she'd fallen overboard. She saw my scrutiny, and the same tell-tale blush stained her cheeks. "Before last night, I had looked forward to sleeping ... because of my dreams. Maybe that is what I need now. To soothe me."

"The dreams where you felt you belonged," I tilted my head toward the deck, "in the sea?" I hesitated to ask because fanciful notions could be useful as a distraction if they didn't engulf her sensibilities.

Jessica studied me a moment longer. Apparently, I passed the test, for she said, "The dream is grand. I hear the music of the sea." Her voice lowered to a whisper, "It is calling me."

A particularly vicious gale slammed the ship, rattling the cabin windows. If the storm was as bad as it sounded, Jessica just might get her wish.

CHAPTER 19

L ate in the afternoon, the wind pushed me, bustle and all, into the salon, where I found Morse sprawled across a sofa in the semi-darkness. Instead of a greeting or invitation to sit beside him, he said something without turning his head or opening his eyes.

"It won't be enough."

"Enough what?" This wasn't the time for games.

"Enough to save the ship, of course."

Over the roar of the wind, the noise from the winch went on, and I suspected it would for hours as the crew tried to rid the ship of thousands of pounds of ore. "You mean that it isn't enough that they are throwing the nitrate over the side?" I asked.

He nodded.

"How do you know?"

He sat up, fixing me with an intense gaze. A chill crept up my arms with the same eeriness as the night of the *séance*. Morse's eyes darkened, and a dull gleam shone from their depths.

I knelt and gripped his hands. "Look at me. In the *séance*, you saw this ship. Didn't you?" I implored him. "You saw us—"

The wind slammed against the salon, rattling the bottles behind the bar. Morse looked through me. When he began to smile, I released him and involuntarily backed away. His chilling laughter sent me stumbling outside into the commotion as they hoisted the nitrate and background to the growing storm.

An hour later, with my sense of unease tamped down but not forgotten, I sat by the hold and watched the crew work. Dusk descended upon the ship, bringing long shadows and wind that sighed our fear. Half seriously I contemplated another foray into Morse's cabin.

Sharing my suspicions about the medium with Browne would not be a good idea. The first mate maintained nothing untoward happened during the *séance* and had no qualms about saying so in strong language. Gently explaining how I'd happened to see Higgins rummaging in Morse's room would be a memorable discussion, and there was no guarantee Browne would believe me. In fact, he wouldn't, just to be contrary.

With a cyclone brewing, Browne didn't need the distraction either. I turned my attention to the deck. Those sailors not engaged in wrestling the nitrate bags to the surface hastily secured anything not nailed down. The wrong kind of excitement tremored in their voices as they worked.

As the sun set, the armies of opal-tinged clouds darkened to a grayish blue ringed in black. Even without a spyglass, an advancing veil of rain could be seen in the distance. Much nearer, the winds became erratic and fitful, throwing bursts of foam high in the air.

I staggered to the bow. The clanking from the chains and creaking of the hull competed with the shouted commands coming from the bridge. Small birds, black except for a spot on their rumps, followed the boat's wake, barely skimming the white froth. As I watched, more and more birds flew to join the others.

One of the sailors, his arms loaded with rigging, paused beside me. He blocked the dying sun, casting me in shadow, and after a look at the birds, he frowned.

"I'd cross m'self, Miss, but my arms are full."

"Why?"

"Them's petrels." He stared at the birds. "They fly with a ship when there's a bad storm ahead." More birds flew to join the others. "The more petrels, the worse the storm."

"Give me some breeches."

I caught the cabin boy by the collar as he ran by. He just stared. I repeated my request, "Bring me some breeches." Rain pelted the deck delicately, as if the storm sprinkled us with innocent intentions.

"Ma'am?" The boy's response blew away into the darkness.

The wind had developed to a shrieking gale as we entered the outer reaches of the cyclone, while the *Passat* plowed forward in a valley of water, and the waves on each side of her climbed as high as the deck.

"Pants ... like yours." I pointed. "Please bring them to me."

"I can't!"

"Yes, you can." I gave him a gentle push toward the crew quarters, "Please hurry!"

"Cory," A growl came from overhead. Browne leaned over the rail of the bridge. "Get back to what you were doing."

"Get the breeches ... I'll square it with him." With a confident smile, I propelled him toward the stairs.

"Return to your cabin, Miss Coulter. Leave my crew alone." Browne withdrew inside the bridge.

"I'm not going to sit and wait to die!" I shouted above the wind.

The cabin boy returned with a rolled-up pair of trousers in his arms. He gave me a wary look before running for the stern. I grabbed the rail and held on as the deck of the ship tilted down. Spray decorated the night like a crystal spider web.

Once inside my cabin, I pulled off my skirts and petticoats. The pants fit, held up with the rope I'd procured from a storage bin. I'd managed to purloin the rest of my new ensemble without being caught.

The wind jerked the cabin door from my hands, and I staggered onto deck. In the short time it took to change, the force of the wind had more than doubled. With a howl like a chorus of banshees, the gales changed direction, and I landed on my side halfway over the rail. A wave rolled up to the ship to kiss me, the white curl at eye level. I scrambled up just as it broke, flooding the deck and soaking my feet. There my luck ended. With a crash of thunder, it began to rain.

Like a drunk, I lurched from bulwark to rail, to locker and rail again, making slow progress to the forecastle where the crew was getting rigged out in their oilskins and hip boots. Browne yelled each man's name as he dug in a locker and passed out the gear.

"Mr. Browne..."

He stiffened and turned. "You are confined to..." He gawked at my clothes.

"Please give me some of those." I stamped my feet. My God, it was cold.

"No." It was Browne's flattest refusal. He threw another set over my head to a final man and tried to close the container door against the wind.

"I'll finish nailing wood over the windows!" I shouted over the gale, pounding a fist on his back. "It'll free a set of hands for you..."

Browne turned, catching my fist in his. "And see you swept over the side? You can't even stand up now."

"Tether me to a bulkhead."

"No!"

I ducked around his thighs and grabbed a slicker.

He shouldered me aside.

"You need help!" I shouted and only had to remember the worry on the Captain's face and the terrified glances of the sailors to know the danger we faced.

Browne retorted, "Not from you." The wind fought him as he tried to force the locker door shut.

"Think, Browne—you know I can help," I wheedled. I could see he was weakening, whether by my argument or because he knew I wouldn't give up. "I'll go in if it gets too bad." I reached inside the locker.

"That's too big," Browne muttered and pulled another set out, but held on as my hands closed around the gear. Through the rain, I could see he regretted it already.

"I'll do as you say," I promised and tugged the slicker from his hand.

"You have no idea..." he began.

If we weren't in a freezing hell, I would have melted at the look in his eyes.

A sharp crack of thunder echoed nearby. I met his worry and said, "We're wasting time. Help me get these on."

He set his jaw and held the jacket open. The *Passat* lurched, and I fell against him.

"Is the Captain going to outrun the storm?" I staggered upright again.

"What?" Browne shouted.

"Is he going to try to use the wind to push us?"

"No! Too dangerous!"

Browne looped a rope around my waist. "You're going inside as soon as you finish the windows. Don't argue." A wave crested leeward and drenched us. I spit out a mouthful of water.

He held up a finger.

"Windows on the salon first. The wood is over there." He pointed to a woodpile and shouted something to a sailor who squished by.

"And send Higgins and Morse out here—we're going to need them."

CHAPTER 20

We only die once and for such a long time.
-Molière (Jean-Baptiste Poquelin)

Latitude 59°17' S, Longitude 67°09' W

Beyond the glow from the ship's lamps, fingers of lightning descended to hiss upon the water, leaving the white froth of the waves as the only color in the surging blackness. As I gazed skyward, needles of rain fell in sheets, blown sideways by howling winds. Then the wind stopped, and the canvasses hung limply before being blown horizontally to their limit and dropped again as the storm shifted and wailed. The darkness made me shiver as much as the rain.

Most of the running lights had been drowned or broken by the waves. Only a set of twin lamps swung from gimbals on the bridge. They could have been incense holders in church, and we were the parishioners praying to the sea gods. I ducked under a wave of water that flew over my head and to the other side of the deck; a prayer would not have been out of line right now. From inside the forecastle, a solitary lamp glowed.

Tethered like a donkey, I couldn't go far. When I reached the salon, I found Morse crouched beside the bar with glazed eyes and cuddling a full brandy snifter. I hesitated at the door, deciding to find Higgins first; Browne may not want Morse in this condition. Higgins could also help sober up the medium.

Dragging my tether like a lengthening tail, I staggered toward the stern, bouncing from the rail to the cabin walls until I reached Higgins's door. As I went along, the deck of the ship tilted in exaggerated angles, and just when I thought I wouldn't fall, it would shift again right under my feet, and I'd grab something to keep from banging my head on the boards.

A jagged arm of lightning crashed into the sea, firing the water as it blossomed to a brilliant green-blue, illuminating the darkened windows of Higgins's cabin. How could the man sleep during a cyclone?

I set my jaw. I was supposed to be hammering wood over windows to keep the sea from invading the salon and cabins. But Mr.-I-only-think-of-my-profits-Higgins needed to be dragged out of his bed to help the ship he'd endangered by smuggling contraband aboard.

"Higgins!" I pounded on the door. Thunder boomed directly behind me. "*Damn you*, open up!" I pounded until my hand hurt. Directly overhead, a piece of spar cracked and broke off. I ducked. The wind carried it high over the water.

I kicked the door. "Higgins!"

A long roll of thunder reverberated overhead. As the *Passat* lurched to starboard, I fell against the door just as the sea brightened beyond belief; like an advancing column of a massive army, a line of lightning split open the sky and marched toward the *Passat,* the effect floodlighting the sea as if a gigantic stage had been lit up.

I wrenched the door open.

The silvery glare from the lightning flashed into the cabin, illuminating everything with clarity. I took a deep breath, confirming

what awaited me here was what I had assumed for the last few seconds but wouldn't admit to myself. Higgins lay on his back with a
knife buried deep in his chest. When a wave broke above the rail
and drenched my back, I breathed again. It couldn't chill me more
than what I had discovered.

His hand felt icy. Eyes like blank marbles fixated on the
stained-glass window, and the Bible had been flung to the floor.
I don't know how long I stood there rubbing my hands together,
thinking that, of all things, he'd be of little use to Browne.

Another crack of lightning shook the windows. I backed out
and nailed the door and window shut. If we hit warm weather
before he was entombed, Herr Higgins would be a smelly mess.
Then an urgent thought occurred to me, and I shuffled around
the corner to the other side and pounded on Mrs. P's door; *the
old biddy had refused to leave her cabin hours ago*. Dear God, let
them be alive.

The door opened, revealing Mrs. P's scowl under a nest of pin
curls. She never looked better. I nearly hugged her. Jessica, eyes
wide, appeared over her shoulder.

"*What* are you wearing?" Mrs. P demanded. "And you have
no hat on!"

What I wore must be more important than dying.

"Get your coat and some dry clothes." I looked to Jessica. "Hurry."
I'd stash them with Morse in the salon. They'd be safer there.

"Miss Coulter." Auntie lifted her chin; she had no intention of
going out in the rain.

I pulled her outside. A trumpet of thunder exploded overhead,
and I pinned her against the cabin wall before the wind propelled
her overboard like a large balloon. Jessica emerged with her arms
full of expensive wraps. The salon was three doors away, a distance
that could have been miles.

When we arrived, I shoved Mrs. P in first, Jessica followed, and
I struggled with the door. As the wind pushed, I pulled, settling for

just holding it shut. The gales rattled the windows and slammed the salon so hard I thought the wall was coming down. It startled Jessica, but she didn't speak. Like a wet bug, Mrs. P scuttled to the sofa and hovered there.

"Where's Morse?" I willed my expression to be calm and not raise the panic level, especially if someone had stabbed him, too. *Why* would someone want to murder the passengers?

A second went by, and then a muffled gurgle came from behind the bar as Morse stood and swayed, drunk as a skunk. I felt so relieved my voice shook. "The safest place is where he is—away from the windows." To Jessica, I said, "It'd be best to get the bottles down from the racks and secure them. Please stuff anything you can under the door." It might help keep the water out.

"Where is Mr. Higgins?" Jessica asked as she began opening bins under the bar.

"He's busy."

For each nail I hammered, I had to swipe water out of my eyes. During the minutes it took to secure the salon windows, the waves had grown higher, and the drenching from the stinging rain more frequent. On my way to the stern side, I shook my head like a dog, so I could see. Oh, if Charles' mother could see me now.

After the next twenty feet or so around the stern, I would be on the other side of the ship. It looked like I would get there but wouldn't have enough tether left to reach all the windows on the other side. Falling twice, I made it to the last cabin, stopped, and nailed wood on Mrs. P's door and window. Lugging the planks took as long as the hammering, and I took to tossing them ahead of me, piece by piece, before shifting position.

An arm slung me over a hard shoulder.

"Hey!"

The first mate just clamped his other arm across my backside and stomped back toward the salon. "Browne!" I kicked until he put me down. He shouted something, but the wind stole it away.

I grabbed his ears and brought his face down to mine. "Higgins-stabbed-to-death. His cabin—" I shouted.

Browne squashed me flat to his chest, his chin in my hair. I would have enjoyed this more yesterday. Or even a few hours ago. I yelled, "I nailed his door shut!" Between the waves, the thunder, and the shifting of the ship, I couldn't think.

"I'll get the others!" Browne's breath felt warm as he growled in my ear. "Into the salon. *Now.*"

"They are already there!"

He shouted back, "Come on!" He tried to shuffle me there, too.

"No." I clutched at his arms. "I want—"

Browne continued to drag me toward the salon.

"No!"

"Yes!"

A towering wave broke directly ahead, washing us to the stern like dolls. I wrapped myself around him, and we stopped at the end of my tether in a swirling pool of seawater. As it receded, Browne scrambled up and again pulled me behind him toward the salon.

"Inside and stay!"

Like the elements agreed with him, the barrage of thunder overhead doubled, echoing upon itself as it coupled with the wind and towering waves. In a concert of premonition, Browne and I stopped our tussle.

With a deafening and blinding explosion, a blade of lightning struck the mainmast, splitting it in two. The concussion knocked us flat. Before we could move, flames ran down its trunk, and the mast swayed between strands of burning rigging. Lines sizzled and blackened in fiery threads as they traveled to the mizzenmast and sails. The huge canvasses blazed brightly in the night.

Browne rolled over me and sprinted toward the mainmast. Two crewmen were already climbing, dragging wet blankets upward, and beating at the flames. As Browne scaled a yardarm, wielding an ax, Captain McQuistan leaned out of the bridge, shouting orders.

In the next few minutes, the crew swarmed over the mainmast, binding it together with anything they could find. When they finished, it resembled a tall, smoking mummy that leaned toward the stern. Into a lull in the thunder, the crew gave a shout of triumph.

But there was more.

The storm, after holding itself to slashes and bursts, released a fury of water that could not be distinguished from the waves anymore. The last of the fire steamed to smoke. Browne bounded toward the bridge. I had intended on following him, but the expanse of deck looked endless, awash in feet of swirling water. It couldn't be done. There was no purchase underfoot; the rain tried to drown me where I stood. It was time to huddle with the other passengers.

I fell twice before reaching the salon door I hadn't nailed shut. It wouldn't budge.

Kicking, pounding, and screaming couldn't be heard above the shrieking storm. Only a suggestion of light came from the barricaded windows as I threw myself against the door. The wind howled in response. I braced my feet and pulled until I slithered off and landed with a splash below the rail.

I didn't cry. I felt like it, but I didn't cry.

CHAPTER 21

About, about, in reel and rout
The death-fires danced at night;
The water, like a witch's oils,
Burnt green, and blue and white.
Rime of the Ancient Mariner
-Samuel Taylor Coleridge

Foot by foot, cursing at myself, slipping and sliding, and blown down, I made it to the first bulkhead and hung on as two of the crew sloshed by. They didn't even see me.

Because of the debris, the scuppers weren't draining the deck. Something metal banged my ankle as it went by. When my tether wouldn't allow me to go any further, I slipped it over my hips and got rid of it. An oily surge of water licked at my knees as the slush inched higher, banking and pitching with the *Passat*.

Something soft wedged between my leg and the bulkhead, floating in the trapped water. I reached for it just as the ship tilted aft. The water cleared away, revealing small sharp teeth and dull red eyes. I yelped and kicked a drowned rat away, stomping through the remaining water until the ship tilted back again. As I climbed above the deck to hang over the water, I tried not to scream again. It didn't help.

As it rode a ferocious roar, another wave swept the deck from the stern. Unwillingly, I went with it toward the bow. More by luck than an ability to see, I caught and held onto the handrail leading up to the bridge as the rest of the water rushed by above my waist, carrying barrels, tools, and pieces of wood. My fingers felt numb, and I had to look at my hands to climb the steps to the bridge.

From this high up, the storm presented a different perspective, a dreadful one. As huge as the *Passat* appeared, she was nothing compared to the swirling vortex around us. By now, all the running lights had been swamped fore and aft. The twin cyclone lamps on the bridge swung in opposite directions with the lurches of the ship. From within the blackness of the storm, the lightning fired sporadic bursts of electric white light across the waves, and the thunder hammered the sky.

The wind had swept the bridge free of all maps and instruments, leaving only Browne and the Captain. They stared, gaunt-faced and grim in the smoky light of the lamps, both holding the wheel. As they fought to keep the *Passat* from keeling over, Browne relayed the Captain's terse orders to the crew in the yards and to those on the deck.

Suddenly, the streaks of lightning were obliterated as a towering wave appeared off the starboard side.

I screamed. Browne pivoted and dove, sweeping us both into a corner.

He held on as the wave covered us and swept through.

Without a word, Browne stood and began securing me to a post with ropes that he looped round and round my middle and legs. He and the Captain both wore shorter tethers than the one I had discarded.

Browne handed over the end of the rope and showed me a sharp knife before he tucked it snugly in my pocket. His meaning was clear; if there was no one left to untie me, I was to use the knife.

"Couldn't get into the salon!" I shouted.

Leaving me with a scowl I didn't deserve, he returned to the wheel.

The frigid air hurt my salt-stained eyes, and my breath left white puffs in the air. Once I stood still, the cold wind whistled through my sodden clothes, seeking entry to my bones.

Browne signaled Captain McQuistan to rest. The gales still drove the ship forward, crashing through immense crests before she fell and climbed again, but the *Passat* no longer swung from side to side in a death knell. The Captain shook his head.

It was as if he knew. Within seconds, the storm increased tenfold, propelling the ship like a runaway train through a tunnel of darkness, the speed and noise incredible. The winds howled from all directions as if Heaven and Hell fought to possess the ship. Thunder boomed, shaking every timber of the *Passat*.

If the ship hit something...

I closed my eyes and wished for comfort ... of Browne. I concentrated all my thoughts to the back of his head, praying he'd get us through.

The ungodly noise stopped, and the wind dropped the ship as quickly as it had propelled it. Through the curtain of rain, I could make out the scurrying sailors on the deck. They looked so much like the drowned rat, only with bleached faces.

Like a celestial hand reached down from the heavens and grasped the ship and shook it, a symphony of lightning and thunder split open the sky and turned the sea into a surreal bowl of violet, green and black, blending into one before separating and fragmenting into a horrific bleak prism.

Colder. The rain turned white.

Two sailors, buffeted by the wind, straddled the icy foremast, legs wrapped around yardarms as they lay prone, trying to reach one of the main canvases which had broken free. Another tear rent the air, followed by a crewman's scream as he plunged to the deck. The canvas spanked the yardarm and then ripped open. The other sailor fell back, clinging to the mast as hundreds of pounds of frozen canvas flapped, flying free. It swung left and lifted straight up in the air.

The sailor nodded, hearing Browne's yells to come down. He nodded again and descended with his eyes on the expanse of sail. The wind shifted. I swallowed a scream as the canvass lifted the sailor off the mast, tossing him into the churning sea. Appeased, the wind roared, and the sail came free, fluttering into the night like a great white bird.

The Captain had the helm again. Browne leaned out of the bridge, watching the waves for any sign of the sailor. His shouts turned to screams.

As if a plug had been pulled in an aquatic bathtub, the *Passat* shuddered and began to slide broadside down a great crest. On the starboard side, a wall of water glistened a dead black as it grew higher and higher.

It was the end. I knew it, felt it.

The mother wave, come to claim the ship, ascended upward in slow motion, towering above the ship. Then it began a downward curl across the *Passat*, swamping the entire deck, reaching insidious and green as the sea *rose*. It washed the crew from the deck, the bulwarks, and masts like specks of clinging lint, and hurled them into the swirling water.

In horror, I watched the sea climb until it crested with the bridge and frothed, licking the walls and the posts, and approached Browne and McQuistan's feet. The sea hissed as it hovered and swirled, embracing the ship like a deadly lover.

The water receded, seeping away under the rails, until another wave approached, rolling lazily, riding the surge, bringing back dead sailors, and leaving them broken and scattered across the deck.

The sea rose again.

Above the deck, up the stairs and to the masts, and level with the bridge, the sea foamed and swirled, surging toward the bridge. I gulped air.

The Captain wore a death mask as he hugged the wheel. The last thing I saw was Browne braced beside me. Water crept up my arms, chin, eyes, and over my head. In a world of green, Browne's hair waved in the water, then blurred to blackness.

CHAPTER 22

In the darkness came moaning ... from far away. Water slapped against wood; the motion was rhythmic, like a baton against a podium. A sickening stench of fish overwhelmed everything as I opened my eyes, peering through my hair and a steady curtain of rain.

I lay on my back and felt the water dribbling from my mouth. Instead of sky, I glimpsed broken yardarms and snapped poles dangling from the rigging; it seemed as if I lay in a bombed-out circus. Bits of tattered sails fluttered overhead. Somewhere a chain banged against wood as the ship rocked violently, and I struggled to sit up. But it was too much trouble... When I peered over the rail, I spotted part of the leeward deck. I ... must still be on the bridge ... a whole canvas lay across the bow and hung over the side and into the water. Again, I tried to sit up and fell back.

Weak light from virgin dawn painted the scene in muted grays and pinks. Just below the bridge, a sailor staggered to a bulkhead, hugged it, and fell again. Swells surged past the rail of the main deck. The froth from the waves rippled, level with the bow, as the ship moved swiftly to the left and swung back again. I closed my eyes and drifted inward.

Something white. Pant leg... more white... I focused to my left, near the wheel.

Captain McQuistan lay on his side, still tethered to a pole. Superstitions always come true; his dead eyes were raised toward the masses of clouds surrounding us. The top of his head had been caved in, and when I saw that his brains had been cleaned out by the sea, bile rose in my throat.

"Browne!" I cried in a hoarse croak that didn't make it off the bridge.

I rolled into a crouch, and then on my feet. I couldn't feel my hands. Too numb, frozen. I patted my thighs. The pats became stinging slaps, and I stamped my feet.

"Browne!" I called again.

Carefully, I worked the knife out from my pocket, mindful that I would be helpless if I dropped it. I didn't feel a cut in my palm until warm blood coated my hand.

The silence, and the absence of scores of voices, sent urgent shivers up my spine. I used both hands, not trusting either to hold on to the knife, as I sawed through water-swollen ropes. Minutes of work produced a few frayed threads.

"God damn it," I worked furiously, "*to hell*!" One loop of the rope fell, then a second that helped to loosen the others.

Other than the heaving waves, the only sound was a chain that smacked the hull every time the ship lurched. I struggled to raise the ropes over my head. They fell onto the Captain's feet, and I stepped over his legs and looked below.

Near the bow, one of the sailors stumbled by on the port side; blood trickled from his arm. It looked like Angelo. He knelt beside the body of a crewman who lay face down on the deck and touched his cheek. The sounds of his sobs came, and with it, the wind rose in poignant harmony. From somewhere aft came a gurgling moan.

Browne.

I swung down the ladder and grabbed the rail of the deck, feeling my feet again. Through a steady rain, I picked my way over dead fish and men, hesitating long enough to ascertain that the crewman I passed was indeed beyond help.

Desperation ate at me as I searched for Browne. The gurgling came from the rear deck again.

My heart stopped. At the base of the forecastle, Browne lay face down in a pool of brackish water. The broken end of his tether curled behind him like a tail.

I started to run and fell over a body that rolled to face the sky, exposing a face so bloated it was not recognizable.

Browne moaned again. I crawled the last few feet. His breaths bubbled the water, and a bruise as big as my fist discolored his temple. But he breathed. No blood. I scooted into the water and cradled his head in my lap. The slush we sat in felt colder than the air.

Browne remained dead weight.

"Come on, Browne. Don't die on me," I pleaded and pushed a piece of sail under his shoulders and touched the bruise on his temple. He grimaced but didn't wake. Slapping cold water on him didn't help. "Browne!" I felt the bruise again, and his eyes opened. Then focused. He crushed me to his chest as his tears warmed my forehead and squeezed me closer. His heartbeat sounded loud, confirming the fact that we were alive.

I pushed back to look at him.

He returned the regard and, after a long moment, whispered, "Like a drowned dog." He seemed pleased.

A *dog*? I would remember that. And remind him of it at opportune times.

"Thank you."

His hold on my arms didn't lessen. I wiped a tear from his cheek and looked deep into eyes that locked with mine, making a memory I'd never forget.

"Can you get up?" I asked.

He did, in one motion taking me with him. He swayed and grabbed a bulkhead. For the first time, he saw the wreckage.

"My crew!" It came out as a cry of pain. He gazed down the length of the ship at the slew of bodies. "Andrews! My men…"

"There are two alive, maybe more." I touched his arm. "The Captain is dead."

Browne winced and set his jaw. The sight of the destruction seemed to strengthen him. Already he stood taller and seemed stronger. I grabbed an iron bar the storm had tossed under the rail.

"The salon—passengers."

He nodded and staggered toward the bow, his steps slow at first, then steadier. He flung debris out of his path before he knelt at the first body.

CHAPTER 23

The rain fell as relentlessly as death, still driven by a strong wind. First, I tried the starboard salon door, but the storm had warped it closed. Faint noises came from inside. I couldn't yell loud enough and didn't bother to try, instead pushing the bar into the jamb and leaning on it. Rain ran down the back of my neck, into the borrowed pants, and down my legs as I repositioned the bar and rammed against it, hearing a satisfactory splintering of wood. The door gave, and I hopped to the side as trapped seawater flowed out in a rush, bringing empty bottles, broken glass, pillows, and crockery.

Devastation awaited me here too, but the objects not broken remained. Overturned chairs and sofas and smashed lamps and dishes covered the floor. Three whimpering people huddled behind the denuded bar.

The place smelled like a fish tank. As I squelched across the wet carpet, Morse's face rose like a pale moon with hollowed eyes from behind the bar. The women struggled to stand. Mrs. Pentifax's pallor looked deathly, and despite wet and stringy hair and a cut on her chin, Jessica had a survivor's glint in her eye. I grinned at her. Mrs. P tottered and grabbed the bar.

"We're alive," Jessica called out.

"Margery? Margery?" Mrs. Pentifax wailed, clutching at Jessica, who turned to me with a look that plainly said she didn't know what to do with her aunt.

"There must be a bottle not broken." I glanced around the room. "Find some and get a little of it down her. We're going to need the rest."

As I looked around, I told myself, *think. We must survive.* Everything appeared soaked, but not a lost cause. "Please strip down the curtains and spread them across the table to dry. We'll use them as blankets." The water had risen to the top of the couches before receding; no one would be sleeping on them anytime soon. I'd get someone to help remove the carpet so the floor would dry.

I faced Morse. "Browne wants you." He hadn't said so, but undoubtedly, he would.

The psychic followed me on deck to where Browne paced by the door to the galley.

"Four men." Browne slammed his fist into the wall. "The rest gone!" He punched the wall again. "Gone!"

"We're alive." I touched his arm. "We need…"

"They're dead." He buried his face in his hands. I may not be the Queen of Tact, but I knew when to leave someone alone—sometimes. I gave Browne his privacy and pivoted to survey the rest of the damage. Christian Morse did the same.

The remaining hatch covers hung open, and the storage bins appeared empty. The storm had cleaned out most of the bulkheads. We needed to find out what was left to eat and drink. Beside me, Morse didn't say a word, just surveying the ship. He seemed as normal, other than his wet clothes and hair.

"We need more men to run the ship." Browne stared at the fallen spars, heaps of rigging, and canvasses draped over the deck and roof of the salon.

"Can we steer?"

He nodded. "We still have the rudder."

Yet the devastation looked worse as the situation became clearer. It wasn't a matter of the damage as much as *what* was damaged and its function. To survive, we had an enormous amount of hauling, mending, and reconstruction to do. The cage the chickens had been in blocked the stairs leading below decks. No sign of the chickens. The overhang above the entrance leading downward had also caved in, and any entry would be perilous, if not impossible. Clearing the debris could reveal more damage, perhaps more bodies.

The dire expectation must have shown on my face, for Browne remarked, "No man would have been below decks during the storm, Miss Coulter. They all died within sight of the sea."

Over the next few hours, the rain continued like an up-ended, bottomless bucket. By midday, it turned into stinging sleet and hail, beating a tattoo on the deck before melting into the knee-high slush the surviving crewmen and Browne stomped through.

With a length of iron, I cleared one of the scuppers, only to have the suction of the release pull more debris banging into my legs, blocking it again. All along the deck, I poked and scraped until enough water drained, and I could see the wood underneath.

The ship lurched aft like she'd been sucker punched. After cursing and standing again, I continued tossing armfuls of ruined and broken things over the side that I recognized and things I felt loathe to touch. When I started on the drains on the other side, the greasy surface of the sea still seemed a great deal closer than before the storm, the churning gales just as strong.

As Browne strode by, I caught his sleeve.

"Are we taking on water?"

"No leaks, but the bilges are weakening. They need pumping out."

"Will it be enough?" The froth that licked the hull appeared soapy and awfully close.

Browne nodded grimly, making me wonder if he would ever smile again. "It will have to be. It'll go slow, but we should keep ahead of it." Over his shoulder, I saw Morse standing under the forecastle overhang as bewildered as a child lost in the woods.

Following my gaze, he said, "We'll give Fancy Pants a few calluses." Browne regarded the leaden sky. "We've got to get started."

"I'll set up camp in the salon; we can preserve heat and kerosene that way."

"You found oil?" He was amazed.

"Quite a bit."

He grunted before tramping over to Morse and taking him away to the pumps.

Humph. A pat on the head would have been nice.

The thunder returned, rumbling across the undulating sea under thick clouds that blocked the light and painted the world gray. The cold had worsened as the day lengthened, and sleet stuck to my hands and hair, crackling in a frozen coating on my clothes. Browne tossed me a set of gloves on one of his passes by, not waiting for a thank you. I sent him a colorful and fun curse and sobered again.

My first project was to inventory the galley and pantry to see what had survived. Food didn't appeal now, but it would soon.

In the storage bins, it seemed like anything moveable—from jelly to a salt cellar—had been stirred into the wet bags of flour and the up-ended jars of lard and sugar by the storm. Saltwater had turned the mess into sludge. In the more protected storage, some tins of dry peas, hardtack, and barrels of salted beef remained, but little else. The find of the day? A box of matches that was carefully stashed in a safer, drier place.

Periodically, I checked on the occupants of the salon, not spending too much time there. If I stopped, I'd never get up again. The temptation from the fire Jessica had built in the grate was the worst.

Mrs. Pentifax's snore floated in an alcoholic stupor from one of the sofas. After leading Jessica through the connecting door from the salon to the galley, I enlisted her as the temporary cook. It took a while to light the stove. Jessica listened to the rudimentary introduction to a soup pot I presented; it wasn't fancy.

The fuel supply provided a singular ray of hope because most of it had been stored under the forecastle. Plenty of wood remained, but it had absorbed its weight in seawater. I aired some lighter pieces under what remained of the overhang between the galley and the salon. I almost smiled when I discovered a pair of large clean tarps, perfect for covering the sofas for beds. The smile evaporated when I had to use a stick to remove a few drowned rats from where they'd ended up. The poor things appeared pathetic until, to my surprise, one wiggled and ran by my boot.

The forecastle came next. Some steps were missing, and only part of the rail remained, which made me wish I'd grown taller or at least had longer arms. Inside, I found one dry bunk and an unbearable stench. Nothing dead, but I couldn't find the source. By pulling and tugging, I got the mattress outside. Halfway to the salon, Browne shouldered me aside and finished dragging it in the door.

"We need to talk." I backed out of his way as he started back toward the pumps.

"Talk," he growled, not breaking his stride.

"About Higgins." I held onto his arm.

He stopped and glared.

"The others don't need to know he was murdered," I said.

"Morse hasn't asked about him yet, but when he does, I'll tell them all the truth."

"They don't need the extra worry. Especially Mrs. Pentifax if she became lucid enough to understand what happened."

"You are not the authority on this ship, Miss Coulter."

I tapped his belly. "No, but I know the truth will only upset them more. Will you listen?" "So, talk."

God, he was stubborn. "Let's get the body out of the cabin while there is still light."

"I need to watch the pumps."

"We'll hurry." I tugged on his arm. "Come on."

Browne split off the planks I'd nailed on and tried the bloated door, putting his back to it. It gave with a creak and tearing of wood.

In the weak light, Higgins's cabin looked the same as the night before, except the blood had mixed with seawater and froze in a shining red pool. No disarray here, only what the storm had done, and no sign of any forced entry but our own. The most unusual item was the armament embedded in Higgins's chest.

I said, "We can't tell them it was an accident."

The purloined articles about the *Moira* and the picture of the vessel I'd seen the other day were gone, and thank God Browne didn't catch me checking for them, or I'd find myself explaining why I was snooping.

He had bent over the body, lifting a stiffened hand, and letting it drop back again. "No sign that he struggled at all. Like he lay still and let someone stick him with the knife."

As we jelly-rolled the body into the bedclothes and dumped it onto a tarp, Browne said, "We should tell them."

"Why?" I added in the trader's shoes and the water pitcher for weight. Browne threw in some soaked books he'd found.

"Because we should." He sounded as "illogical" as any woman, but I didn't say so.

"Mrs. P is in shock, and Morse is like a sleepwalker. Do you think Jessica needs to hear that there is a maniac with a knife running wild?" As we began sewing the tarp closed, I held up the string we sewed with. "What is this made of? It is much thicker than sewing thread."

"Cat gut."

Oh ... I tried to hide my revulsion.

Browne hadn't given up. "Nothing to worry about. Whoever killed Higgins most likely died last night."

"We don't know for sure. How can we?" I knotted off the thread and got to my feet. "It won't hurt to lie." I kicked the shroud. "Say he fell overboard."

With a ghost of a smile, Browne sighed. "You are an infuriating woman."

I waited. In the tiny cabin, there was only room for us. And Higgins's remains. If he felt trapped by my insistence, so be it; I didn't mind arguing over a dead body.

"All right, Miss Coulter. We'll do it your way." He backed out the door with one end of the bundle. "We'll say he fell over."

CHAPTER 24

ARGENTINE SEA
Latitude 40°38' S, Longitude 58°39' W

A rumble of thunder, silence, then a sudden deluge.

The storm broke as Shaw finished carrying the last of the galley slop out; sixteen trips with a double-slung bucket over his shoulders. Farley danced along beside him, his mouth going like an auctioneer's. Just one swing of a bucket and over the side the red-headed devil would go. Shaw was convinced Peech had wished the Irishman upon him as a special kind of torture.

When they arrived at the rail overlooking the surging sea, the urge to send Farley over the rail wouldn't go away. Shaw felt anxious about his thought, but not a bit ashamed, as he eyed the runt again. If he hit him square on the back of the head with the bucket … he'd have to move quickly to hoist the bastard the rest of the way over. Yes, Richard Shaw, upstanding, churchgoing, and law-biding employee of Lloyds of London, considered murder with a clear mind.

The hair on the back of Shaw's neck rose, and he pivoted. From inside the bridge, Borodin's enigmatic stare met him, and then the scarecrow shook his head slightly. Shaw felt his face flush and swiveled to see if Farley had also read his intentions. No, the runt just babbled on. More rain splattered the deck, and Borodin drew back inside the bridge. Shaw sighed.

"So, what did you do for bloody Lloyds?" Farley asked as he bumped over a pile of planks Shaw had stacked yesterday and sat down.

"Just paperwork." Shaw lied.

"Eh? Why did you come over here?"

"It is none of your business. However, I have relatives near Panama."

"Rich?" Farley's face lit up.

Shaw shook his head.

"Borodin says you know ships."

"I don't," Shaw said. "I'll have my dinner now."

With the evening weather bad, Borodin and Farley delegated the watching of Shaw to an unfortunate veteran with one eye and a distinct limp. Each trip Shaw made to the head had a thumping accompaniment. Last night, in the wee hours, he had finally slept and woke with the first hint of dawn. His bunk and clothes were wet, an instant reminder of his final and necessary act from the night before. Before Shaw could dwell upon it, he felt the prickling sensation of being watched and opened his eyes.

Borodin stood over him, staring. Shaw stared back and, after a moment, said, "Yes?"

Another minute passed with only the sounds of the men working and walking the decks floating through the open door. Borodin contemplated Shaw like he'd never seen him before.

"Get your boots on."

When Shaw stepped onto deck, he thought the *Hussar* lay becalmed. But a few of her smaller sails remained up, and he felt the delicate caress of a wind freshening. He hurried to the side, and as he touched the rail, the thought of rescue turned sour; they rested at anchor less than a league offshore, facing barren cliffs nearly as tall as the ship. No village or town lay there. All along the coastline, jagged limestone emerged from the waves like rows of protruding teeth.

The dark, swirling water indicated a tremendous current ran underneath the *Hussar*, surging toward shore and generating waves that exploded in plumes of water. The agitated sea writhed and danced in demented swirls; there'd be no swimming to shore from here. Shaw cursed.

He had been a prisoner for over two weeks! But he still had hope and continued to study the coastline that seemed as wild and primitive as any found in an adventure book. Nor did he see any huts or boats or smoke from cooking fires, only the large-winged birds that wheeled above the cliffs before swooping to the surf and soaring up again.

"Fritz says you stopped off at the bowsprit last night." Borodin leaned against the rail, studying him.

Shaw nodded grimly without comment. In the hours after midnight, the ship had been buffeted by a healthy wind when he'd gone to the head. Old Fritz the Peg Leg thumped along behind him, sticking to his trail like a lame, nasty dog. When he'd started back, Shaw discovered what the sadistic scoundrels had done.

As his revulsion turned to anger, Shaw grabbed the nearest ax and strode to the bow. His geriatric keeper made outraged noises as Shaw swung the ax twice, three times, and the woman's corpse came loose from where the bastards had tied her. As he gazed at what they had done, Borodin's words came back to him from the night Shaw had found her tied to the wall in the crew's quarters. "You can't help her now, any more than you could a week ago."

When he had flung the ax to his warder's feet, the other pirates on deck became aware of something unusual and came loping up. Shaw ignored them and climbed hand over hand to the end of the bowsprit until he hung thirty feet above the leaping waves. Spray drenched him as he untied the corpse the rest of the way. Yes, she'd been dead many times over. And even if he'd killed a dozen of them to rescue her—where could he have kept her safe on this godforsaken ship?

And now, bathed in sunshine, Borodin stood beside him, reminding him of it all over again. Shaw squeezed his eyes shut until the image of the woman dissolved. She had become a grotesque masthead, and he could have sworn her accusing eyes bored into him as he finished untying her and let her fall into the rushing waves.

When he looked again, Peech's scarecrow still stood beside him. Borodin gazed at the shoreline as if he were searching for a landmark, yet when he talked, it seemed his mind wasn't on landmarks. "There's always been a ceremony of death. It has been said the dead are alive, and the living are dead. She was dead the minute we saw her, Mr. Shaw."

"You are murderers." Shaw refused to visualize again what he'd seen. He was beginning to hate himself and his logical mind, which had turned him into a coward.

"Nothing changes, Mr. Shaw. Would you rather she had been put ashore still alive?" Borodin's voice hardened. "She'd have been killed by her tribe. Tainted from the outside."

"You cannot justify what happened."

"No." Borodin faced him with eyes open to slits. "And you are not in a position to judge, are you, Mr. Shaw?"

Shaw looked away from the pirate. No, there was no answer, only escape.

He stared at the distraction in front of them. "Why are we here?" He couldn't see beyond the ridge of cliffs bordering the shore. There was no inlet ... nor bays to moor in. No signs of habitation, not even a fishing boat.

"We're going ashore."

A gust of wind blew Shaw's hair in his eyes. "Why?"

"Captain says so. We go when he's ready."

Which meant noon, maybe later, depending on when Peech had passed out last night. "What's there?"

"No more questions, Mr. Shaw. You'll be going with us."

CHAPTER 25

Hell is empty, and all the devils are here.
-William Shakespeare

A gull cawed.

As a quartet of pirates rowed beside him, Shaw craned his neck, tracking the bird until he lost it in the glare of the sun, thinking it would be nice to pretend he was on holiday. Perhaps a pleasant boat ride, followed by a picnic. With a sigh, Shaw knew the wish for just that, a wish.

He did enjoy blessed quiet at last; Farley had been left behind. Only the crash of waves against the rocks accompanied them. Two more pirates sat at the bow. One cradled a loaded rifle, and the other trained a spyglass on the unwelcoming shoreline.

Peech, belligerent and hung over, sat in the rear, squinting against the glare off the water. A knife was strapped to his belt along with a bag of shot, and he appeared formidable, even more so because he didn't try. As he flexed and relaxed his hands, his tattooed arms rippled with suppressed muscles. By his side lay a decorated machete, probably picked up in an upriver raid. Another machete lay on the other side of Borodin—just out of Shaw's reach, in case he had the urge to hack them to pieces and row back to Rio. A mystery to Shaw was a pile of empty burlap bags on top of more rifles. What did Peech expect to find ashore?

And how would they land? He could only see a line of rocks, exploding surf, and the towering cliffs in front of them.

Borodin held a spyglass to his eye, and his lips were pressed so tight they puckered his face. The tension in the man delivered a trickle of dread to Shaw; a simple raid wouldn't rattle Borodin.

Sweat ran down the faces, arms, and backs of the rowers. Shaw glanced aft. Behind them, another boat laden with a party of pirates followed along, their oars dipping deep in the waves. The crashing and pounding from the sea against the rocks grew louder, the current swifter. Borodin lowered the glass and slid over to replace the pirate sitting at the tiller.

The rocks, carved sharp by the unending surf, loomed closer, and the sun burned hot, as if they'd entered another equatorial zone. Over the last week, Shaw had shed a layer of burnt skin and the pallor of London, and now he followed the example of the pirates, removing his shirt.

As the boat drew closer to the coast, seaweed snaked upward through the agitated water. Silver-striped fish darted through the tendrils that tickled the underside of the boat, becoming a tangled forest that moved with the current. When a pirate pointed to a ridge of pink coral, Borodin nodded Buddha-like, and Shaw's anxiety grew. The coral would be razor sharp and like an ax to wooden hulls.

Now that they neared the shore, Shaw observed what most passing ships wouldn't be able to; below the cliffs, shallow caves dotted the shoreline under natural limestone arches reminiscent of Roman bridges. As he tried to see into them, the waves grew higher. Shaw couldn't remember a starker, more forbidding coast.

Peech had the spyglass and studied the caves, his thick neck turning degree by degree. In Shaw's fantasy, the bastard seemed to have a favorite point of reference in a rock formation atop a cliff that resembled a kneeling woman.

The tension in the boat increased as the current pulled them along. The pirates were no longer rowing, but holding tight to their oars just above the waterline as Borodin steered. In the distance, the *Hussar* floated behind them, a menace and symbol of safety.

With a loud rending, they hit a submerged rock. The pirates at the bow stabbed the water with oars, pushing them off again. The following boat saw them, skirted the rock, and swung around, missing their bow by inches. Peech stood and screamed oaths at them. As he sat again, their boat lurched into an eddy, and Shaw nearly toppled out when the current seized them. The swells had become ten-foot waves propelling the boats toward shore.

Through a curtain of water, Shaw glimpsed the cliffs. Then they dipped into a trough and skimmed toward land, riding a tunnel of rushing water. As they scraped along a line of coral, they heard a rending of wood as their boat bumped into more rocks. The fingers of coral below them multiplied, and before them, the overlapping waves collided with the rocks, exploding in geysers of spray. One of the pirates tried to protect the rifles as they scattered across the bottom of the boat. When Shaw reached for one, Peech kicked him in the head, and he fell against Borodin.

Shaw wiped blood from his nose and peered through a burst of white stars until he could see again. He didn't even know why he'd reached for the rifle, but he didn't wonder long because of what happened next.

A crackling concussion and a chorus of shouts jolted the air as the boat behind them spun broadside into the rocks, breaking open and dumping the pirates into the churning waves. Shaw held on as their own boat caught a wave square on. When he could see again, only pieces of kindling remained from the other boat and a suggestion of faces and arms in the whirlpools below. Shaw sputtered, trying to respond as a Christian witnessing death, even for evil men—but he couldn't formulate the words. Peech could.

"The hell with them!"

As if the tides could hear him, their speed increased, slamming the boat like a bullet toward the cliffs. Borodin gave up the tiller to hold on as they twisted and turned, bumping into the rocks, tilting hard over, and then shooting forward again. Shaw couldn't see the *Hussar* anymore through the waves and spray.

Suddenly, they fell into a perfect calm. Floating, hardly moving as their boat neared the mouth of a cave. In concert, as if they'd rehearsed it a dozen times, Shaw and the pirates ducked, and the boat slipped under a jagged arch barely above the prow, the arch looking for the world like a toothless mouth gaping open.

The cave had swallowed them. Dank, mossy walls of black obsidian framed the cave as it expanded into a large chamber where light ribboned the water from the cracks in the ceiling. They floated in a fern-lined amphitheater where Shaw had no trouble imagining ghosts whispering and dancing in the air around them.

"High tide, Mr. Borodin?" Peech asked, twisting to survey the chamber through the gloom.

"Aye, Sir." As Borodin spoke, the boat drifted under a beam of sunlight; the effect christened Peech's henchman and turned his face into a study of shadows and planes. His eyes gleamed with uncharacteristic excitement that frightened Shaw more than the ferocious waves and the cold hearts of the men he traveled with. What were they doing here?

Shaw turned around. On the cave wall, indistinct shapes loomed, becoming clear...In row after row, *corpses* hung on the walls, rising from the water. Shaw gasped as each tier became visible. They had been crucified on the obsidian walls! Feathers decorated the bodies and protruded from grinning skulls. Some skeletons had the bleached quality of age while others still sported tufts of white hair ... and their faces seemed alive...

The shiver started in Shaw's toes. Then his knees jumped and jittered, and his shoulders shook as his scream bounced between around them, dissipating upward. Peech backhanded him, and Borodin caught the back of Shaw's pants and yanked him into the boat again. A face full of fetid water cleared his mind. Shaw subsided, gulping air.

Peech said, "If he screams again, cut his throat."

Borodin nodded assent as the pirates skimmed their oars over the surface, moving the boat to the far side of the cave. Shaw's breathing slowed to normal.

From the gleaming black obsidian walls and the ivory bones of the dead to the golden streamers of light falling from the ceiling, the scene looked horribly beautiful. To Shaw, it seemed as if the skeletons appealed to them, greeting them with outstretched hands, lending the scene an eerie quality Shaw never hoped to feel again. He looked closer; pearls, opals, rubies, and slivers of gold decorated the dried seaweed slung like garlands around bony shoulders and woven into rib cages.

"Notice anything, Mr. Shaw?"

Peech's bantering startled him. Shaw looked again. Wordlessly, he shook his head. The dead descended in row after row into the green-black water so close to them that he could have reached a hand to touch their feathers. What did Peech expect him to see?

"The walkway, Sir," Borodin pointed. Carved into the rock at the highest tier, a narrow walkway encircled the edge of the amphitheater.

"Do you see the way in, Mr. Shaw?" Peech asked in a kind tone.

If Shaw didn't know any better, he'd have sworn Peech was intent on corrupting him into his evil world. Why else would he ask him that? The bloody murderer was a bloody nightmare, not his friend. Shaw glanced around the cave. The circular paths met before an arch the height of a man and led into the shadows where the meager light couldn't penetrate.

As soon as they docked before the opening, a pirate pounded a stake into the limestone. The pirates not only seemed to know where they were going but what to expect.

With Peech in the lead, they disembarked, and Shaw and Borodin brought up the rear. As Shaw scrambled to stand on the ledge, he brushed against a corpse whose fingers felt like dry branches scratching his bare back.

"Hurry up, you bastards." Peech's distorted voice floated back from well inside the shadowed opening. "We have to get out again before low tide."

Shaw's last sight of their boat, and he freely admitted it was a fond one, disclosed the tide already receding, inching down the slick cave walls. Borodin had left a long line of tether. They would need it; even as Shaw watched, the retreating tide revealed another row of skulls adorned in wet feathers. When he spied a snake swimming into an adorned rib cage, he hurried faster into the passageway.

The walls narrowed, and as they walked through single file, Shaw became acutely aware that the pirate he followed hadn't bathed since Rio. Yet he wasn't offended; at least the fellow was alive enough to secrete offensive smells. Shaw also felt a bit naked—the pirates carried axes, machetes, and rifles. As their prisoner and unwilling voyeur, he strode along empty-handed.

Within minutes, the dank smell of the passageway evaporated, and the walls became less slippery. The salty sea scent that he was so used to was replaced by air that grew fresher and warmer and perfumed with a strangely cloying scent of flowers of a type that Shaw had never inhaled before. The uneven rock path they trod grew steeper, and ahead of them, the darkness lightened.

Three paces more, and Peech stopped so quickly that they all piled into each other. A few grunts and a murmur in their private language were exchanged. As Shaw opened his mouth, Borodin whispered, "Quiet. Otherwise, we're dead."

Shaw clamped his jaw; he didn't expect Peech to be up to any good. Over the pirates' shoulders, he discovered a curtain of greenery and bright sunlight. No birds chirped or other woodland sounds … until he heard a muffled chanting.

Borodin hissed in his ear, "You stay here."

"Then why did you bloody bring me?"

"Quiet, Mr. Shaw. The Captain says you watch. That's all. Don't go for the boat—you'd never make it back through the rocks." Borodin's whisper broke off at a signal from Peech. Without apology, he shoved Shaw to the ground and climbed over him, following the others.

CHAPTER 26

It is natural to die as to be born.
-Francis Bacon

As Shaw stood again and stared out the opening, his breath caught.

Idyllic, narcissistic; his first thoughts could only be described as pure sensation, like a prurient dream he shouldn't acknowledge seeing or enjoying.

Under a canopy of trees, he spied Indians—dozens of them, naked except for elaborate headdresses of exotic feathers. They leaned against trees, reposed on benches, or fornicated on expanses of velvet-like grass. Their hair was bleached of color, and their eyes were just as colorless under white lashes. With skin so pale, so translucent, their blood vessels seemed like red lace traveling over the shadow of their bones. The soles on their feet and hands glowed a rosy pink.

Shaw felt no embarrassment, only fascination; the women had full, ripe breasts, broad hips, and they walked in a swaying, unconscious sensuality. He had never seen women like this. He'd not even heard about them. On a carpet of grass, a tiny child-woman rolled from side to side, her laughter echoing in cascading peals of merriment.

Shaw sniffed the air. The source of the perfumed smell seemed to come from the thousands of white flowers with blood-red centers. They dripped from a profusion of bushes that carpeted the wide area between ponds, trees, and what appeared to be a shrine. Captain Peech's strange traveling cruise had turned surreal. And erotic.

All the colors, scents, and sights seemed heightened, and the picture before Shaw was intense and overwhelming. To his left, a group of Albinos reposed in a mound of entwined bodies and legs. Most of them appeared young with luminous, silky skin, and Shaw found himself drawn again to the pixie-like woman. Then something new caught his attention.

Two women, holding hands, stepped into an azure pool in the center of the glade where an Albino man floated on his back, a beatific smile on his face. He reached an arm to one woman, stroking her hair. The other woman emerged from under the water and grabbed his foot, tickling it. He splashed crystalline water at her and gracefully turned and dove underwater. Shaw blinked, wondering if he was imagining it all.

The air grew warmer, and he wiped his brow as the scene wavered, then refocused to his distinct unease; on the far right of the glade Peech and the pirates crouched behind a blind of unnaturally green foliage with knives in their teeth, their rifles and machetes ready.

Peech scurried further into the glade, darting between clusters of odd-shaped, obelisk stones, followed by the other pirates. Borodin remained behind the foliage, his rifle trained on the nearest group of Indians.

Shaw's sense of right and wrong warred within him. Borodin had said that Shaw and the rest of the pirates could die only minutes ago. But what about the Indians who so innocently played and frolicked in front of him? They were unarmed in every sense of the word. Could he protect them? There would come a time soon when he would sacrifice himself to prevent Peech from killing. He started forward and faltered to a stop. Either he didn't have the courage, or he hadn't seen enough evil.

In the next few moments, Shaw discovered why they'd dared to come ashore through the forbidding rocks and why Peech had taken such a risk. Behind the Indians and the obelisks where Peech crouched, the sun shifted and seemed to concentrate on a specific spot causing the stones to shimmer. Shaw blinked. The stones gleamed as they formed features and solidified, becoming lifelike statues of gold. Most fascinating, they had the faces of infants.

Peech and the other pirates did their best to hide behind the statues. At his signal, the pirates sprang forward. When they touched the golden babes, a tremendous screeching tore the air, rupturing the peaceful idyll. The women wailed. As the Albinos cried out, their skin darkened, becoming otherworldly as the cacophony grew louder and a sharp wind arose.

With the statues tucked under their arms, the pirates turned to run. From all directions, the screaming Albinos rushed toward them as Peech leapt over shrubs and splashed through pools. The other pirates ran after him.

Like the Indians, the trees and bushes had darkened, and their twisted branches waved demented arms. Then a tree shimmered, just as the stones had; Shaw gasped as it changed into a wolf. In seconds, the remaining trees changed, too, the animals rising on their haunches and howling. Borodin splayed a string of shots into them, felling the Albinos and wolves that chased Peech and the pirates. When the pixie-like nymph took a blast in the face, her dying cry penetrated Shaw—more than any other sound he'd ever heard.

A pirate cried out as a wolf jumped on his back and buried its teeth in his neck. The perfumed air turned acrid with gunpowder and death as Shaw backed away from the glade, running back into the dark passageway. He had no trouble hearing the barrage of rifle shots, growls, and pounding of feet that followed him.

Shaw burst out of the tunnel and skidded over the ledge above the grotto. As he fell, he clawed at the slick wall for the tether, instead finding clouds of feathers that floated with him as he slid through the first layer of impaled skeletons. Shaw grabbed the rope, swinging face first into the wall and into the arms of a corpse that became animated at his touch, embracing him. Whether intimately or aggressively, Shaw didn't know; he just screamed. And he bloody well didn't care who knew it.

He twisted out of the grasp of the corpse and loosened his grip on the rope, half falling and rappelling downward until he landed in the boat. From above him, Peech's shouts came, growing louder. Along with the commotion of the chase came a series of echoing shots blending with the agony of the dying Albinos. Suddenly, Peech's ugly round face loomed over him.

"Catch, boyo!"

Peech flung the golden babe over the ledge, falling end for end, into Shaw's arms. It nearly went through the bottom of the boat. As Shaw rocked backwards with it, he couldn't help noticing how cold it felt to his touch, as dead as the nearby corpses. Repulsed and fascinated, Shaw scooted to the bow, laying the statue on the floor of the boat.

Peech started down the rope, hand over hand. With a shout, another golden babe was tossed over, missing the boat and sinking fast into the water. A second pirate started down the wall after Peech, just as Borodin made the ledge above them. Shaw could see his back and the flash of his cutlass as he fought off the screeching and clawing Albinos.

"Jump!" Peech roared.

Borodin plunged the cutlass into an Albino woman, using her as a shield, and shoved her into them. Then he jumped for the tether and came down fast, landing hard as the other surviving pirate cut the line free. Without thinking, Shaw took up an oar along with the others. They rowed furiously as the tide drained away, and above them, the high-pitched screeching of the Albinos clamored with outrage and grief that resounded in the cave.

Over Peech's shoulder, Shaw saw something made from night-mares—the corpses on the walls began to move; their skulls pivoted on bony necks, and they jerked like puppets in their excitement.

"Keep rowing!" Peech yelled in his face.

As their boat neared the mouth of the cave, Shaw's oar struck something hard. He dipped the oar again. Something pulled on it from underneath the water. All around them, ivory arms emerged, then dozens more corpses swam to the surface, clawing their way through the water. The bodies on the walls flailed and struggled until they detached themselves and fell into the water to join the others. Peech elbowed them off his back, and another slithered into the boat. Borodin's oar caught it full on, and he swatted it off.

With his face ribboned in blood, Borodin rowed, ignoring the furor, and he rowed hard. Shaw increased his speed, matching him. They shot into the passage, skimming along, fleeing the tumul-tuous onslaught that echoed behind them.

As the boat squirted out of the cave, it caught the outgoing tide into the inlet, leaving behind the Albinos' grief and outrage as it faded away. When their boat caught the current, Borodin left the oars and grabbed the tiller. Still terrified, Shaw rowed, not believing they'd made it, and he wouldn't be certain until they boarded the *Hussar*. Repeatedly, they fought their way to the crests of the waves, fell back, and climbed again, edging away from the cave.

"The rocks, Mr. Shaw! The rocks!" Peech bellowed.

Shaw scooted forward, stabbing an oar into the frothing, churning waves, each time receiving a jarring response from what lay just under the surface.

The afternoon sun had deserted them. With a bleeding sunset sitting on the horizon, the *Hussar*—so forbidding and evil—had never looked so beautiful. A larger boat of pirates, dispatched to meet them, drew near. Shaw spied a huge rock straight ahead. He yelled, and Borodin swung the tiller, but not in time. As if he speared fish, Shaw hit it square on with the oar, and they veered away. A line slung to them by the other boat sailed over their heads. Peech snared it with an oar, and in minutes the other boat had them in tow, heading back to the ship.

Shaw stared at the golden babe that lay at his feet. What had they done?

CHAPTER 27

My priorities had logic to them; find out what we had and make sure it stayed dry.

Only a few hours remained until sundown. Like an exhausted sentinel ringing the discordant bells of doom, the clanking pumps from the bowels of the *Passat* accompanied me everywhere on the ship. At one point, I rested, watching the men taking turns at the pump and noting each one broke into a sweat in the freezing air after only a few turns of the handle. Angelo, with his arm in a sling, took a turn, followed by a sullen Morse.

Periodically I looked in on Mrs. P, of whom I'd become protective and fond. With her sagging jowls and dazed expression, she just sat still, deflated, and wrapped in a shawl. Her wire-rimmed spectacles had washed out the cabin door the night of the storm.

When Jessica arrived with a cup of soup and seated herself before her aunt, I went back on deck. The idea of food did not sit well with my stomach.

By the late afternoon, the rain and sleet had abated, leaving the wind to beat the waves into a frothy meringue a chef would be proud of. The blanket of black clouds still covered the *Passat*, promising more rain. As I looked over the rail, I sighed; a day of pumping and we only floated a few inches higher.

That reminded me of something I'd meant to do.

With the loud droning from the pumps as accompaniment, I approached the hold and made a quick check for Browne's where-abouts; he would disapprove of my mission. Without the vigilance of the steward, the Captain, or anyone who kept records of cargo, there was no telling what was down there. Something unimportant before could be vital now. Natural light was fading rapidly; it would do to hurry.

A moldy stench billowed out as soon as I laid the door back. I pulled on the rope ladder, testing it. After taking a last breath of fresh lung-freezing air, I turned around and started down the ladder.

It certainly was a mess. During the storm, the mounds of cargo containers had fallen over, splitting open and crushing whatever lay in their way. The remaining eight-by-eight-foot crates that had been wedged in stacks meant to sway with the ship now leaned at precarious angles. Browne would kill me if he knew I had come down here. I shrugged; Browne was busy. And obnoxious.

Under a halo of eerie light, I clung to the ladder a few feet above the bottom of the hold and twirled in a slow circle. The cavernous room had a reputation as a dark and unhealthful place at the best of times, and with stagnant water fermenting in the bottom, it smelled worse. Pieces of wood and flotsam floated inches below my feet.

Something moved in the water on the starboard side, eddying the surface. As I wondered if I'd have to share my ladder with a rat, the oily water smoothed out again.

Without warning, something blocked the light from above. Heaps of water-logged rigging tumbled down, knocking me into the fetid slush. I cut off a scream when I hit the water, creating a splash that ricocheted off the walls.

The hatch slammed shut; whoever had thrown in the rigging had withdrawn. It was much darker... I felt panic rising in my chest. Didn't he hear me scream? The bastard.

"Hey!"

No answer.

I struggled to my feet. Water lapped at the tops of my thighs. "Help!"

The rope ladder dangled about a foot above my head and to the left. I took a step toward it and fell face-first across something that rose in the water, something I'd freed from where it'd been wedged.

It turned over.

Daniel Murphy's bloated face bobbed just below the surface, his shoulder bumping into my hand. Small teeth had already nibbled his eyes. His mouth gaped open as if grinning at my fear as I shrieked and flailed in the water, shrieked more, and jumped for the rope.

Light flooded the hold again. I caught a glimpse of Browne's face as he started down the ladder. My screeches became whimpers, and I grabbed his hand. He jerked me up and under his arm, then pushed me through the opening. I belly-crawled across the deck and lay still until Browne scooped me up and held me. It seemed I was crying.

"Murphy—" I pointed. "D-dead." I buried my face in his chest. Browne's arms were around me, but I could feel him leaning over, trying to see into the hold.

"What were you doing down there?" he growled.

He cared more for what was decomposing underfoot than what blubbered in his arms.

"What were you doing down there?" he repeated.

"Someone threw ropes on top of me and k-knocked me into the water—"

"Ropes?" Browne raised his brows. "We *need* rigging. None of the crew would throw them down there."

"Someone threw ropes on me!" I shouted. Nothing could stop me from crying faster than being called a liar. "Heavy ropes." I tried to get loose from him. "Let me go!"

"I'll talk to the men." He stroked my hair.

I knocked his hand away. "Don't treat me like a child."

"Why would anyone throw ropes into the hold?" He brought me to my feet.

"Maybe he couldn't throw a knife that far!"

"Calm down. I'll talk to the others. Maybe they didn't know you were down there."

"Assume anything you like. It was done on purpose."

"Miss Coulter—"

It sounded like the beginning of an arrogant lecture. "Save it, Browne."

I felt a warm hand on my shoulder.

"I wouldn't want anything to happen to you."

"Thank you for bringing me up." I shivered and took a deep breath. While he was a bit mellow, it seemed as good a time as any to tell him. "Browne?"

He released me and took a step back. Damn it if he couldn't tell when I was about to say something he didn't want to hear. I waited until his curiosity got the better of him.

"Yes, Miss Coulter?"

"You said you released Murphy from irons before the storm hit."

"So, I did." His eyes narrowed.

"He didn't die in the storm." I pointed at the hold. "Someone slit Murphy's throat."

As Browne climbed down the rope ladder to retrieve the body, the rain returned in a fury. I grabbed a tarp and tried to cover the opening. The bellow from below, because he couldn't see, made me remove it. Twenty minutes later, the downpour had washed the stink from the hold off my clothes, and we'd pulled Murphy's body up and onto the tarp.

Daylight, or gray-light, began to fade. While avoiding where I had found Murphy, I continued to salvage what hadn't broken, stopping to sip a cup of soup-a-la-Jessica. I still wasn't hungry but recognized that I couldn't go on ignoring food indefinitely. When she returned to her aunt in the salon, I scrounged in the galley for salt, dumping in a big scoopful. That should help. As I stirred the pot, the bits of dried beef and peas drifted around like the pieces of the *Passat* that still floated with us. I closed my eyes to the image and gulped the rest of the cup.

Mrs. P had taken to wandering like a blind sheep, bumping into furniture and out the salon door where she could fall overboard. Jessica learned to stay with her. The vacant look in her aunt's eyes indicated more than the loss of her glasses. Until we were rescued, there was nothing we could do for her besides keep the stove lit and stir the pot. From the many copies of the Bible we had, Jessica had taken to reading it to her. Before I left the odd comfort of the salon, I scrounged until I found a tin of oregano. Into the pot, it went.

With a cup of tea and another of soup, I carefully walked with the roll of the ship to stand under the bridge. Browne's shadow moved from fore to aft, and I could hear his cursing, mostly the same two-word Olde English invective, over and over again. A strip of a soggy chart sailed over the rail.

"Browne!"

"What, Miss Coulter?"

He sounded harassed. He needed to be harassed.

"I've got your tea and soup."

"I'm not thirsty or hungry." He leaned over the rail and took them.

"What's the matter?" I asked.

He cursed, pivoted, and left me standing on deck. A minute later, I noted that in the short time it took to climb up there, the man who wasn't hungry had drained the soup.

"What's the matter?" I repeated.

He glowered. "Curse it! I can't find my charts or instruments—" He flung a hand around the bridge.

Granted, it was untidy. "But with the cloud cover," I looked in all directions to see if anything had changed and confirmed that if we hadn't been floating in it, one couldn't tell the difference between the sky and the sea. "How can you expect—"

"I want to know where we *are*, Miss Coulter."

"Obnoxious, ungrateful, arrogant swine."

While I muttered endearments to the first officer, I stepped around a pile of debris I hadn't removed and entered the Captain's cabin. His sextant, ancient but usable, was mounted on the wall. From a footlocker, I unearthed curious-looking maps and other instruments I couldn't recognize. Maybe the swine could. I gathered them up and returned to the bridge.

After dumping them on the chart table, I turned to go. Warm hands grabbed my shoulders. I sneezed.

The hands dropped. "Damn it! Get some dry clothes on."

"What the hell for?" To prove my point, the rain started again, pelting the murky water and splashing across the deck and the parts of the bridge that no longer had a roof. "You're as wet as I am—and a hell of a lot more bull-headed!"

An hour later, I leaned over the rail, too exhausted to move but unwilling to admit it. If we'd had a sun, this would have been the moment it gave up in a blaze of orange and red.

A thin, almost imperceptible line of gold remained, separating the clouds on the horizon from the darkening water. At this very moment, it wasn't raining. I pushed away from the rail and straightened, feeling every cold, constricted muscle. The highlight of the afternoon had come when I'd found two intact lamps besides those that hung from gimbals in the forecastle and bridge. Finding more wicks would be for tomorrow.

I glanced back at the water and stopped.

Big, bluish, and smooth, what I spied looked longer and wider than the *Passat*. A whale? It flipped over. And *glistened*...

"Ice!" I screamed.

Two crewmen came running, and Browne lurched out of the galley.

He pivoted and scanned the area. Not too far away, more of it floated, lumpy and submerged near the jagged peaks that rose from the deep water like horned sea monsters.

We had drifted into an ice field.

"Holy mother, Jesus, Mary—" Angelo fell to his knees and crossed himself. The other sailors, Casey and Green, didn't say a word. The terror dancing in their eyes could have been seen from across the deck. They looked to Browne, who recovered first.

In a few strides, he reached the main cabin and started unstrapping the iron poles lashed to the wall. He roared orders, and the two remaining sailors came running from the forecastle.

"Two of you at the bow. One on each side." He turned, "Miss Coulter, you'll be the watch."

I regarded, without enthusiasm, the remaining mizzenmast that poked up into the clouds. Browne urged me ahead of him and gave me a boost.

Feeling every muscle that wasn't already screaming, I climbed. But I couldn't—wouldn't—go to the top. Sweat trickled down my back and froze to my shirt, and it tickled. Lucky me. What remained of the mast swayed like a drunk when I'd only ascended halfway. The perspective from here had a unique quality. Perhaps it would help detect a passing ship, but Browne's directive was to watch the water near us for ice. He shoved a pole in Morse's arms and sent him to the stern.

We spent the next fourteen hours in this position. As much as I hated climbing up, I abhorred going down and not knowing if we'd hear a sudden rending of our hull and then sink.

Around midnight, Jessica ferried cups of god-awful soup to everyone. I think she added sugar. After a few sips, I tossed the rest. From the immediate swearing, Browne must have been tramping by on the shadowy decks below.

The invasive cold and the stamping of feet on the deck kept me awake. Then Browne's bass rumbled, floating upward in song. Angelo's tenor answered in the same cadence, repeating the ditty. Morse was silent, but the others joined in, out of tune but consistent. The song grew old long before they quieted. Instead of taking comfort from their chanty, I realized how alone we were and how vast the ocean could be. When Browne called up asking if I would sing for them, I told him that if I did, I would cry.

As their singing faded in and out, depending on how far away they walked, I swung my feet for circulation and regularly shifted position on the frozen and uneven crossarm. I certainly stayed awake. Developing a rhythm where I twisted and turned like a marionette without strings to keep an eye out helped. So did seeing the ice as it lurched unpredictably in a black sea. Once, an iron pole connected with something hard, followed by a long chilling scrape that wasn't repeated.

As a soggy dawn crept upon us, I leaned against the mast and shivered. The rain had returned an hour before.

With the glass to my eye, I gazed at a gradually lightening sea in which the *Passat* was dwarfed by the blue and white masses of ice. Like medieval castles, crystallized minarets crowned the ice floes, and spires and pinnacles decorated others. The irregular peaks raised thinning ice branches to the sky, where they shone in the light. My mind played tricks on me too; Some of the bergs were massive, like ships of ice with empty masts not unlike our own. What if frozen ships existed inside them?

The sun rose higher through a curtain of light rain, and the ice glistened as the sea turned from black to an intense, clear green.

The *Passat* rested a few hundred feet from a berg that rotated in the current and bobbed just under the surface. Of all things, it resembled a smooth and enormous baby's behind being rocked from side to side with an invisible hand. The berg drifted slowly to the east, with the *Passat* trailing behind it like an unwilling toy wagon.

I looked straight down into the water. How odd ... Shapes moved below. They weren't fish. They *moved*, not *swam*. The water became clearer and—

My first scream split the silence open. Too terrified to reason, I screamed again and again and wrapped my legs around the mast, clinging to it, and screaming with my eyes closed.

The mast shook violently, and a hand yanked my foot. I tumbled down.

Browne caught me and jumped onto the deck.

Echoes of explosions, gunshots ... but there weren't any.

It was the ice.

I screamed into his chest.

He whispered fiercely, "Loud-noises-break-up-ice!"

The crackling barrage echoed, triggering others, echoes on top of echoes, as the ice fractured.

Browne covered my mouth, cutting off my scream. I couldn't breathe and struggled to free myself. He clamped tighter. "Stop!" Browne growled into my ear. I went limp, starting to black out from a lack of air. His hand dropped, and he studied me as I gasped for air.

"I saw... saw—" Whimpering, I buried my face in his chest again and shuddered, once more reliving what I saw in the water.

"What did you see?" he asked, and I felt him edging toward the rail.

Too—horrible—I shook my head, not wanting to look again. My ear rested on his heart as he looked over the side. The steady beat did not change; he didn't see anything. A morsel of hope dawned. Perhaps I didn't see anything either? Was I just succumbing to irrational fears from exhaustion or fright?

Browne straightened and slung me over his shoulder. In three strides, he opened the door to the salon and dumped me onto a mildewing sofa. Mrs. P wriggled out of a chair and started for the door. Jessica caught her and led her back.

Browne spoke over my head, "Get some dry clothes on her. She's hysterical."

Of course. And I faint, too.

CHAPTER 28

Light poured through the salon's portholes. At first, I thought I'd slept a long time, but then remembered the latitude-shortened days; we probably had no more than nine hours of light per day.

The clouds and rain had retreated. During the seven hours I slept, the sun must have appeared, if only for a bow and curtain call. With a good stretch of my back muscles, I tottered to the salon doorway. We no longer trailed the iceberg; instead, the *Passat* sat still, suspended in the ice field like a waterlogged moth caught in a cage.

It was beautiful, if hopeless. A mantle of red and gold bathed the furthest bergs while the ice sparkled benignly, denying it could fatally injure ships. I avoided looking over the side … that must have been just a different kind of fish I'd seen, one that my fevered brain had invented. But one that inexorably reminded me of what I'd seen during the *séance* that I wouldn't allow myself to think about.

Browne approached and shoved an almost warm cup of tea into my hands while eying me for an outburst or other signs of feminine irrationality. I ignored his scrutiny and gazed to the south, where snow-capped peaks and glaciers rose taller than the Andes.

Much closer, the ice resembled a surreal chorus line, framing the sea in all directions.

"Thank you." If he didn't mention this morning's incident, I wouldn't.

The smaller icebergs drifted within a few leagues of the *Passat*. On the lee side, two crewmen patrolled with long poles balanced on their shoulders. Just as Browne had done earlier, Angelo stood by the bridge watching me, and I did my best to look calm by willing myself not to worry about what I saw. As Browne stomped by, I asked, "Have you ever thought about death? What it means?"

His answer came easily. "Of course. We all die." He waved an arm toward the water. "We may die very soon."

"What I meant was," I sipped the tea, "Do you fear death?"

"I don't think of it. Not worth the time."

"But it must be faced." I risked a quick look into the water and up again. The mystery of what I had seen seemed so close, yet I was afraid to know more. In some ways, the storm we'd just gone through wasn't nearly as terrifying. "We don't know what death is."

"Morbid thoughts for a lady."

"Do I look like a lady?" I tried to laugh. My hair had more salt than dried beef, my hands felt as rough as shoe leather, and I dressed like a cabin boy—a dead cabin boy.

In contrast, Browne appeared handsome and aggravating. His dark hair could use a good brushing, but I made allowances considering we were in the middle of a catastrophe. He also seemed to be in fairly good humor. "I found Higgins's contraband yesterday," I said.

"Under the nitrate?"

I nodded.

The more I scrutinized Browne, I determined that he was tired. The bruise on his forehead stood out in stark contrast to his pale skin. "You need sleep. If I could throw you over my shoulder, I'd dump you on a moldy couch, too."

He shook his head. "Later, maybe. What was under the nitrate?"

As the sunset painted us in a film of pink, I pictured Murphy's face and swallowed hard. "It was more under the body, the part I saw. There were gunny sacks in crates that had broken open."

"What was in them?"

"Rifles. Scores and scores of rifles."

"I figured something like that," he growled. "Higgins is dead anyhow, damn him. Murphy too, or I'd whip his ass. Their greed could have sunk us."

As he spoke, I thought about the conflicts between Germany and France. The idea of supplying thousands of men with the means of killing each other should have been abhorrent to anyone, even Herr Higgins. Nearby, a house-sized chunk of ice cracked off the ice shelf and fell into the sea, sending spray hundreds of feet into the air.

"We're still sitting heavy. But the bilges are pumped, and they'll hold for a while if we can get out of here." Browne eyed me, almost with his old twinkle. "We might survive, Miss Coulter."

"You think so, Jack? After almost dying with you, I would think you could use my given name."

He laughed and turned me toward the stern. "Angelo is patching a sail together from the pieces left by the storm." As we watched, he dragged more rigging from under the debris and knelt beside it.

"You should have said something. I found a whole canvas this morning."

"Where?" Browne's eyes gleamed with hope.

"I'll show you." I wasn't averse to taking advantage of his optimism. "After you sleep." With the removal of the bodies and general disruption in routine, I hadn't had time to tell him yesterday. "Also, kerosene, boxes of matches, too. Some stores." Before this, I never would have thought the sight of a bag of sugar could be exciting.

Browne rubbed his hands together. "We'll jury a sail tomorrow and be able to maneuver if a wind comes up."

"Can we avoid the ice?" If we ran into one of those frozen mountains, it would put an end to my whining about salt in my hair.

"She's a big ship, but if we aren't going too fast, we can." An infant breeze ruffled his hair. I fought the urge to run my fingers through it. He eyed me. "Want to talk about what made you scream this morning?"

I tried to smile. At least he didn't use the words "fainted" or "hysterical."

The water around the ship darkened as the night wrapped around us.

"No," I whispered. Again, a fragment of what lay beneath the waves came back.

Browne slung a warm arm over my shoulders. "What was it?"

Such familiarity, but at least he was warm.

I shook my head. He wouldn't believe me. In fact, I doubted I believed it. "Where are the others?" It would be nice to think that there were many sailors still with us, but I knew better.

"Voss and Carey are asleep in the forecastle. Jones and Green are on watch."

"I should learn their names." It seemed easier to recall the faces of crewmen who were no longer with us than to feel guilty because they had died. That led to nagging questions I had thought about all day: *why were we spared? Why not them?*

"I'll make sure they introduce themselves." He yawned.

"Sleep, Browne." He looked dead-tired. "I'll wake you for the watch." Perhaps it was cheating, but I used my familiarity with him to touch his chin and win my point. "You need to sleep."

"I will." He nuzzled my hand. "If you tell me why you screamed."

Always a contest. "Give it up." I snatched back my hand and pushed him toward the salon.

CHAPTER 29

By the pricking of my thumbs,
something wicked this way comes.
-William Shakespeare

Against the ice, the sea appeared blacker at night, and as I paced the deck, I realized the temperature had dropped further, each breath a puff of smoke in the frigid air.

After about six hours, I'd tried to wake a nearly comatose Browne, who grinned wickedly and attempted to pull me onto the sofa with him. From across the salon, Jessica blushed and resumed trying to get her aunt to eat. Mrs. P's condition looked unchanged; her spirit was still lost. In contrast, Morse appeared invigorated by our predicament as he quickly marched by the door toward the bow.

Tonight, the Englishman strode the deck like he'd been born to it, his expression alive and jubilant. It would have been more natural to fear our chances for rescue, yet he showed no sympathy for the dead or even for his fellow passengers. His one comment had been, "Accidents happen. Higgins shouldn't have been about the deck during the storm. He wouldn't have fallen over." The medium apparently believed the false story we'd told regarding the trader's demise.

Hours after Browne arose, I still paced the deck, all the while aware of a deep and distinct fear that seemed to watch me from the shadows.

When a noise came from the bridge. I trotted to the rail below it. "What's wrong?" I kept my voice low. Browne moved around inside, cursing, dropping things, and throwing pencils.

More mutterings and the crash of something big against the wall.

"What's wrong, Browne?" I hissed, nodding politely to Voss as if nothing was wrong when he passed by on his round.

"Damn clouds," his grumble came. "I want to get our bearings."

"Leave it and come keep me company." Companionship, no matter how caustic, was welcome. The ship seemed enormous, which made my loneliness much more defined; I'd sung in halls smaller than the deck of the *Passat*.

"No."

He was hiding something.

"I'm coming up."

When I made it to the bridge, Browne ignored me. In fact, he wouldn't look at me as he fumbled through the makeshift navigation pieces.

"What's *wrong*?"

"Nothing." He shuffled papers at a table where a navigator had once sat making careful notes about the ship's course and location. As Browne continued to avoid my eye—his nervousness became tangible. A trickle of awareness and then a shiver ran across my skin on icy cat feet.

I grabbed his arm. "What *is* the matter?"

The same haunted look swam in his eyes as it had our first night at sea, bringing back how desperately he and the Captain had wanted to be through Cape Horn. And when.

Browne looked away.

Jessica hadn't sung out the time from the salon door recently, a duty she'd inherited because of the proximity of a mantle clock and an absence of live cabin boys. I watched Browne. He resumed shuffling through the charts and looking at the sky.

"What's *wrong*?"

Maybe it was the growing dread in my voice. He faced me. The fear in his eyes finally made the connection complete, the Captain's superstition, the murders, and the palpable worry in so brave a man as Jack Browne.

"What day is this?" I demanded.

He flinched.

All Hallows Eve. It had to be.

I staggered and turned. The rifle noise in the *séance*, the rushing water, the screams... "God—" I pulled at Browne. "We've got to stop *him*—"

"Stop who?"

As Browne spoke, the lamps on the bridge dimmed, and a long scream pierced the air. We rushed to the rail. The scream came again, answered by a grumbling report of breaking ice from much too close.

The deck appeared eerily deserted. Then the door of the salon flew open.

With a bloody knife clenched in his teeth, Christian Morse emerged carrying the limp form of Mrs. Pentifax. The heat from her body steamed in the frigid air, and her throat gaped open, gushing crimson.

"Browne!" I cried. Before we could move, Morse slung Mrs. Pentifax over the side like a sack of potatoes. From far below, the splash came, and in the murky water, ominous shapes swam to the surface, circling.

Browne cursed and pushed me back as he grabbed for the ladder, but this time I moved faster. He vaulted the rail to the deck, shoving me behind him.

The two sailors on duty at the bow thudded a few feet away. The ice grumbled.

Browne's eyes never left Morse. "Back to the bow, men!" He barked. "There's ice close."

The sailors retreated. I wondered where the crew from the stern were and why they hadn't responded to the commotion in front of us. It was a fair guess Morse had visited them with his knife but didn't dare to cross under the bridge and be seen.

Beyond the salon roof, deep bluish masses of ice glowed in the night, looming high above the ship. Morse disappeared inside the salon again. Browne started forward and stopped when the psychic had returned, dragging something pale.

"Browne!" I pulled at his sleeve. "Oh, my God..."

Stripped naked and her hands bound, Jessica lay at Morse's feet.

Browne took a step closer.

Morse brought the still-wet knife to her throat and inserted the point just under her chin. Browne froze. I faded back, intending to go around the bulkheads and come at him from the rear.

"Don't, Miss Coulter," Morse called. Then he laughed. "Get back where I can see you!" he waved the knife. "Move!"

"Let the girl go, Morse." Browne held an arm in front of me.

The meager light from the lamps swung with the roll from the ship, causing Morse's eyes to shine from the shadows before fading again. He grabbed a handful of Jessica's hair, pulling her to stand.

"So pretty." Morse's timing was as good as if he'd been on stage. "Pretty." He ran the knife tip under the rag tied over her mouth. A line of blood dribbled off her chin. Browne took another step toward them.

Morse brought the knife to her throat.

"Sir. First Officer. Sir—" Morse's manic laugh echoed across the deck. His eyes danced to the music in his head, and his voice dropped to the chatty tone he'd used when we'd sat in the café so long ago in Celize, sipping orange juice and discussing the voyage.

"Please lower the skiff." Involuntarily, I looked at the small boat strapped to the side at the forecastle. When Browne didn't move, Morse drew the knife from Jessica's chin to her other ear. "Now!"

Browne bestirred himself, slowly at first, then faster, probably realizing that we could be rid of the madman by giving him the skiff. In five strides, Browne reached the forecastle, the sound of the chains binding it loud in the unnatural stillness as he worked them loose. When the boat began its descent, I looked over the rail, wishing I hadn't. The watery surface bubbled like a caldron over a fire. *What was going on down there?*

Seconds more, and the boat swayed level with the bulwarks. Morse shouted, "Into the boat, Miss Coulter!"

I didn't understand, risking a look again into the water. Why would I get into a small boat to float in that frigid sea? Why didn't he get in?

With the knife in his teeth, Morse lifted Jessica over the side, dangling her by a foot. I didn't move, which infuriated him. Again, he waved the knife, slicing the air with each word while the venom in his eyes warred with the madness.

"Into-the-boat—Miss Coulter."

I looked at Browne, back to Jessica, then Browne again, and stepped to the rail.

"Wait!" Browne's said, his voice ragged.

"Now!" Morse yelled.

I scrambled into the skiff, causing it to buffet wildly.

"Swing it over here." Morse leaned over the rail, searching the water below.

With a death grip on the sides of the boat, I peered over the top, refusing to be frightened while suspended more than thirty feet above a churning sea and while I tried to figure out how to stop him. He murdered a defenseless old lady! Morse was much more than a foppish medium. It had been part of his acting. A whimper came from Jessica as she hung over the water, crying softly.

"Pull the girl back in, Morse," Browne growled and took a step toward him.

Morse lifted Jessica higher and then slammed her face first into the hull. The crying stopped.

Faintly at first, within the silence around us, the eerie noises I had last heard in the *séance* returned. I glanced in all directions but couldn't see the source. This time, the voices sounded clearer … the chattering, the desperation of men, hundreds and hundreds of them. But where did they come from? I watched while Morse cocked his head to listen. Although faint, he heard them too. The moonlight hit him, causing his face to stand out starkly in the darkness.

"Greely," I whispered. Instantly and terribly, I recalled the newspaper article and the words Caparilli pronounced upon the sole survivor from the *Moira*: "'He is insane.'" And for all I could tell, he was immortal.

The psychic had heard my whisper. "Bitch!" He spat at me with his eyes full of hate. The ring of cold from the night of the *séance* returned, encircling my neck, squeezing. As I gasped, another piece of the mystery fell into place; Morse had just demonstrated a power no psychic possessed.

Chattering.

From the sea below us, the noise grew louder.

This time Browne heard it too; the puzzlement showed in his eyes. He adjusted the chains, and the skiff edged toward Morse. He still thought we could somehow get rid of the madman. I wanted to stop Browne, but the cold held me with an icy hand. Behind him, Angelo and Voss had returned.

The knife in Morse's hand gleamed, and as the boat swung closer to him, his attention bounced from the skiff to Browne and then to the water. Mine remained on his grip on Jessica's ankle, the only thing that kept her from a long fatal fall into the frigid water. What happened next made things much more interesting.

A reverberation came from the depths, sounding like undersea thunder. The psychic listened and then slapped Jessica against the hull as he cackled.

"Let them go, Morse." Browne edged closer to the rail, dividing his attention between the fiend and the growing chorus emanating from the sea.

The reverberation deepened.

From deep below, it began.

Quietly. Then, tumbling like an avalanche, voices echoed with other voices from thousands of men, their murmurs overlapping, threading together, growing stronger. Into the rumbling, the sliding and clanking of chains arrived, competing with the breaking of timbers and grinding metal. The growing clamor of rushing water overlaid it all. Above everything, *chattering*.

Over and over, the wind rattled glass until it exploded. Water pounded wood, doors slammed, and terse voices peeled away into a void, returning in shuddering waves of anguish. The rush from a monstrous flood of water heralded the screams emanating from a graveyard of shipwrecks and the agony of men who knew they were about to die. As their panicked screams competed with the thunder from below, Morse's eyes deserted me, and he listened, allowing the band of cold holding me to fade.

The cacophony exploded as the doomed men jabbered in Spanish, Dutch, Chinese—in every language they cried. Their screams pleaded, and commanded as their words coursed and prayed in a dreadful choir, shriller still, then burgeoning until I thought I could see them ... and feel their pain and futility.

I covered my ears. Louder. As they shouted in a concert of fear and confusion, the pounding of running feet and anguished pleas fused into a single voice that echoed, repeated, and grew.

Only one!

Chanting.

Come with us, only one! Only one!

Morse gave a shout of triumph and let go of Jessica's foot. She fell in a twirling spiral of flailing legs as Morse jumped into the skiff. The boat rocked wildly, nearly dumping me out.

The point of his knife pressed against my breast. He grabbed a handful of my hair and shook me. "It's mine! You fucking bitch—mine!"

I tried to speak, but the chanting roared, resounding in the frosty air.

Come with us, only one!

Morse had waited, and he had plotted. He'd kill many more times to have what lay in the water below—what I'd only glimpsed that night in the *séance* and now could see and hear. The veil betwixt the living and the dead had lifted, just as Captain McQuistan had so fearfully predicted.

Morse laughed. Blood still smeared his lips. "Only one! Only one!" he repeated and turned to Browne, who leaned over the rail. Angelo stood by with the chains braced in his hands.

"Take us down!" Morse ordered. When Browne didn't move, he jabbed me with the knife. I gasped, and my shirt grew wet with blood.

"Morse!" Browne pleaded, his eyes locked with mine.

"Lower it! And I'll let her go." Morse sent me a sinister smile, enjoying his lie because he saw that I knew it for one. In a calmer voice meant to appease Browne, he added, "After I'm down there. You can throw down a rope for her."

When the skiff hit the water, I would die; Morse would cut loose from the ship, no longer needing me as a way down there. The band of cold again held me prisoner. I couldn't warn Browne.

"Morse!" Browne yelled.

"Lower the boat!" The knife sliced my cheek, bringing stinging pain as hot blood gushed off my chin.

Browne waved an arm, and the chains clanked together. The boat descended. "Bastard!"

In a deafening wave, the voices grew stronger, and the jabbering rose to a crescendo ...

Come with us, only one!

A long scrape came from under the reverberation, as if an enormous door opened, and the sea roiled. The skiff hung above it as the water cleared to an intense green...

I screamed.

Thousands of skeletons, sailors and boys, their bones bleached white and their skulls rigid in agony, swarmed like fish in the water underneath us. *Chattering.* Below the writhing forms, in mounds of collapsed hulls and timbers, lay a vast undersea graveyard of ships surrounded by broken masts. Mountains of coins, rubies, and gold gleamed from within it all.

"Leave her be!" came Browne's agonized cry.

The boat dropped lower. I pressed my hands to my wound, stopping the blood, wishing I could stop the death cries of the sailors. Above it all, it sounded like ghostly cannons rumbling and more explosions as the ice broke up. Christian Morse released his hold on my hair and leaned from one side of the boat to the other, ready for what he had dreamed and killed for. The band of cold left me.

The last chains fell away from the skiff as we hit the water.

Morse slashed and sawed at the ropes binding the skiff to the *Passat.* I reared back and kicked him in the face. He fell flat, and his head hit the side of the boat as the first ivory hand snaked inside. Icy fingers touched my arm. I twisted away. Morse's bloodied face lost the greed, and he began to yell. I didn't have to kick him again. Boney arms and grinning faces crawled on top of him.

I kicked another dead sailor back into the water.

Come with us, only one!

Browne rappelled down the side of the hull, tossing a coil of rope half in my arms, the rest into the water. Dead hands tugged on it as I struggled to climb. Browne scrambled up and regained the deck, pulling me after him.

Behind me, Morse's screams escalated to shrieks as I bounced against the hull and swung high in the air, kicking off the outriders who clawed at my feet. The psychic's yells became muffled under the scraping of bony fingers and the scrabbling of arms and legs that sounded like an army of insects.

Browne pulled me upward. Nothing sounded better than his swearing.

I couldn't help but look down. The sea churned and boiled under the layer of dismembered bones and hollow-eyed faces that writhed and darted in the water, all the while jabbering.

"God Almighty!" I screamed as Browne grabbed my hand and yanked me up and over. As the chattering horde crawled up the hull of the *Passat*, the sound of nails scraping wood sounded much closer.

From the salon came an ominous sign. The clock struck the hour, slowly intoning twelve bells.

Midnight. All Hallows Eve.

A long and deep reverberation came from far below. As the veil thickened and began to close, the water darkened. Like dead flies, skeletons fell off the hull of the *Passat*, splashing back into the sea. The frenzied army of the dead swarmed the skiff and pulled Morse's bloodied body into the water, and they still chattered as they dismembered the boat and slithered under the surface. Without the brilliant light emanating from behind the veil, the sea rapidly changed to black once more.

The chattering repeated, fading.

Come with us.

Only one!

CHAPTER 30

Like the fish of the bright and twittering fin,
Bright fish! diving deep as high soars the lark,
So, far, far, far, doth the maiden swim,
Wild song, wild light, in still ocean's dark.
-Herman Melville

Falling.

Jessica gulped air as the sea rose to meet her. Like a school of fish, flickers of ivory moved in the water below. Riding a terrible clamor of voices, she plummeted headfirst through a wreath of bubbles and into the sea.

Arctic water seared her skin, and something scraped her arm. In the murkiness, she recognized the shapes as bones, feet, pelvises, and legs. A laughing skull with pits for eyes swam with her, its jaws snapping and hands entangling her hair. She plunged further.

As numbness overcame her, a thin stream of blood trailed behind her like a red ribbon. She saw herself from a distance, traveling past the skeletal hands that reached out of the blackness. Seconds more, a layer of sharks crowded the water; the sea's silent sentinels had arrived with their frozen eyes and gleaming teeth.

The sharks followed her descent, their velocity as great as her own. One brushed against her shoulder, and Jessica lost her last breath in an involuntary scream as she filled her lungs with sea-water, coughing and swallowing more.

Her vision clouded as the cold claimed her, reaching from her feet to her thighs and coursing through her veins and into her bones. Was this death—poignantly painless and cold?

The water changed to an intense clearness as she sank still more rapidly, leaving the sharks behind. Fish with bulbous eyes and vibrating gills appeared next, displaying flashes of brilliant colors. Then chunks of wood banged into her, and strings of sea-weed brushed her face as pink-bellied shells drifted by like colorful toys bobbing in the current. Roaring filled her ears. The chanting vibrated around her and undulated, melding into the water, and although she tried to hold on to it, logic deserted her. When Jessica opened her eyes, her memories had evaporated; everything she'd ever held dear she left further and further behind. Every sense became the sea.

The cold intensified, and the last of her bonds slipped away as she fell deeper still; wanting speed, she kicked her feet as the music of the sea, mysterious and pervasive, became tangible. Into it, the voices came again, chanting and screaming.

Come with us. Only one.

The water changed to a deep and beautiful green and enveloped her in serenity. She hadn't been afraid when she entered the water nor when she stopped breathing. And now, directly below her, an enormous shadow loomed dark and mysterious as the water cleared to the density of air.

Broken timbers, fallen masts, and an ancient sail lay on the bottom of the sea. Clouds of iridescent fish swam in and out of the portholes and the decaying wood. The center of the ship was like a chimera, indistinct and mysterious before it faded into darkness and disappeared into the deep shadows in the center of the wreck.

Around her, the chanting grew stronger and the music of the sea louder. Jessica extended her hands to a point, unerringly becoming an ivory bullet aiming toward the target.

Come with us. Only one.

The water shimmered, and from inside the ship, a veil of light blossomed and spread like an open vein in the darkness. The wooden deck dissolved as she passed through, the veil closing behind her.

Only one.

I cried.

Weak and womanly, I cried into Browne's chest. Sobs shook me as I kept looking over the side to see if the skeletons still clawed their way up the ship and if they still writhed in the waves and chanted from under the sea.

"Jessica—" I blubbered, knowing she must have died horribly. "Mrs. P," I sobbed again.

I felt the ship roll. The skeletons were climbing up the side! I screamed, feeling my mind come apart. Browne held on, murmuring words in my hair that sounded far away.

They were reaching for me—for all of us! We were going to die! I climbed over Browne, "Let me go! Let me go!"

Then I could remember no more.

I sniffed. Fishy mildew. When I opened an eye, inches away were pink flowers, the pattern on one of the salon sofas.

My bloodstained shirt was spread open. Browne sat beside me and dabbed something onto the wound on my side. I grimaced. That was what had woken me. My jaw ached, and I wondered why. From outside came the crackling and grumbling of breaking ice, sounding far away.

"Browne..." I winced and pushed his hand away. He regarded me warily, which served to bring it all back.

The shudder started in my right leg, then the other, as the rest of my body convulsed. I felt so *cold*. Browne covered me, holding on until it stopped. I lay still. Minutes passed, and he made no move to get up.

"Can't breathe, Browne."

He sat up, looking contrite. As he should. I rubbed my jaw.

"Did you have to hit me?"

He capped the bottle of vicious-looking liquid but didn't take his eyes off mine. "I thought you were going over the side out there." He stared some more. "You were hysterical. I'd do it again if I had to."

If he didn't look so serious, I would have said something. We held the stare for a long time until he blurred because the tears came, sliding unchecked down my cheeks. He used a fingertip to wipe them away.

"How long have I been lying here?" I asked.

"About eight hours, maybe more. I got some laudanum in you to calm you down."

That reminded me of the last time he'd decided I needed laudanum. This time, the situation required it.

"What did you see?" Browne asked and aimed a thumb outside.

Perhaps this time, he would believe me. I took a deep breath. "An enormous graveyard. It must be of all the ships and men who have died in the Horn. Thousands of them." My hands started to shake, so I grabbed his. "Only they weren't dead. Or I should say at rest."

He nodded. "Go on."

"The water was murky. You saw it."

His eyes hardened. "I did. And heard what was down there."

"The skeletons came from under us. Did you see them?"

"Yes."

"And the wrecked ships? And piles of gold?"

Browne nodded. That alone made me feel better—I wasn't crazy.

"Morse saw this?" he asked.

"He expected it. That was why he did it."

Browne rubbed his chin like I would love to. "He knew it was there. Didn't he?"

"Yes, like me, he saw some of it in the *séance*, but I think Morse understood what it was and where it was." I touched his hand. "Remember the story of the *Moira*? I just attributed the experience to that. But ... Morse—"

"Morse was after the treasure from the *Moira*?" Browne's brows headed for the ceiling in disbelief.

"No. Something more; he wanted the treasure from the hundreds of wrecks, too. Many more ships, much more treasure. That wasn't just a few artifacts we saw. Morse expected to find this... I couldn't understand until..." I took a deep breath, and Browne squeezed my hand. "Yesterday morning, I saw them, the dead sailors."

"When you screamed from the top of the mast?"

"Yes."

"You thought I wouldn't believe you." Browne's lips tightened despite his facade of calmness.

"I knew you wouldn't."

"We'll talk about that." He stroked my hand. "When you're stronger."

That sounded like the threat of a good debate. Like the old Browne. "What did you hear last night?" I asked.

"Thundering. Voices. From down there." He glanced out the door and looked thoughtful.

"The water changed color then. Like a gate opening in front of an enormous light." I couldn't describe it any other way.

He nodded. "And Morse thought he'd plunder the treasure when it opened?"

"Yes. And since you are in the mood to listen… Morse was John Greely."

"We don't know that."

It probably wasn't the best time to tell him about my snooping and finding the Caparilli article. Instead, I said, "If we were in Rio or anywhere, we could find out. There's a trail of information in the newspapers. Morse thought he'd get the treasure, and he came back for it, not the artifacts," I said.

Browne stood up to gaze out the porthole and then sat down again.

"You know, all the reports about the *Moira* that said someone survived weren't all superstition. Greely existed."

"Maybe. The Captain thought that enormous light we saw under the water, and maybe the skeletons, were real." Browne scratched his chin, remembering. "The Captain believed that whenever there is a place of mass death—things happen. He might have known more and just didn't say. Superstitious." His eyes grew speculative. "Maybe he heard it from another ship who heard about it. A hundred years ago, this probably happened to another ship on another All Hallows Eve. Only they didn't have Morse aboard."

His speculation faded, and it wasn't hard to decipher why. Browne looked sad. I touched his hair. "I'm sorry about the Captain."

He growled, "Morse was insane."

"Agree, and I feel so sorry for Jessica and Mrs. P. And the others, even Higgins."

"That was flat-out murder. Poor girl. And her aunt and the other passengers. And my men." Browne's eyes blazed, and he grumbled a curse under his breath. "Murdering bastard—I should have known."

"You couldn't have." I shook my head and then shivered. "You meant that he killed the others? Carey, Jones, and Green?"

Browne's expletive was my answer. Morse would have slaughtered us all, one at a time, if he could have. But he needed an incentive for Browne to lower the skiff for him. Now that I thought about it, he would have needed Browne to bring it up again unless he thought he'd row for days to reach land. I waited as another shudder passed through me. It was chilly here. My shirt still hung open, displaying my ruined corset. When I tried to close it, Browne took off the sweater he wore and helped me into it. It felt warm and smelled of him.

Weak light filtered through the windows. "You are going to be cold," I told him. The fire in the hearth had been rebuilt but needed stoking. As he opened his mouth to deny it, a shout from the deck sent him running out the door. I managed to run too, but not as fast or steadily.

Angelo and Voss, the two remaining crewmen, patrolled the deck, checking for ice. I hoped that was all we would see. Voss had issued the alarm.

"We're caught in the current, Sir. Thought you should know."

The *Passat* did move, though slowly and with a decided list to starboard. She had such a haggard, defeated air about her. The jury-rigged sail lay in a heap by the mizzenmast, and Angelo hopped around it, attaching rings and rigging. Browne turned and hesitated.

"How do you feel?" He looked me over. "You aren't big enough to fend off ice."

Aware I was about to say something stupid, I answered, "I feel fine."

"Good. We need a watch up top."

"Uh-huh," I sighed and began to climb the mast. Cass Coulter; world-renowned singer, destroyer of society's finest, and lookout boy on a lost ship wearing a dead cabin boy's boots.

The current lasted a few minutes before the *Passat* drifted to a stop. I remained up top. One look at the sea and I agreed we needed a lookout.

The field ice, bigger than islands and probably bigger than small countries, still covered the southern horizon. Not too far to the east, chunks twice the size of our ship broke off from the giant flows, creating thundering explosions that echoed to us and would forever stay in my memories.

As the bergs hit the water, the spray froze onto the sides of the parent glacier. The ice dipped and shouldered into the field, splintering off more segments that bobbed in the sea; they would make their way to open water, some moving to the east or drifting west, the rest floating toward the *Passat*.

If I didn't like those mobile destroyers of ships, there were many much closer. A few bergs sat in the water within a league of us, glistening like ice castles in a hot sapphire pool.

The top of a mast is a lonely place. For hours, I was left alone with the images of Morse carrying Mrs. P out of the salon and followed by the horrible moment when Jessica plummeted into the sea. Could I have done something? Yes, I should not have let the implications from the *séance* stand and acted after Higgins and the doctor were murdered. For God's sake! There was something *wrong,* and I did nothing. When my recriminations turned to tears, I had to hide my face from Browne and the others; there was nothing they could do about my guilt or to bring them back.

From all indications, it was noon. I huddled into a ball, careful not to tumble off the spar I sat on. If it weren't so cold, it would all be a beautiful dream. The clouds hung over us like a heavy gray blanket with a few moth holes letting in spots of weak sunlight.

After a while, the *Passat* appeared to be drifting away from the field ice, but the same current that carried us also brought the smaller bergs. According to Browne, the water was deeper than our anchor. We could rig up a sea anchor, but to use it, there had to be a breeze. I'd seen the contraption; it consisted of a brace and two types of back sails. When positioned against the wind, it held the ship steady. However, as Browne said, there wasn't any point in sitting still in the current; a traveling berg would probably ram the ship.

On that cheery thought, I sneezed, and it began to rain.

CHAPTER 31

With tragedy, time is relative. Certain things seemed immensely important. Perhaps only as a balance against the forces we could not control.

As an example, before the end of the first day, I somberly disposed of Morse's last two victims. He had killing in his heart and sleeping men at his mercy. They'd never made it to their duty stations. I wrapped each body in the corpse's own blood-soaked bedding, weighted it, sewed it closed, and tugged it over to the side. Angelo helped, crossing himself before and after touching the shrouds. Voss, the other remaining crewman, refused to help or make eye contact.

Through it all, day and night, the rain emptied from the heavens in an incessant downpour. Yet, there was a damnable absence of wind. Browne stopped on his rounds to remark, "Blow us to this bloody place. Blow us to pieces. But it can't blow us out of here."

With more than enough fresh water from the rain sails, I kept us in clean clothes. Angelo had taken over as much of the cooking as his injured arm would allow and oversaw my efforts, which could have been worse. He also reported we had food, despite Morse's sabotage. With no one watching, the madman had dumped the staples that he thought crucial over the side. Important they were, but he didn't realize that without fresh vegetables or fruit, scurvy would be upon us within weeks. Finding another cask of salted pork elicited a groan. Salt! My skin flaked with it. Salt water, salt pork, salt in my hair and on my face. Salt!

By the third day, most of the icebergs had drifted away, and the icefield appeared no closer than before, evidence that the current had dragged us around in a circle.

A weak sun blessed the *Passat* at dawn of the fourth day. By using the glass, everything within five leagues could be seen. All of this I spied from my usual perch on the mizzenmast. The situation was laughable; to anyone looking, I would resemble a scrawny robin with messy feathers.

Browne resorted to using the ship's bell to detect ice by timing its echoes. If the sound bounced back too soon, the *Passat* neared substantial ice. He and the remaining two crewmen kept an eye out for submerged sleepers, but the situation had lost its urgency. In fact, it had become tedious.

"Land!" I yelled at Browne. Black, snow-peaked mountains loomed in the north, beyond the ice field. "What is it?"

From his position under the bridge, Browne frowned and lowered his glass. "*Tierra del Fuego*, maybe Isla Hermite. Hell. I don't know."

Before he could again curse the loss of the charts and maps, I asked, "The compass?"

"With the armory of rifles that we've got in the hold, I'm surprised we didn't sail backwards before now." He started off on watch again, more of a stomp than a walk. "We've only drifted a few leagues east in four days."

I controlled a more refined curse and brought the glass up again. To the north, things appeared clear, and a bank of black clouds advanced from the south. Maybe there would be wind. Not a gale to rip apart our pitiful sail, just enough to move us along.

At sundown, my wish came true. Patchy clouds moved across the horizon like plump ethereal dancers, and a baby breeze freshened as Browne emerged from the galley with tea. He handed me some and headed for the bridge. By the time the stars came out, perhaps we would be under sail.

"We might have to take the canvas down," Browne said as I joined him on the bridge.

"Why?" The *Passat* needed to move, not sit here and die.

"Because we'd all be up all night with it, Miss Coulter." He watched the clouds. "Think about it."

I looked at the sky, trying to justify Browne's assumption. I still didn't like his attitude. I'd met a jackass in Carson City just like him. Yet, he could be right; I knew enough about ships to know it took a helmsman, a lookout, and many more men to handle a vessel of this size, even with one small canvas above her. We numbered enough if I counted. All our travels under sail would have to be a group effort.

The breeze deserted the ship by morning.

As I walked the deck, each step brought a creak from dull boards that had once gleamed on this proud ship. Life now depended on wind. With a private chuckle, I remembered when it depended upon applause, my voice, and the on-time schedule of trains. Not anymore. Today's agenda was to pack the personal belongings of the dead. I also wanted to start a journal about our voyage and the deaths.

Browne interrupted his cursing at his navigation efforts long enough to suggest I look for an extra journal in the Captain's quarters. He had taken over the ship's log but had no aptitude for narration; I had watched him labor over the single notation from a compass reading.

Opening the door to the Captain's quarters released musty air riding atop the faint scent of the Captain's aftershave. Poor man. I blinked to keep tears from forming. The Captain had been so superstitious—it turned out with cause—yet very sweet and dignified. He had been a very personal man, and it felt strange, as if I stole part of him by stepping inside. Shaking off the feeling, I set the lamp on his bedside chest and, for the first time, really scrutinized the cabin.

This was where the ship's theme of church and whorehouse had originated. The pious demeanor of the stained-glass panels faced the garish red of the wallpaper, and the plush and worldly bedspread went well with the picture of an opulent nude that hung over it. As I stood with my nose nearly touching the stained glass, I studied the details, noting the artist had depicted an angel in a rather flamboyant style. Interesting. Also, the folds of her robes hid a collection of small skulls. How strange.

Suppressing a shudder, I glanced to my left and back to the panels—the face of the angel and the nude were one and the same. Curious, but not as much as those chattering skeletons from the other night.

By comparison, the stained-glass panel in Higgins's cabin depicted an angel holding an infant in one hand and a torch in the other. In here, the angel held the infant, but the torch was upside down. Skulls replaced apples in the trees behind the angel. The panels reminded me of Tarot cards.

The upside-down torch and the air of serenity seemed to say our mortality isn't sudden. Nor is it to be feared. Expect death, just as the solemn and accepting countenance of the angel did. Perhaps I did understand. Could it be that, like a looking glass upon his soul, Death and the angel portrayed the worry that so often accompanied the Captain? It was something he could not accept.

I gave up wondering, sat at the desk, and tried his pen.

Log: November 4, 1851. Notations by Miss Cassandra Coulter To whoever should read this, please do not expect a precise seafaring account. It will not be colorful, and it won't be pretty. A diary of sorts, perhaps. But not a romantic tale. I have concluded that the sea is not romantic at all. Browne, and hopefully others, at some point, would read this. Therefore, I would be careful of what I wrote—declining to pull down my pantaloons by means of the pen for all to see.

There are four of us surviving our ordeal. First Mate Jack Browne, Mates Arnold Voss, Angelo Vitius, and myself, Miss Cass Coulter, recently of Washington D.C. We are of the opinion, our chances of survival are good if we are found soon.

At that point, I lay my head on my arms and became weepy and sentimental as my thoughts turned to waltzes on warm summer evenings, silk gowns, and soft petticoats. The smell of roses filled my senses, and I relived stolen kisses along the Potomac as the boats paraded in a majestic line. The sound of champagne corks popping seemed real, and the sharp smell of gunpowder, too, as firecrackers lit up the night.

I closed the log and ran a hand across the tooled leather, the sound like rocks scraping the bottom of a ship. My nails were broken, and my palms dry and reddened from climbing up the mast, hauling wood and dead bodies. So feminine.

Browne knocked on the door and bustled in, carrying buckets of water. More stood behind him, steaming in the arctic air.

"What are you doing?" I took a swipe at my tears.

He strode across the room, produced a key, and inserted it into a door in the corner. When he got the door open, I gaped. Beyond his rear end stood a large, claw-footed tub that took up most of the little room. I thought I'd never have another bath after we lost the other tubs in the cyclone.

"Your bath, Madame." Browne bowed.

I should have been suspicious of him. But all I could do was murmur "thank you" over and over again as he poured the buckets into the bathtub.

CHAPTER 32

B liss. The water I lay in, luxuriated in, and reveled in, could not have been finer if it had steamed from silver pails in the hands of virile young men warbling love songs.

I closed my eyes, and the soap bubbles became feathers wielded by angels, caressing my skin and moving between my toes. I held capfuls of them in my hands and dribbled the water over my arms, watching it sluice off and fall into the tub again.

Bubbles. Thousands of them winked at me before they popped and became part of the water once more. I stretched. Lying naked in a dead sea captain's private bathtub could be construed as callous. It should have sent chills racing up my spine. Instead, it restored my femininity. The morbid collection of skulls, silver-edged knives, strings of colorful beads, and even what looked like a shrunken head positioned above the tub seemed enjoyable. But everything good must come to an end. I did wait until the water had not only cooled off, but gave me goosebumps before I got out.

As I dried off, I examined myself, feeling my ribs easily and the prominence of my hipbones. If we existed on pea soup and dried pork much longer, I'd be outright skinny. Just the thought of food made my stomach growl, and I could taste a plate full of rare roast beef decorated with fresh greens.

The arctic air gradually replaced the steam in the tiny room as I combed and dried my hair. A discreet knock came from the cabin door beyond the outer room.

"Miss Coulter?"

Damn it. I opened the door into the main part of the cabin and looked for the clean clothes I'd thrown over the Captain's desk. "What do you want?" I called.

The clothes weren't there.

"I want to come in and see if your wounds are healing properly."

Sure, you do. Browne didn't sound dispassionate and medical; he sounded like the smug rat that had stolen my clothes from where I'd left them. He had probably slunk around while I lay half asleep and submerged in the bath.

I demanded through the door, "Where are my clothes?"

"Under my arm," Browne said. "They are what you might call insurance."

"For what?"

"For you inviting me in. You'd turn blue running across the deck to get more."

"Jackass."

"What was that?"

"I called you a jackass!"

I looked around the cabin. The wardrobe looked empty; Browne had removed all the uniforms and other clothes.

"You underhanded—"

"Miss Coulter?"

"Go away, Browne."

"'Fraid I can't do that."

I ripped a blanket from the bunk and wrapped it around myself, feeling the wind whistling under the door. But I couldn't stand there forever and freeze. One of the traits of a jackass had to be his stubbornness. I jerked the door open.

"Give me my clothes."

Browne frowned as he spied the blanket.

"Give me my clothes," I repeated. "I've got to get dressed." I reached for the clothes. "My watch starts soon."

Browne gently pushed me back as he came in, shutting the door. His expression appeared blandly deceptive, like fluffy clouds under a voracious storm. He tossed the clothes onto the desk behind him.

I kept a tight hold on the blanket and waited, never realizing how small and still the cabin was until now.

He leaned back, crossed his arms, and rested his rear against the desk.

"The wounds are healing." My voice sounded like someone else's, the words unimportant as I reached for my clothes.

"No redness?" He drew a finger across my jaw. "I need to see." The playfulness left him replaced by a seriousness that warmed the air more than the steam from the bath had done.

Faintly, the sounds of the ship filtered into the cabin, along with the gentle slapping of the waves against the hull. After all the weeks of searching looks and wondering, it came to the feelings I'd suppressed, along with the always unanswerable questions. Browne's eyes held the same honesty I'd dreamt about and the maleness I'd raged about, but the arrogance and proud disdain had departed, bowing to quiet respect. The contest had ended.

I held the blanket open.

For seconds, he didn't move. I breathed again as he knelt, and his hands gently examined the pinkish marks Morse's knife had made above my breast and the two near my middle.

"No infection," he murmured.

"No infection," I repeated, breaking the silence while the sensations his thumbs induced reminded me that we were alive. My trembling fingers entangled his hair.

He kissed his way upward, his breath warm and touch slow. A tremor passed through him as I opened his shirt.

Browne lay on his back, breathing heavily, his hair tickling my nose. As I kissed his brow, I wished the *Passat* could fly into a port, any port, or to an elegant hotel and drop us in a feather bed. Our current accommodations couldn't be much different; we lay on a narrow bunk without room service. But we did enjoy a freezing wind whistling under the door. And, of course, little chance of survival.

"Browne?"

"Huh?"

I hated to disturb the beatific smile on his face. "Do you know where your pants are?"

I adjusted to another position on my backside. The spar I sat on was as narrow as a bigot's mind and studded with bolts that protruded in odd places. Permanent indentations on a rear as lovely as mine would not be pretty.

It was cold tonight. The ice field still lay a few leagues to the south and west, and storm clouds surrounded the ship like a malignant down blanket. I hid a cup of warm tea under my arm and pulled my slicker close as I scanned the surface with the spyglass. Raindrops as large as silver dollars splattered the deck, magnifying into bluish crystals.

To the right, between the bulkheads, we'd stretched out the canvasses again. If tonight's rain came down as hard as yesterday's, all the water barrels would be full and guarantee many more soaks in the Captain's claw-footed tub. The patter of rain turned into a downpour.

Browne strode by, balancing an iron pole on his shoulder. He didn't look up, although he knew where I sat. We weren't speaking.

For two days, in loud whispers and hisses, our argument rose and fell like the swell under the ship. We tried not to disturb Voss and Angelo, but they couldn't help but hear enough to take sides after hearing Browne's idea of a whisper.

He wanted very badly to repeat our lovemaking. Although a very pleasant experience, more-than-pleasant experience, I declined. Browne then asked if I would sleep in his cabin. I declined. The argument heated up at that point.

Without a doubt, Browne was a great sailor. He knew the wind, the sea, and his ship, but he had a complete disregard for the process of reproduction. Our coupling, occurring as it did on a particular day, may have—here I shuddered—may have produced a little sailor. This did not bother Browne, but it terrified me. And until I knew the outcome, there would be no visits to his cabin, and bath time would occur behind a locked door.

Consequently, we floated becalmed in name only. Browne fumed. He stomped. I avoided the most innocent kiss, knowing it led to more.

As he passed by again, I thought I heard teeth grinding.

CHAPTER 33

There it was—a prize in the brine.

I straightened and withdrew my hand from the barrel. After shaking off the salt and wood shavings, I held a piece of dried beef as big as a shoe and hard enough to whittle into a jewelry box. I tossed it into a pot on the stove and duck-walked the barrel to the side before tipping it up to dump the salt into the sea, then rolling the barrel to where the others lay. The empties would make kindling.

I hesitated.

They could also float.

The thought kept me outside the galley, staring at the dozens of barrels. What if they were strapped together—for instance, around the sides of a raft? Unbidden came a clear picture of the *Passat* abandoned and floating in the distance as we climbed waves, drawing inexorably away from her.

The thought saddened me very much. I sighed and went back to picking through the dried beans; weevils had furrowed through the bags of flour, and I didn't want the little buggers in my soup.

According to Browne and his sextant, we'd drifted another few leagues east. As I stood in the galley door and peered through the gaps in the midship bulkheads, I could still make out the glittering ice fields to the south that spread like an elevated and endless skating rink. The image triggered a memory of ice skaters swathed in red and blue mufflers singing Christmas carols as they skated in front of the Capital. I shook it off and concentrated on separating the beans.

The beef wouldn't be eaten, instead softened and chopped into chunks of bait. For the distance we'd drifted, I could stomach fish caught in these waters; the dead bodies were leagues away. I shook the cleaned beans into a jar and started on the next bag.

It began to rain, but I didn't see it anymore. Like a river, the days ran together. The raindrops, the endless sea; it all felt the same. My skin had dried and become powdery in the constant wetness. In Jessica or Mrs. Pentifax's effects, I might have found a vial of crème, but it felt too much like robbing the dead, even over so paltry an item. Wasn't it enough that their deaths still repeated in glorious color in my nightmares?

More rain fell in a fast staccato on the metal bulkheads and the deck. It seemed the day had sloshed by, perversely lengthening as I grew more irritable and convinced that the inanimate objects on the ship walked into my path by design. To show its compassion, the rain worsened, pelting the roof of the galley until it sounded like I stood inside a tin can.

A shadow blocked the doorway of the galley. After letting the handful of beans slide through my fingers, I turned.

Browne stood in the opening. Our supplies had dwindled, and he'd lost more weight in the last few weeks. He'd also lost the confident and sarcastic humor I had grown to count on to ward off despondent thoughts.

"What do you want?" To my ears, I sounded like a fishwife. Frustrated, I turned back to the beans. My elbow hit the pot. Dried beef and water splashed to the floor, soaking my leg and boot.

"Damn it!" I dropped to my knees, grabbed the pan, and slammed it onto the galley counter. As I crawled under the mess table, tears blurred the piece of beef.

Browne plucked it from my hand and threw it onto the counter. We held a long stare until he opened his arms, and I buried my face in his chest. For minutes, we stood that way as my tears soaked his shirt. It was the first time we'd touched in more than a week. I stroked his face. He kissed my fingers until I stood tiptoe to press my lips onto his.

I pushed him away; he tasted of salt. Everything was salt and water. Everything. I felt the tears return.

"What's wrong with me, Browne?" I asked.

"Nothing." He leaned against the galley wall and pulled me close so we could view the sea as it swelled and swayed, cold, gray, and endless. Sunset tried to burn through the distant storm clouds as he tightened his hold.

"I'm surprised you haven't gone hysterical on me before." He kissed my ear, and I elbowed him. "Seriously, you'd make a great sailor."

"So now I'm a sailor?"

"Of a sort. And a soldier. You don't complain."

"It wouldn't change anything." And I did complain ... to myself.

"No." I felt him lose the bit of humor he'd regained. His voice dropped flat, "It wouldn't."

I turned and made sure I had his eyes. "We're going to make it back."

He smiled and pulled me closer. "We could—"

"We could finish our chores." I touched his lips. "There is no one I would rather—" I whispered in his ear. "But you know we can't."

"I don't care." He growled.

I slipped from his arms and pushed him out the door.

Day twenty-two, after the storm.

I sat on a barrel and listened to Angelo talk as he and Voss sewed portions of sails together. The idea of wind under these leaden skies seemed ludicrous. I sniffed the air; within the hour, we'd be shaking the rain from our eyes.

As the days went by, the southern spring drew on, a prelude to Christmas. We still had the cold, but the frigid conditions mellowed for these few months. The difference would be enough to allow the ice field to melt a bit and chunks to break off and begin floating our way while we sang Christmas carols.

"Why do we sit here?" Angelo asked the question of Voss, but with a glance my way, he knew I listened.

Voss grumbled, "There is always wind in the Horn." He gazed across the water. "Something is wrong. Something bad."

"Do you think so too, Angelo?" I asked.

He nodded; his expression as grave as Voss's. "It is true. There is always wind. Where is it?" He spread his arms wide. "Where? It is like we wait for something."

"We're waiting to die," Voss spoke the words softly.

Angelo uttered automatically, "You're crazy."

"The *Passat* is cursed." Voss slapped down the canvass he worked on and stood.

A deep growl came. "That is close to blasphemy, Mr. Voss." Browne joined him beside the rail. They were both of a size, standing nose to nose. Browne added, "The *Passat* is a fine lady."

I agreed: a fine ship. But, sure as hell, she rotted under our feet. I'd spent the last few days watching the mold grow and avoiding the stench of the hold.

Voss dropped his chin and glanced at Angelo. He mumbled, "No disrespect, Sir." He knelt and went back to sewing the sail. Angelo squinted at Browne and picked up his needle.

I needed to get back to work, too. In the last few days, I'd cleaned out the lockers that belonged to the dead and missing sailors, packaged their personal effects, and become morose over little things like photographs. Each engraving of a wife, a mother, or a child made their deaths personal. One sailor had posed by his horse; they both looked a mite smitten.

Insignificant possessions seemed to gain importance. I'd find myself grasping a Bible worn smooth from use and smelling faintly of human sweat. By holding it, I would relive what the owner had hoped and prayed for, and inside would be the inscription to a dead son or grandson. At that point, I would wipe away tears for someone I didn't know.

The *Passat* held surprises despite Morse's attempt to rid her of sustenance. In the Captain's quarters, I had discovered a cache of malt liquor, and under the steward's bunk, a trunk had held tins of sugar and matches.

The hold yielded the most interesting thing still left on the ship. After the water had been pumped out, what I'd fallen over that day lay exposed; we had enough rifles and ammunition to take over Belgium. Or we could defend ourselves. As it was, only boredom and fear threatened our dreary existence.

Browne still frowned at the back of Voss's head like he waited for more of a fight. I could give it to him.

"Teach me to shoot."

No reply, no indication that I'd spoken, but a muscle twitched in his neck.

I crossed the deck and stood in front of him. "Teach me to shoot, please, Mr. Browne."

"No." It was his flattest refusal. His lip curled, and I was reminded of our early days just out of Celize when he'd been all business.

"Short of tying me up—" I could wipe that look off his face. "You can't stop me."

"Miss Coulter, you cannot disobey my order."

"I am not one of your sailors. I'm a passenger." I retrieved one of the rifles I'd stored behind a locker and held it up. "There are four of us. We need to know how to defend ourselves."

"Against what?"

"Anything. I should be able to use a rifle. God knows it isn't less ladylike than any of the rest of this." I swung the rifle around, and Angelo ducked to the side. "If I could shoot from the top of the mast, it would be most effective."

"You'd be easy to pick off, the first to go."

"You don't know that." I tried to sight down the barrel.

Browne removed the rifle from my hands. "The recoil would throw you off. You'd fall to the deck." He glared. "You are a most irritating woman, Miss Coulter."

"Thank you." I smiled. It was Browne's kind of compliment.

"You pester me." He had brought the rifle up to aim across the swell of the waves.

"We should be able to defend ourselves," I repeated. "We can't outrun an enemy anymore."

"What makes you think of an enemy? We're more likely to be rescued by a whaler or cargo ship." He ran a hand across the stock and weighed it in his palms.

"Perhaps. But we're helpless, just sitting here."

Browne held up a hand.

"Does that mean you agree?" I asked.

"That we're likely to be attacked? No. But I'll teach you to shoot."

"Do Angelo and Voss know how?"

"We can all handle a gun, but," he sighted on an imaginary target across the waves, "It would do us all good to do some target shooting." He stopped me as I started to wrestle with a box of ammunition. "We have to clean the guns, and you need to learn about them. Then you'll shoot."

"All right."

"First," he looked out at the sea, considering, "we'll get in some fishing. Gunshots would drive the fish away."

CHAPTER 34

Never interrupt an enemy when he is making a mistake.
-Napoleon Bonaparte

RIO DE JANEIRO

"No word again, Sir."

As the secretary to the American Ambassador to Brazil summarized his report, he stood at attention, heels together, and gazed through a bay window to a distant point above the jacaranda trees that ringed the walls of the estate. It was a magnificent view. Across the city and downhill beyond a teaming slum of starving peasants, the Bay of Rio de Janeiro glimmered in the late afternoon sun.

Ambassador Byrd left his desk and joined his secretary in staring over the rooftops to the bay. It was a clear day, and he could see for miles.

After a moment, he murmured, "The sea is an infinite mass, the last frontier of the unknown."

"Yes, Sir." The secretary tried to remember where he'd heard that before. He also hoped the ambassador would get to the point soon.

"Mrs. Byrd is getting restless." The ambassador sighed.

The secretary nodded, understanding explicitly from past performances how Mrs. Byrd could be restless. In its simplicity, he considered the description of Mrs. Byrd's impatience more evocative than the one about the sea.

Mrs. Pentifax, sister to Mrs. Byrd, had charge of the ambassador's daughter, and their ship was overdue, having left Chile almost four months ago. Aside from his concern about the situation, the secretary had complete sympathy for the ambassador. When he said his wife was restless, the ambassador needed more than sympathy.

"Did she specify what she expected you to do, Sir?" Perhaps they could send someone from Chile to look for them.

"She certainly did," Ambassador Byrd said. "She wants something done." He sighed again and resumed his seat behind his desk. "The 6th Fleet has two warships docking here tomorrow."

The secretary stared, wide-eyed.

"I've come up with a legitimate reason to send a warship to Cape Horn. Possibly to send five hundred men to their deaths. Or to find what remains of my daughter." He stood again and began to pace. "When the *Passat* failed to come around the Cape, I assumed the worst." He met the secretary's eye and hardened his voice. "I am a realist, Jeffrey."

"Yes, Sir."

"I know my daughter is dead. And my sister-in-law." He strode to the windows and back. "I've known it for weeks!" he shouted.

"Yes, Sir."

The ambassador's voice grew fiercer. "But an effort must be made, and through luck, an opportunity has arisen."

"The wire we received yesterday? The one from Lloyds of London, Sir?"

Ambassador Byrd nodded. "Yes. They had insured the missing ships, and now their investigating agent has gone missing also. He was in Rio many weeks ago, last seen leaving a restaurant by the wharf. A ransom demand by pirates has been made, and the negotiations are to be concluded in Chile."

"Do you think he is still alive, Sir?"

Ambassador Byrd shrugged. "Perhaps. The *USS Henry* will be a week behind the pirates and the captured Lloyds' man, a Mr. Richard Shaw. Officially we'll be sending the warship to look for Lloyds' missing ships, but they'll also be looking for my daughter and the remains of the *Passat*."

"A ship of that size will have to be outfitted. I believe that takes a least a week alone."

"Provisions have been made for a special operation to outfit her, and a fresh crew is standing by. She'll sail day after tomorrow!"

CHAPTER 35

DRAKE PASSAGE

Latitude 58°41' S, Longitude 60°23' W

The sun angled in from the galley window, hitting the cutting board directly, and twinkled in the eye of the fish as if it were still alive.

I had no problem scraping the scales off of it. Twice, though, I'd stuck the point of the knife into the pearl-like skin of the fish's belly and twice cringed and backed away. Angelo laughed. We stood side-by-side in the galley, staring at the rather large bass.

"The feesh is already dead, Miss." Angelo's accent that made some of his vowels long. His eyes twinkled. "The feesh won't be any more dead if you gut eet."

No, I thought, but it wouldn't be pleasant.

Catching the fish had been fun, the pull of the line exciting, and the fight well worth the exercise. Browne and Voss shouted advice and sidestepped while I leaned back and shuffled fore and aft until landing the damn thing. At close to twenty pounds, Angelo declared it a prize and helped take it off the hook.

That was hours ago. On the galley cutting board, it just looked like dinner. I held the fish up and realized the eyes reminded me of those on a doll I once saw in a store in Manhattan. I slapped it down again and gritted my teeth as I made a deep slash, opening its belly.

"Oh!" Fish guts and blood spurted out. I'd never seen so much blood in something so little. And said so.

"But," Angelo turned from stoking up the fire, "we have even more blood than the fish."

As I rubbed my shoulder and rotated it a few times, I decided I didn't want to know what the bruises looked like.

Spent cartridges littered the deck like confetti. For three days, we'd been target shooting from midships near the gunwale and could continue a long while with the amount of ammunition in the hold. There were still enough bullets down there to last into the new year. Where had Higgins intended to sell all the weapons?

"All clear?" I called out.

Two echoes came back from the stern. I concentrated and squeezed the trigger. The tins on the top of the bulwarks jumped in succession, and the recoil tattooed another design on my shoulder.

Browne came up behind me and kicked the casings out of his way, the sound like tinkling bells. "I'd rub some oil on that if I were you, Miss Coulter." He pointed to my shoulder. "Or I could do it for you." A smile went with that, reminding me of his good humor before the storm.

"Thank you, anyway." I found a broom and started sweeping up the casings. Voss joined us.

"We can take care of the rest." Browne watched as Voss released a volley of shots.

I dumped the casings into a cask and scooped the remainder into another.

"Might as well throw those over; we don't need them." Browne started to lift the cask.

I stopped him and held a handful up. "We could use these."

"How?"

I asked, "Will we have to abandon ship?"

Browne's eyes narrowed. "Perhaps."

"We have wood to build a raft. Those casks," I pointed to the corralled herd of barrels midship, "would help it float."

After a minute of eyeing the barrels, he conceded. "All right."

"But the raft would leak where the wood joined together."

Browne nodded.

"We melt the shells." I rolled a single shell between my fingers. "And coat the inside of the raft. It would be watertight."

"It would sink like a stone."

"Not if we used it just in the cracks and we add extra barrels around the outside."

Browne's frown looked permanent. I wrapped my arms around his waist and squeezed.

"It might work."

He looked at the casks, then at the casings. "We'd need a hot fire to melt the brass."

"And we could use paintbrushes to put it on with."

"No. It'd cool too quickly. It will have to be poured on." He aimed a frown at the casks.

Around us, the sea looked calm, the towering waves we'd ridden a memory. Into the image, I inserted a small raft ringed in casks and surrounded by crests of white water and shuddered. Yet it meant survival. "It would work, wouldn't it?"

"Maybe."

"Then I believe you should kiss me, Mr. Browne."

CHAPTER 36

Latitude 57°48' S, Longitude 69°01' W

Still wearing his dress whites, Admiral Villiers watched Rio recede, happy to be plowing through waves again. He glanced at the blazing sun above them; such fine weather for hunting something wicked, such as pirates. A day—maybe three—was all he could tolerate on land before he felt the need to feel the wind and salt against his face again. The urgency of this assignment made his reunion with the sea even more exhilarating.

He'd kept track of the piracy reports and the losses. Whoever was operating in these waters had grown bolder, and the request from Ambassador Byrd couldn't have arrived at a better time. In less than a week, they might be closing in on what he termed the Hell Ship—the one that killed just to kill. Also, he had the element of surprise, for now. The *SS Henry*, the crown of the American fleet, had cannons that would blast the pirates out of the water—if he could get close enough.

"More speed, Rogers!"

To himself, he added, "We'll find the bloody bastards."

Admiral Villiers lowered the spyglass and made another notation on a chart. The navigator's figures and his numbers agreed. Courtesy of a strong gale, they were doing better than fourteen knots an hour continuously for the last two days. If they maintained the pace, a confrontation with the pirates could occur before the Horn. A situation possible and most desirable; Villiers was not eager to contend with stormy conditions and the buccaneers at the same time.

A cry from the dog watch went up. He had always secretly envied the enlisted men responsible for the watch. That high up, they were spectators to the most spectacular sunsets that bled more beautifully than a painter's pallet. They also had first sight of the enemies they faced.

All along the decks of the *SS Henry,* a chorus of orders rebounded. Villiers leaned over the rail of the bridge, as keyed up as the rest of the crew, enjoying the first sign of excitement since they'd left Rio.

"What is it, Jenkins?" Villiers returned the salute.

"The 'nest," the petty officer pointed upward, "says it is what is left of a ship, two leagues or more off the starboard, Sir."

Admiral Villiers shaded his eyes and scanned the white caps before issuing orders.

"Comin' about. Man sighted! Over there Bosun!"

Though a flurry of signals bounced above his head, Villiers half-listened as he peered through a spyglass and swept the indicated area, section by section. The shadow from a piece of wood caught his attention. Then a cluster of floating debris. Among the wreckage, he saw a man's face. Or part of one.

The bell of the *SS Henry* resounded. One of the enlisted kept it ringing as they closed in on the target area. Close up, there was no doubt they had found what remained of a destroyed cargo ship.

Although a mite unusual, Villiers sat fore in the skiff as his crew rowed toward the debris. He believed in knowing first-hand what they were up against, and this looked to be a solid clue. He had to squint against the glare of the sun to distinguish the shadows from the wood and flotsam.

The sailor in the water did not raise his head. Strips of peeled skin striped the face and shoulders. Two of the enlisted jumped out of the skiff and pried the sailor loose from the block of wood that he'd clung to. From the way the man had lain across it, Villiers assumed he was dead.

The man was brought to the side of the skiff, rolled in, and laid flat on the bottom of the boat.

"Dead?" Villiers asked.

"Not good, Sir," Ensign Dalton replied.

Villiers left his seat to bend over the injured man. Almost imperceptibly, his chest rose and fell.

Moments later, the skiff bumped the side of the warship, and many hands scrambled to haul it upward. When it came level with the deck, other crewmen lifted the survivor onto a stretcher.

"Into the shade with him," Villiers ordered.

The man's eyes had swollen shut from his days in the sea and the blazing sun. Above his elbows, where the waterline had been, every inch of skin had blistered two or three layers deep, and the flesh looked a pulpy, pinky-white. His lips were a mass of scabbed blisters.

"A little water. Not much yet," Villiers said.

A soaked cloth touched the man's lips. He jerked and made a cawing sound as water trickled into his gaping mouth.

Villiers had seen castaways like this before; he doubted this one had much time.

"Squeeze my hand, lad, if the answer is yes. I must ask you some questions." Villiers knelt beside the stretcher. "Do you understand?"

Ensign Dalton bathed the man's forehead as Villiers spoke.

"Was it pirates, lad?"

A squeeze.

"How long ago? Two days?"

A slight shake of the man's head.

"Four?"

A squeeze.

"Thank you, lad. When you're stronger, we'll require more details. Rest up. You are in good hands." Villiers tried to sound comforting, knowing it was only for the man's peace of mind. Or maybe his own. He signaled for the stretcher to be taken to sickbay, certain the injured man would be dead before dawn.

The man's finger waggled. One of the enlisted leaned over him.

"He said, 'Horn', Sir."

"Lad?" Villiers again held the man's hand.

The effort to speak probably cost the survivor his last few hours. "...*Ascencion* ... men ... dead. Rammed!" He gasped out the last word. "Pirates ...black ship ... horn..."

"In Cape Horn?" Villiers knew the Cape was more than a week away.

The sailor raised his hand, extending a shaky finger. He poked the air. "Horn ... ripped ... open."

The dead sailor was sewn into a weighted canvas shroud, and the remains slipped over the side at sunrise. Villiers and the chaplain spoke a few words before the crewman from the *Ascencion* joined his mates at the bottom of the sea. In the long run, he'd bet this man suffered more than the rest of his crew. A drawn-out death, not as quick as a bullet. Word had come of his death an hour after dinner; he'd never regained consciousness.

With the echo of ceremonial gunfire still ringing in his ears, Admiral Villiers turned away from the sea, grim-faced and resolute. He'd added the sailor's scanty knowledge to the rest of the reports and felt his blood boil. Although several pirate ships operated the waters of the Caribbean and each side of the Horn, he felt sure the ship they chased was responsible for the other deliberate destruction he'd encountered. The sailor from the *Ascencion* wasn't the first to survive, but he'd described how the mystery ship so successfully sank her prey. He'd blast that confounded horn off that pirate ship if he got close enough.

To the south, the remnants of a storm decorated the far points of the horizon. Villiers smiled. Might not his quarry have been detained for a day, maybe two? He could hope for more. With a good wind blowing and the *SS Henry* under full sail, Villiers could smell pirate's blood.

In fact, he could taste it.

"Admiral Villiers!"

"Yes, Rogers," Villiers lowered his glass. It had been hours since they sailed away from the wreck of the *Ascension*, and at the moment, he studied the jungle coastline, seeing a large cat, perhaps a panther, streaking across the sand and back into the shadows of the dense greenery. Just as swift as the cat, they gained speed over the waves to chase their quarry.

"The course, as mapped, Sir," his lieutenant said, clipping the words in military style. He shuffled papers, awaiting a chance to get them signed.

"Thank you. Ahead, with all possible speed."

"Aye, Aye, Sir!

CHAPTER 37

DRAKE PASSAGE
Latitude 57°96' S, Longitude 68°49' W

At last!

Hallelujah, Hallelujah!! Praise to the goddess of Menses. Oh, bless her, buy her a bushel of absorbent cotton, oh bless her.

I had had nightmares and day frights fraught with morning sickness and a protruding belly, not to mention an inadequate diet, relentless rain and cold, and then childbirth. I wouldn't need any stimulus to be afflicted with nausea—the *Passat* would shift and sway constantly. No, thank you! The idea of a child on a doomed ship terrified me ... until now.

Dear Menses, you have arrived!

As the days went by, the urgency of survival lessened, and little things became noticeable. In particular, Voss worried me. Not while he worked the ship, but otherwise.

Like a slow leak in a hot-air balloon, his rationality seemed to seep away as his behavior became more peculiar. It manifested in the way he clutched his spoon, as if he expected it to be snatched from his hand when he ate. Small noises caused him to jump, drop a hammer, or kick over a bucket, and his forced laughter always arrived late, without humor.

In odd moments, I found him staring across the sea, always to the north, and his face did not appear calm, not at all. Perhaps he dreamt of being on land again. The rest of the time, he seemed furtive and grew increasingly nervous with each passing day. If Browne noticed, he probably assumed the man's behavior was nothing more than to be expected under the circumstances.

For the last few days, our efforts had been concentrated on building the raft, and under Browne's guidance, the planks had been sawed, measured, and hammered together. The brass casings, after several experiments, grew shiny and white as they melted over a roaring fire. Only a small quantity could be melted at a time, then poured in and spread thinly before hardening in the frigid air.

The result was an uneven, shiny floor covering the bottom of a fifteen-by-ten-foot wooden raft with the brass tamped into the crevices and up the sides. Satisfied, Browne declared it was time to attach the empty casks.

Like clusters of buds on branches, the casks sprouted and grew from the sides of the raft, enlarging its circumference greatly. I left the men to their hammering and again accessed our provisions. How much we could take on the raft depended on the weight and the room the provisions took up. I made a list: one bag of beans, twelve tins of tea, three bags of peas, three tins of sugar, a handful of raisins, nine pounds of smoked fish, more fish cooked and salted, and enough tobacco to pollute Antarctica. By the time I rejoined the men, Angelo had left them to patrol the decks, mostly out of habit. Although still bitingly cold, there was no wind; the ship lay becalmed and out of the current, which would have brought the orphaned icebergs near. I judged the hour to be noon, and a pallid one, under a heavy blanket of clouds that shut away the sun.

We'd fashioned a pitched roof and crude benches in the center of the craft wide enough to seat four, two per side, with storage for supplies underneath.

"What are those for?" I pointed. Hooks poked out at several points just under the upper side of the raft.

Browne stopped hammering long enough to say, "Buckets."

I assumed to bail water with. "And that?" I pointed to the top of the makeshift mast to a sort of metal basket a few feet wide. It served no purpose I could see except as a spot for an errant gull to squat and hatch eggs.

"A fire at night to help another vessel spot us, Miss," Voss said as he flattened another nail.

"And not to run us under," I surmised.

In his most sarcastic drawl, Browne said, "You're picking up sea talk just fine, Miss Coulter."

"Thank you." I pinched his cheek, not the one with the crop of whiskers that scratched my face every time I got close. The men, by some tribal agreement, had stopped shaving as soon as they began construction on the raft.

Voss walked a water cask to the raft and loaded it in. Two more were already in place. At the sight, a realization struck home, a sad one.

"We're leaving the *Passat*." I studied her battered masts and drooping rigging, the damaged storage bins, and smashed bulkheads, then remembered how she had shone in the sun that day in Celize.

Browne slung an arm over my shoulders. "I'm afraid so. She is rotting under our feet, and we'd be hard-pressed to sail her if a decent wind came up."

"We can't leave her." I had grown to love the ship; creaks, smells, and all.

"If we stay, we'll grow weaker. And we'll die."

"Surely someone will find us."

"It's been weeks." Browne looked painfully somber. "We can't wait much longer."

I remembered persuading him to build the raft. Now he couldn't wait to sail away in it. "Are you afraid of dying, Browne?" The question came from nowhere, but like most lovers, we thought in similar patterns. He didn't hesitate to answer.

"No." He looked across to the ice fields. "But we don't have to wait for it."

I sighed. It was time. "When will we leave?"

"Before the week is out. We'll start to suffer from scurvy soon after that, and there's no telling how long it will take to reach shore."

"Doesn't scurvy make your teeth fall out?"

He nodded. "It also brings on depression and severe weakness. A hundred years ago, whole crews withered and died on long voyages just because they didn't have fresh vegetables."

"I thought it was lemons or limes they needed."

"They're good, especially the lemons." He puckered his lips like he could taste one. "But potatoes and onions—raw—do the trick, too."

Like jewelry on a faded dance hall queen, the brass rail of the *Passat's* bridge shone through the grime and dirt. "I'll be ready," I murmured. Browne didn't need to know that I could already feel the depression he talked about and some of the weakness.

"Good." He turned and called to Angelo. "We're going to weight the raft and launch her over the side to see if she floats."

With her square lines and solid beams, the raft looked buoyant. But was she seaworthy if the high swells came back? Or a storm? While I wondered, Browne, Voss, and Angelo drew lots to see who would ride the raft down and test the oars once she hit the water. Angelo grinned and hurried to get his rubber boots.

Since the storm, the *Passat* rode even lower in the water. All day long, the sea lapped against the hull only fifteen feet below the deck. As they prepared to lower the raft, the clanking chains around it brought back the night of All Hallows Eve. Vividly. I shook the images away and concentrated on Browne's profile, shutting out the rest. As if on a string, he turned, his expression saying he remembered with me.

The raft sported a pulley system of ropes attached to the ship. Angelo could lower himself by hand without our help if he chose. The three of us would use it when we abandoned the ship.

The raft hit the water on one side and then leveled off. Angelo regained his feet, smiling big and trying not to fall again. "Leaks?" Browne called out.

Angelo dutifully toured the square bottom, shaking his head. "No, Sir. Watertight." He undid the harness, and the chains flew back, smacking the hull, swinging out, and then lying limp again.

"Keep one line on her, and let out some slack," Browne shouted, his hands full of lines. Angelo waved assent and cast off the tether to the ship in his hand as it unwound from the raft's mast. He took up the oars and angled the craft out a few feet before running from side to side to check her buoyancy.

A thrill on tiny feet ran up my arms. She floated! And with the tiniest of breezes, she would sail.

For some reason, I happened to look at Voss. Standing beyond Browne, he gazed at the craft, not with pride, but with an expression I couldn't understand. Envy? There shouldn't be any; if it mattered to him, he could always take the raft down again after Angelo returned.

While Angelo braced the tether, Browne pulled the raft back to the *Passat*. With the craft snug against the hull, Angelo caught hold of the chains.

The rain—which had held off for hours—arrived at sundown. For an hour, it came down, then quit. Stars twinkled, glittering attendants to a new moon as it ascended in an inky sky. My reverie from the starboard rail came to an end with a curse from a familiar voice directly behind me.

"Oh, Hell."

Browne stood with hands on his hips and glared at the raft. As Angelo reported, with its shiny brass bottom, the raft was watertight. When filled with a good foot of rain, it resembled a large bathtub.

I wrapped my arms around his waist. "Should have pulled a canvass over it, Browne."

He responded by shoving a bucket into my arms.

Half an hour later, we leaned against the rail, winded. The raft was empty. I'd developed an appreciation for the rigors of bailing water ... and a new blister. Browne unfurled a portion of an old sail, and we covered the bloody thing.

CHAPTER 38

There is one knows not what sweet mystery
about this sea, whose gently awful stirrings
seem to speak of some hidden soul beneath.
-Herman Melville

A noise, like wood rubbing wood...

As I drifted back to sleep, the noise came once more, and I sat up.

Moonlight poured through the salon windows, riding the night sounds of the *Passat*. The creaking and shifting repeated as if the ship slept fitfully. Yet no matter how faint, the other noise did not belong. I pulled on more clothes and crept to the door, fully awake; we never slept soundly anymore—or without our boots on. Christian Morse had robbed us of that.

Cold night air slapped my face. Instead of the noise that had drawn me outside, I detected a faint clink of a chain from the fore section. Or midship. Browne had come off watch when I'd retired, making his usual offer to share his cabin. Angelo slept in the fore-castle behind the salon. That left Voss on watch.

From the breeze that teased us nightly, ripples undulated around our hull before becoming swells a short distance away. The ship swayed with gentle movement, and when a faint vibration passed under my feet, I became alert and headed that way at a trot, careful not to make any noise.

As I passed Browne's cabin, he bolted out, nearly knocking me over the rail. I grabbed the tail of his shirt and lurched along behind him until he thudded to a stop.

The raft was missing.

In its place, pieces of wood, tools, and a single rope littered the deck. Beside the rail, the chains had been coiled in neat mounds as if whoever removed them wished to be quiet. Browne bounded to the side rail.

"Hey!" Browne shouted.

Voss had used the rope pulley. He had just reached the water, and we arrived in time to see the raft dip and then right itself. As he swore his outrage, Browne raised a leg to the rail, planning on going over the top, but I held onto him.

"Voss!" Browne yelled and tried to swat me off.

In the growing swells, Voss struggled to control the raft. Just as Browne reached the lines tied to the deck, Voss cut them, and they blew free.

"Voss!"

It was as if we weren't there; the man we'd gone through a nightmare with wouldn't even look at us. Bathed in the moonlight, his face glistened with exertion. By now, Angelo had hurried up to us, wearing only trousers. His hair stood on end as he shouted more curses at Voss.

"That doesn't help," Browne snarled and cast about, looking for a way of retaking the raft. As he scrambled around the deck, Voss unshipped the oars and pushed away from the *Passat*, finally looking up to where we stood.

"Why?" Angelo cried.

As Voss rowed in a steady rhythm, the raft emerged from the shadow of the ship into the open sea. When he answered, his voice sounded like a stranger's as it carried to them.

"The *Passat* is cursed—as you are. I cannot wait!"

The moonlight caught him just then, and I could see that he couldn't. His internal fear had consumed him; calculation painted his face the day we tested the raft. From the noise Browne was making beside me, he wasn't ready to let Voss go.

"Here—Angelo," Browne said. He'd tied the longest line he could find to a spar and the other end to his waist, ready to jump into the frigid water. In the freshening breeze, the raft had already pulled maybe thirty or forty yards away before Browne straddled the rail.

"The rope isn't long enough!" I shouted. "The raft is already beyond you." I grabbed Browne's arm.

He shook me off, cursing and measuring the distance, his face flushed red. I'd never seen him so angry, not even during our most heated arguments. He started undoing the tether—and if I knew him—so that he could jump in and swim out anyway. Angelo began to argue with him.

A sharp noise and then a shout made us turn back to the raft.

The call came from Voss, and it wasn't born of triumph—it was horror.

The moonlight clearly defined the raft, each keg and bolt, and its brass bottom shone. Below the raft, something large agitated the water. When Voss ran to the aft end of the raft to crouch behind the mast, the breeze nudged him further from the *Passat*. Browne made a sound in his throat as the thing broke the surface.

A long pearl-white tentacle as wide as a man, flecked in blue and purple, and studded with suckers, curled upward above the water. In a graceful, slow arc, it flexed down again across the fore end of the raft. Voss screamed as more tentacles emerged in explosions of spray, encircling him and waving in the air above the raft.

"Oh, God," I whispered.

A bulbous and grotesque head rose from under the surface as another tentacle slid around the raft and hugged it like a toy, drawing it close. The top of the head was as high as the sail and wider than the raft. As its unblinking black eye watched the craft, I could have sworn it also studied this ship. Voss brandished a knife, hacking at the tentacle that lay across his legs.

The giant octopus finished wrapping itself around the raft and began to descend.

"Between its eyes!" Angelo shouted.

With a curse, Browne darted to the forecastle and back, flinging rifles to us. He raised his and shot. Seconds more, Angelo also had. One of the shots hit the creature just as mine went wide. We continued to shoot as Voss' arms waved futilely, and until his screams changed; the tentacle had slapped him, shredding him open.

The raft was drawn inexorably downward. The rifle slipped from my fingers to the deck.

"You poor bastard." Browne leaned over the rail; his face drained of all color. "Damn." He drew me to his side, and I clung to him as the raft disappeared into the churning water. A keg shot into the air and then settled on the surface, testimony to midnight horror.

CHAPTER 39

BETWEEN RIO GALLEGOS AND THE FALKLANDS
Latitude 51°33' S, Longitude 67°38' W

By noon, the last of the Sunday prayer services had ended, and Admiral Villiers left the chapel to walk slowly back to his cabin. Unlike most admirals, he did not spend his days secluded, only appearing for exercises or disasters. He enjoyed the sea, reveled in the feel of it, and usually wouldn't miss the view from the bridge. But for now, he could do with a bit of solitude.

Rain laced with pellets of ice fell over the decks, melting to slush, and thunder arrived in loud reports, decorated by fingers of lightning. This was a small storm, an appetizer. As Villiers stood inside the doorway of his quarters, the drumming of the rain overshadowed the ship's noises, which were considerable.

He shut the door and turned up the flame in his table lamp before picking up his pen and thinking. Above his desk, the only picture in the room captured his thoughts; it was not of war or ceremony, or wife and family, but a picture in oils depicting a fantastical water scene.

Amid white-capped waves, mermaids rode seahorses with their breasts modestly covered by conch shells. The reins of the seahorses were of gold mail, their harnesses studded with rubies and pearls. Skulls and bones floated on the water. Center of the picture, a scaley and fearsome sea serpent devoured a ship, sails and all, including the crew, who were eaten whole or fell into the foaming vortex below. In the froth, a sea lion with bared teeth swam toward an infant washed from its mother's arms. On the left far side of the canvas, and discernible through the waves and mist, was a man's face watching the scene in terror.

To Villiers, the man's face was his own.

CHAPTER 40

DRAKE PASSAGE
Latitude 52°28' S, Longitude 66°29' W

"We can build another raft."

Browne didn't respond. He hadn't said much throughout the rest of the night. I sat on the overhang of the bridge, my boots dangling over the deck. Behind me, Browne propped himself against the navigation table and peered at the charts under the candlelight. Several times, he gave up and stared at nothing. If someone had asked if I knew where we were, I'd respond that we floated in a watery Hell, trapped by fate that wouldn't let us go.

However, that didn't mean we gave up.

"We've got wood. More kegs. And some supplies left." As I watched the sky, the night began to lighten, just perceptibly. In another hour or so, it would be dawn.

"Be quiet." Browne didn't look up, but I could tell he listened by the depth of his frown.

I'd gotten a response. A rude one, but a response.

"If I do, I'll fall asleep."

"Then go to bed, woman!"

That sounded more like the old Browne. I got to my feet and stood beside him, pretending I knew what the charts meant. The markings on them became clearer as the sky lightened, displacing the stars. Browne sighed and threw down his pencil.

He rubbed his face and finally looked up.

"We can build another. And we might have another clear night," I said.

He shook his head and tapped the barometer. "More likely, another storm."

"Do you have an idea where we are?"

"Yes."

"Would Voss have made it to land?" On the map, the hand-drawn specks designated islands that appeared to be fairly close.

He pointed at the specks. "Perhaps. If he'd figured sailing due north." Browne eyed the map. "If so, he might have hit Tierra del Fuego."

"What's wrong with that?"

"They're islands as bleak as the backside of the moon. Maybe a few turtles. No supplies."

"Oh." I thought about it. "If we rebuild, where would we sail?"

"Nosy, aren't you, Missy." Browne frowned. "A bit more northeast. We'd try for Isla Homos, a bit east of Isla Hermite Island. There's a whaling outpost on the island's east side. There'd be people and supplies."

I let the visions of beef and bread float by for a second. "How long would it take us?"

"With luck, a week. Maybe more."

"So, we rebuild?" I hugged him.

"You are a sneaky woman."

I bit his ear. "I know."

Browne nodded, either agreeing with me or the situation. He didn't look happy. "We rebuild."

"Good. We have an hour before dawn and your watch."

He looked up. "So?"

I pulled on his hand, enjoying his expression as the realization dawned on him. "I think the Captain's tub is big enough for two."

CHAPTER 41

The evil that men do lives after them,
the good is oft interred with their bones.
-William Shakespeare

Latitude 55°23' S, Longitude 64°07' W

"*Tierra del Fuego* lies 50 leagues due east." Borodin pointed off their bow.

In the three days since the assault on the Albinos, Borodin's wounds hadn't healed. Jagged streaks of red still striped his face, shining wetly in the sun.

The *Hussar* sailed south, tracking no particular course. Shaw suspected Peech of trolling for ships to plunder. The pirate seemed in no hurry, changing their direction by a few degrees, first one way and then another, then steering the ship in a wide arc back to the original line she'd been sailing.

"Will we have enough provisions to round Cape Horn?" Shaw asked Borodin. Standing side by side, they'd contemplated the sea for a half-hour in silence. If Shaw had to converse, not fraternize or approve, but converse so as not to become insane, he had to talk to them.

A sly and rare smile creased Borodin's face. "Knew you weren't simple. You know ships."

Shaw shrugged. "And my question?"

Since they'd rowed out of the cave together, leaving behind the Albinos and their dead, Shaw had realized a sort of camaraderie with Borodin—of terror shared and not forgotten. Not one of moral affection. Borodin wouldn't hesitate to kill him and enjoy it. Under Peech's command, Borodin obeyed, yet he seemed separate, examining each atrocity before committing it.

"We'll get through the Horn." Borodin tossed a handful of fish scraps to the gulls. "Or we'll be like them, happy to lick the deck if it takes too long."

"So why are we sailing in circles? Why not set a straight course through the Horn?"

Before he turned and walked away, Borodin looked through him, reminding Shaw eerily of the malevolent eye of the giant squid.

Two more days and the *Hussar* abandoned its aimless trawling for treasure, and Peech ordered the bow of the ship to point due south. The weather cooperated with strong gales that grew colder as each league disappeared under their bow, and the crew's cheeks glowed red from freezing rain, not liquor. With the sunset, they dropped anchor.

Shaw had requisitioned a mangy peacoat, a stained sweater, and heavier pants. Knowing the cold weather would soon be upon them, he'd already washed and dried two blankets, convinced he could see the teeth marks of the rats in them. A week ago, he had found caulking and spent a day patching the walls of his cabin to keep the cold out. It took several evenings to remove, repair, and re-hang his door. Farley eyed the work with interest and put Shaw to work in the salon.

For the last week, Shaw's nights had gone better. Exhausted, he ate his meal and then paced the deck until the cold drove him inside and into a deep sleep. He'd discovered that there wasn't a single book or newspaper on the ship. None of the pirates seemed to mind at all; it might interfere with their destructive habits. Shaw kept to himself and tracked where the *Hussar* sailed as best he could, and each dawn bled more of the white glare from the Antarctic in the distance.

Shaw had seen little of Peech since the raid on the Albinos. Farley's unsolicited opinion was that Peech needed time to be a papa to the golden babe. Shaw assumed the bastard spent the time drinking until another unfortunate ship crossed their path.

A couple evenings ago, he'd stood on deck listening to the nightly drinking until the offkey singing had hushed. One could have heard a mouse stomping as a drunken Peech predicted an enormous treasure lay in the icy waters before them. Wonderful, Shaw thought. They'd never dock in any port if the pirates prospected for fortune.

The evening meal, a kind of stew with chunks of fatty meat and floating pieces of potato, rolled in Shaw's stomach, keeping time with the back-and-forth sway of the *Hussar*. He sipped his tea and studied Borodin, propped against the next bulkhead. The man looked ill; not only did Peech's scarecrow appear pale, but he hadn't lit a cigar. The deep scratches Borodin had acquired from the Albinos began high on one cheek and almost touched his other eye. Even in the shadowy gloom of the evening, Borodin's eyes glittered from fever as he returned Shaw's regard and then went back to watching the sea.

The wind had turned frigid and constant as they sailed south, and most of the pirates stayed below or in the forecastle. Only those on watch moved about the deck huddled into their coats. Shaw finished his tea and began his evening promenade. Borodin trailed a few steps behind, always a reminder of his status as prisoner. Shaw didn't feel compassion for the man; another keeper could be assigned if he needed to rest.

"How far to the Horn?" Shaw's question faded away as a particularly vicious wind whipped by. Borodin ignored him. Shaw increased his pace. As they neared the area opposite the Captain's quarters, Shaw felt a frisson of dread pass through him quickly, like a moth flying in and out of a halo of light, or perhaps it wasn't there at all.

Borodin may have felt it, too. He hesitated, and his voice seemed wary. "Tomorrow, if the wind holds."

In the next few seconds, Shaw had no time to think as awareness and sheer animal fear shuddered through him. The sensation became an icy hand around his heart as Borodin froze, crouching low on the deck, and Shaw did the same.

The air thickened, tinged in an unholy red at the far edge of his vision. The cold intensified, became palatable and solid, and Shaw felt the hair on the back of his neck prickle and wave. He soon knew why.

Beyond the point where the night swallowed the running lights of the *Hussar*, a line of pale shapes hovered above the waves, floating toward the ship. Fear weakened Shaw's legs, and he tried to scream. As they drew closer, something familiar and frightening reached him; the cloying perfume from the flowers that he'd last smelled in the idyllic amphitheater and that grotto of animated skeletons.

Then he saw them, the Albino women, shimmering white against the night as they approached the ship, toes trailing in the froth of the waves. Their translucent skin contrasted starkly with the red glow inside their bellies. As they wailed, their mouths opened like black holes, their laments piercing and otherworldly.

Shaw couldn't move. An inarticulate noise came from Borodin, and he bolted aft into Peech's cabin. The wailing became sobbing as the women drew closer.

The Albinos hovered only a few feet from the deck when at last Shaw felt his feet move, he was somehow at the far end of the row of cabins when the women floated over the rail. Their arms were raised in entreaty … their cries heart-wrenching. Shaw understood. No matter how frightening they were, he understood the wanting, elemental and maternal.

He heard a thump. From inches away, Peech's face filled a porthole. Farley peered, open-mouthed, from the next one.

The air pulsed and thickened with the keening, bleeding until it began to rain cascades of white flowers that covered the decks, the bulkheads, and the sea. Peech's eyes bulged, and he backed away from the porthole as the women crossed the deck and passed through the cabin wall.

Shaw couldn't help it. He edged closer to look inside the porthole. Borodin stood there, his back to Shaw, and although he couldn't see everything, Shaw could hear. Above the wails, Peech's voice rose in anger, not fear.

With outstretched hands, the Albinos advanced to the far side of the room where Borodin wielded an ax from side to side, defending himself, not Peech. The wails grew more plaintive. Behind the pirates, the foot of the golden babe protruded from a nest of wine bottles.

Peech bellowed like an enraged bull and pulled a long sword from his treasure pile, backing away until he stood in front of the babe. Farley danced to the side, swiping the air with knives in both hands. With a roar, Peech lunged at the Albinos.

In a cloud, they swarmed the bastard, propelled him the length of the room, and slammed him into the wall. Peech lay still, but Shaw could see a hidden gleam in his eye as he watched the women.

Farley dropped the knives, grabbed the babe, and ran behind the sofa. Borodin shouted something. The runt shook his head.

The women turned on Farley and in seconds, engulfed him. He screamed once, twice, and then emitted a long, drawn-out shriek. The room filled with bitter smoke as his skin flamed, shriveled, and fell away.

The Albino women lifted the Irishman, still clutching the babe, and turned, floating back through the cabin wall that no longer seemed solid. As Shaw watched, they drifted over the rail and across the waves under the rain of the white flowers, their toes again trailing through the froth of the sea as Farley's screams faded into the night.

CHAPTER 42

*At the end of life death is a departure, but at life's
beginning a departure is death.*
-Victor Hugo

Like an alabaster statue, the Queen glowed in the emerald water, framed by a forest of kelp, and haloed in bright light. A carpet of pink shells littered the sand where she reclined on a seaweed bed, and surrounding her, ancient shrines rose hundreds of feet upward through the myriad of sea life.

"A kiss, my pet."

At the command, a shark nuzzled her hand and brought his snout from her ear to the base of her throat. The shark left his mistress, circling to the object at her feet. Impaled on a bar of coral lay a man, his once handsome features bloated and eyes nibbled out—a delicacy not to be missed.

"Amuse me." The Queen commanded.

The shark dove toward the man, swerving off at the last second, teeth gleaming. The man made an involuntary movement to escape, and the Queen clapped her hands, clearly delighted.

Shaw awoke, wondering if the dream was really a dream.

Chapter 43

Latitude 58°.41'S, Longitude 60°23'W

"**S**ecure the raft," Browne commanded.

Lightning flickered on the horizon as the wind stole Browne's order away, blowing it upward into the bank of charred clouds that hung over the ship. I fought my way up from the salon and started looking for ropes—rigging—whatever the hell it was called. I'd come a long way from the delicate passenger he'd tried to shoo into the salon. Now, he didn't hesitate to shout orders and expect me to hop as fast as any seaman.

In the last few days, we'd almost built *Raft II*. Voss had shown decency and left about half of the fish, the beans, and the tea. We had more water than we'd need for a year. At the same time, Angelo seemed subdued, resigned, and I hoped not superstitious. To that end, I made a point of speaking to him with as much confidence as I could summon. No glint of insanity shone in his eyes, but very little hope did either.

Browne's prediction proved true. It looked to be a nasty blow, and we were taking no chances; I had nailed wood over all the windows and lashed down what remained of the supplies and clean bedding high up the walls in the salon. Distantly, lightning flickered, punctuating Browne's orders, as I flattened the last nail over a board covering the Captain's window. This action obscured the disturbing picture of the woman with the hourglass. An omen, perhaps?

Angelo and Browne stowed what was left of the large canvasses. They no longer fit the shorter mast we had. Instead, the smaller makeshift sail was lowered, furled, and stashed like a bag of diamonds. We couldn't afford to lose it.

Although still afternoon, the storm darkened and blurred time. Was it after 4 o'clock or much later? The *Passat* complained like an old woman. As the swells grew, they lifted and dropped her again, and the hull creaked, a stark reminder of the vessel's frailty. Browne came running up the deck, ready to seal off the hatches leading below. While becalmed, we'd applied pitch to the seams and crevices, doing our best to make her watertight. From the look of the purple clouds and distant thunder, we'd soon know if it would hold.

Little was said as we donned oilskins; each of us harboring private thoughts from the last time we'd worn them during the bloodbath of All Hallows Eve. A shudder rattled through me as I stared at the salon door, remembering Morse bursting through it carrying Mrs. Pentifax. I slammed the storage locker door. There wasn't time for this ... this ... useless remembering.

Stowing the navigation equipment and charts had been a priority hours ago. Browne said he had verified our position. I groaned. God knew what it would be by morning. I wanted to stamp a foot and shake a fist at the sky; we were about to lose all sense of place.

With the wind, the cold descended upon us like an unwelcome guest, bringing back memories of the cyclone's destruction. The stinging rain turned to sleet, and small shards of ice battered the ship like a fusillade of bullets. Dormant for so long, the sea churned whitecaps, strewing them across the seascape and streaming ribbons of frothy lace everywhere.

Fear wouldn't embrace us this time. We were hardened to it. And we already knew the force of the sea, the raging noise over a world upside down, and the stark brilliance of lightning when it broke open the sky. Now, we knew it alone.

I held on to the rail as the *Passat* dipped and twisted to a new position before sliding into a trough. She climbed sluggishly to the next crest as the curl of a wave broke above her, flooding the bow. The ship was so ungainly and heavy; we could not steer her or outrun the wind. Nor help her.

As the rain grew colder, slush and ice crusted the deck. I had kept the bulwarks clean of debris this time, and we had much less to break loose and block the drains. Still, the wind did its best to shear off what it could, never being satisfied.

Browne had attached my tether early on. In minutes, the seas climbed higher than our decks, but so far, the *Passat* hadn't been swamped. Or, as Browne said, "Pooped." I fell over a barrel and clutched my side at the pain. Then I moved quickly and stood again. Browne did not need more to worry about.

For the next few hours, we became part of the storm, moving with each gust and thrust as it worsened. Just after midnight, the three of us met on the bridge. Without a word, Browne began lashing me to a post. While the storm raged, Angelo secured himself, and Browne took his place between us. There was no need to describe the bleakness we knew.

The *Passat* keeled over so low to starboard; the waves licked the deck.

Colder. I tried to smile at Browne but couldn't move my lips. His eyes, always so expressive, looked pained at my attempt. The wind rose, growing furious at the empty deck and the ship that didn't resist. Like a metronome, the *Passat* swayed in a watery crib. The wind shrieked, clawing for a body to drown in the for-ever icy water.

I woke to Browne undoing my bonds, my head resting on his shoulder. When I kissed his neck, it was like kissing a popsicle. He responded by dropping my ropes and holding me close. Just as he kissed me, a call reached us.

"Sir!"

Through a veil of soft rain, I spied Angelo at the bow. He carried one of the ice poles, and I could see something I didn't want to beyond him.

"Hell!" Browne dropped me and raced for the stairs leading down.

When the curtain of the rain lifted, it revealed an ice world, glistening and deadly. I fought a heavy, morose feeling inside. And worse, I knew the storm had blown us back to the same spot we'd been on All Hallows Eve. Long ago, I had memorized the position of the mountains in the distance after sitting there for weeks.

We checked the water for submerged bergs, finding none. Browne needed to be satisfied. I climbed the mast and hung there with the spyglass to my eye. Nothing floated in the water. From its location a few leagues to the south, the ice field seemed as beautiful and deadly as before. But the feelings the ice aroused were different now. I wasn't afraid to die, but I'd be damned if I would. Death would have a fight on his hands.

"No ice!" I called down and put the glass to my eye again. The edges of the field appeared softer; it was spring here, and the ice had started to melt. Before I lost my nerve, I looked straight down into the water, half expecting a submerged body. All appeared serene, the sea a deep gray-blue streaked with green. No dead bodies, animated skeletons, or treasure.

As I remembered Morse, a chill crept up my arms, and the glass shook in my hands. I had to hold it between my knees or drop it.

Chapter 44

Latitude 60°34' S, Longitude 62°52' W

After the storm, nothing changed. For almost a week, we'd drifted within sight of the ice field accompanied by the wind and chilling rain, which had grown constant. As our supplies dwindled, I caught several assessing, non-personal looks from Browne. Tonight, it seemed he inspected me for an indication of hysterics or the first signs of scurvy. While I didn't feel great, my teeth didn't wiggle. Yet.

As I leaned over the *Passat's* rail and gazed into the water, I wiggled my boots. I'd been standing here long enough for my feet to go numb. Without having to turn, I knew Browne had joined me at the rail.

"A beautiful sunset," he said.

I agreed. After so many days of rain, with only black clouds for company and lightning for illumination, this night seemed special.

The air had an infinite clearness; the clouds removed to a distance beyond where the spyglass could see … and to where the shadows of the world ended. Even with the intense clarity, I could not spot Noir Island, the closest landfall by Browne's calculations.

Last night, a long discussion had ensued over whether our raft would make it that far.

I enjoyed watching the streaks of pink, gold, and violet blending into a cerulean sea. Using the spyglass altered the view, making it softer, like a Renaissance painting. And since the sea's surface wasn't diluted by haze, it gleamed almost blindingly.

"We need to check for ice. Clear weather won't stop the bergs from traveling." Browne squinted into the glare.

I sighed. "You can give me a boost up." Of course, he'd take the opportunity to do more than that, which was a fine idea.

The sunset seemed even more spectacular from high atop the "stump," as we called it, of the mainmast. Under the dying light, the ice masses glittered as if painted with slivered diamonds. Some of the peaks to the south were of an immense height, their perpendicular walls like tall buildings. Below them, flat ice fields resembled stark white lakes that extended for hundreds of miles. Further away, beyond the ice fields, rose the frozen mountains of the South Shetland Islands, towering in their awesome height and beauty.

Browne paced the deck. And whistled. His form of strutting. So subtle, Mr. Browne. I had enjoyed last night also, but I didn't flap my wings and crow. Angelo would probably avoid my eye, embarrassed for both of us.

I watched the shadows on the Shetlands lengthen, their purple turning to black under the glistening fog-shrouded peaks. Idly, I brought the glass east to the horizon. If the air had not been so clear, I would not have seen it.

Puffs of gray, like fuzzy balls, concentrated in a mass where the water met the sky, and then came a flare of gold and more bursts of gray. In seconds, a much larger eruption of orange sparks lit the semi-darkness. From this distance, it looked like the water exploded in bursts of fire.

"There's something—Oh God!"

Browne whirled and trotted to stand below me, following where I pointed the glass. "Damn it." He ran to the bridge and retrieved the other glass.

In sharp relief to the glimmering light, the outline of a ship engulfed in flame was mirrored on the black water. A distant ripple of thunder preceded a faint explosion that haloed the sky above it. A reverberating boom echoed faintly across the water as the ship blew up. Immediately and unbidden came thoughts of our own stores below.

A large shadow floated beyond the flaming ship. I squinted through the smoke, and with the light from the burning ship, I could just see it; like a ghoul, another vessel hovered there, illuminated by flames as she slowly turned.

"Dear God," I whispered.

The other ship was coming this way.

Rendezvous

CHAPTER 45

"Sir!"

A quick rap on his door brought Admiral Villiers to his feet, still clutching his pen.

"Come in."

His first lieutenant stood at attention. A gleam of excitement shone in his eyes for the first time in weeks. "Twenty degrees off the lee side. Extreme distance. One ship burning. Another moving swiftly away, heading dead south."

At last. They were slower and bigger, but Villiers and the *SS Henry* had surprise and plenty of gunpowder on their side. "Are we on their tail, Lieutenant?"

"Aye, Sir."

"And Lieutenant," Villiers held up a restraining hand, "no lights. We want to surprise her."

CHAPTER 46

Over the next few hours, the other ship sailed closer. She gradually slowed and stopped, an indistinct dark mass that waited a few leagues away.

"Who are they, Browne?" I stood beside him on deck, leaning into the security of his side.

"It's too dark to tell."

If nothing else, the last few months had taught me when Browne was lying. Nothing as tangible as his face turning red, a hesitation, or a fancy lie. Whatever it was, I knew he lied.

"Who are they?" I tried to get the glass from him.

He held the glass above my reach. "Just a ship. They've stopped. Probably they have no wind. Like us."

"Browne, you lie. No—don't say it. Do I have to get the other glass?" I met his glare with mine.

He frowned and raised the glass again. "They aren't friends."

Against the evidence of what I had seen, I still said, "Maybe they couldn't help the other ship, but they might deliver us to a port." I reached for the glass and succeeded in taking it from him.

"They're pirates, Cass."

His first use of my name, coupled with the worry in his eyes, melted my self-delusion.

"Pirates," I repeated.

"They burned that ship. And now they want a look at us."

In the still air, a tremor licked my nerves. I could barely see the other ship, but had no trouble imagining what walked the decks.

"You don't want to think about what they'd do to you."

"I could hide."

"Where?" Browne growled. "They'd find you anywhere on this ship." He spoke determinedly, but if I knew Browne, he wasn't defeated.

"I'll be in the water."

"You'd freeze before they stopped looking. And Angelo and I would be dead."

"They have no reason to kill you. Give them what they want."

Browne tucked the glass under his arm and moved us into the shadows, a reminder the pirates had glasses, too. "They burned that ship. No witnesses."

"They killed the crew?"

"Yes."

"But I thought there weren't pirates anymore. The Royal Navy and the American fleet stamped out piracy. I read of it."

"They caught the ones who were stupid enough to get in their way. Those governments only looked because the shipping companies insisted. But," he gazed at the darkened ship as they, too, waited silently for dawn, "they never die out."

"What are we going to do?"

"To begin with, we'll make sure they don't see you. We don't light any lamps and make as little noise as possible."

Weak sunrise filtered through the galley window onto the counter where we usually dissected fish. This morning I lay atop it on a rolled-up blanket and cuddled a rifle close like a lover. Or a child. My last thought, before I'd slept, asked if I'd ever see Browne's child. I determined I would and that she would be the apple of his eye.

The sunrise hadn't awoken me. Browne had tapped a finger on the metal wall of the galley, and in a stage-whisper, said, "Get up!"

On my hands and knees, I peeked out the crack in the door. For the first time, details of the other ship could be seen; she was painted black, and the tops of her sails poked through the fog like sharp mountain peaks. When I saw that she floated only a few ship lengths away, fear raced through me with urgency. Not the kind we had known the night of All Hallows Eve, but of distinct danger.

Like we had rehearsed for most of the night, I crouched on the table just under the porthole. We'd broken out the rest of the glass, making it look like the storm had done the damage. Boxes of ammunition and several more loaded guns lay within reach. Browne, appearing as innocent as he could, stood alone and unarmed on the other side of the wall.

I rubbed my hand over the rifle stock. What had started as sport now became our only chance. We'd oiled our weapons and double-checked what we could. It took hours, but we removed all traces of my habitation, from hairbrush to the red dress I'd worn the first evening at sea, leaving no sign I had made it through the storm. We'd done the same for Mrs. Pentifax and Jessica, leaving only the men's belongings for the pirates to see. All of this had been accomplished in the dark amid whispers and urgency. My stomach rumbled, whether from nerves or hunger; I couldn't tell. But another look outside proved it to be a moot point.

The pirate ship drifted closer, looming out of the morning mist that swirled around its deck and snaked into rigging and sails. An eerie thought came; the pirates' silence mimicked our own, and to keep that many men quiet took a terrifying presence.

I watched the ship for several minutes, hearing nothing except the sloshing of waves against her hull. If Browne hadn't woken me, we wouldn't have known of her arrival. She drifted ever nearer as the fog thinned to reveal dozens, no, hundreds of men in bright pants and shirts on her deck as they swarmed up masts and perched on yardarms.

The other ship matched the *Passat* in size but appeared taller because she still proudly displayed her canvasses. She seemed so much stronger. The envy I felt almost overrode my fear as I remembered how the *Passat* had looked the first time I saw her in Celize and of the weeks we'd sailed under her proud lines.

Browne paced with his hands in his pockets and his head bent. Waiting. He was a fine man, noble and brave. "Do I love you, Mr. Browne?" I whispered and wiped away a tear that had escaped.

The *Passat* rocked in the swells from the pirate ship as the vessel drifted closer.

I smelled mold, the constant reminder that with each day, the *Passat* rotted from stem to stern. Last night, we made the right decision. There was no other way.

By now, the pirate ship floated so close that her masts obliterated the sky. She looked for all the world like a dark bird of prey. On her decks, I spied scores of more pirates with tattooed chests and mangy hair held back by bandannas. Short knives were strapped to their waists, and some held guns. The low murmur from the pirates grew louder. On their bridge, a muscle-bound man issued orders and herded a single pirate ahead of him down the ladder to the deck.

Perhaps I should have said prisoner. The man looked too clean and unspoiled. He also wore glasses like those favored by accountants, and his hair was combed, unlike the rest. Most telling, the muscled man led him to the deck and held on to his arm. They were joined by a tall, gaunt man with cruel features apparent even at this distance. He studied the length of the *Passat*, seeming to stare too long at the galley where I lay.

The muscled man pushed the clean man in front of him as they neared the rail. By now, only the width of a ship separated the pirates from us. Any closer, and we could smell them, and I had no doubt they stank. The muscled man smiled at Browne, and it was a terrible smile, like a salivating snake to an injured mouse.

A new wave of pirates arrived on deck, and even more posed by the masts and off the yardarms. They watched the *Passat* without saying a word.

"Bit of trouble?" The muscled man shouted, looking over our ship like a trader would a questionable offer.

"Storm," Browne called back.

The muscled man continued to scan every inch of the *Passat* with narrowed eyes. He would know how many men it took to run the ship. "Sounds like a spot of bad luck. Any of the crew left?"

The gaunt man had joined the muscled man, flanking the bespectacled prisoner. If ever I had seen cold evil, the skeletal man embodied it. He looked ill, too; streaks of bloody scratches ribboned his face. I ducked down further as his gaze traveled my way. Not being able to see our danger magnified sound, including the creaking timbers and the swells slapping both ships.

"None." Browne's voice carried clear and strong. I edged up again. If we got out of this, I'd never forget any of it, and I'd make sure Browne didn't either. I rested the nose of the rifle on the lip of the porthole and watched from the shadows.

"What are you carrying?"

"Nitrate," Browne shouted. By now, he stood just outside the open galley door.

"Ah." The muscled man rubbed his chin, maintaining his hold on the prisoner. I had no doubt that he was indeed a prisoner as distinct fear and anger warred across the man's face. Any second I expected him to shout a warning to Browne, and he would probably die for it.

"So that's all, eh?" The muscled man sounded disappointed.

"Yes, sir. Just that, and the passengers' effects." Browne stiffened, and I followed his gaze. Another swarm of pirates had climbed up from below deck, their numbers swelling by many score. That didn't frighten Browne; it annoyed him.

"I'm the First Mate. Who are you?"

A swell of derisive and surprised laughter rippled through the ring of pirates. The muscled man growled, "Captain Peech!"

The prisoner, at last unable to control himself, yelled something to Browne.

"Bastard! Enough of you!" Captain Peech swore and flung him over the rail and into the sea. At the same time, the gaunt man turned slightly, bringing up a rifle, swift and sure.

Like I'd been taught, I held my breath, drew a bead on his heart, and nailed him. Then I fired off a round that caught Peech in the arm. As he recoiled and spun around, I got him in the ass. All hell broke loose on the pirate ship as Browne dove into the galley under a fuselage of shots.

"Damn, I'm a good shot!"

"Shut *up,* Miss Coulter!" Browne dragged me by the arm, gathering guns and keeping low. As arranged, we went out the back door and down a waiting rope ladder to Angelo, where he sat in the raft, oars at the ready ... we might be able to get away, but shouts and gunshots peppered the air.

As we dropped into the raft, Browne and Angelo started rowing. An errant bullet zinged by my ear. When I turned around, I saw that the pirate ship had come to straddle the end of the *Passat,* bow to bow, giving the pirates a partial view of the raft as we rowed away. If they cared to look.

"How far do we have to be?" I asked.

Browne didn't answer but kept rowing. We heard a commotion of running feet and shouting as the pirates boarded the *Passat*, tramping across her decks. More bullets whizzed by. We were not their focus; most of them looked for treasure and any crewmen, so they weren't picked off like the gaunt man had been.

"Get down!" Browne hissed. I belly-flopped and peeked over the ring of casks around the raft.

Above the din the pirates made, a voice of authority cursed and raged. It had to be Captain Peech. The asshole wouldn't be sitting down for a while.

"Browne!" I pointed.

Curiously and without any wind, the pirate ship moved north as if propelled out of the way by an unseen hand. Where it had been, the water between the ships bubbled, becoming agitated and foaming.

"Mon Dieu!" Angelo gaped.

Under both ships, the sea swelled into a ridge and rolled; the rest of the ocean lay as flat as glass. Was it a whale? Four whales and a sea monster? The two ships drifted toward each other again and stopped moving.

I gaped. In front of the *Passat*, a school of swordfish spurted up from the surface like heralds of an advancing party. A column of purple seahorses emerged next, jetting just above the water on their tails as they circled the area. I shook my head, and the image remained the same. A school of sharks joined them, racing in pairs between the vessels, their speed whipping the water and sending up plumes of spray.

Browne stopped rowing and blurted, "Mermaids?"

Yes, and mermen. Easily dozens of them, the men broad-shouldered, green-haired, and bearded, their skin the color of emeralds. They cavorted with the other sea life as they swam, their scaley tails slapping the water. It all reminded me of an aquatic ballet. A strange one.

The water lightened in the new morn, causing the sea to sparkle like a pool of diamonds. From the middle of it, the head of the man thrown overboard emerged. He didn't resist as the mermen and mermaids guided him off to the side, and more mermen surfaced, mounted upon seahorses that sped through the water. I squinted. They took their places as if they stood guard in a circle, just like a stage. Through everything moved fish of all sizes, their scales shimmering in the sun.

The scores of pirates who'd invaded the *Passat* leaned over her rails, jabbering and rushing back and forth to peer at the scene below. A spear was flung into the melee of sharks.

From the shimmering depths, the water undulated, and frothy bubbles rose to dance on the surface. I shivered.

"Angelo, do you hear that? Browne?" I whispered.

"Faintly." He began rowing but still watched. "Like singing."

From beside him, Angelo said, "Perhaps it is angels singing."

Like a choir, voices blended with ethereal music that grew stronger. The sound became palatable in its energy, building to a crescendo that seemed to reverberate within the waves. On the aquatic stage between the ships, a head of golden hair emerged, studded with jewels, and braided in black seaweed. Angry blue eyes blinked away seawater as she rose from the waves, nebulous and naked.

Jessica.

She rose higher. Regal and perfect in beauty, she regarded the ships, the raft, the pirates, and finally, the prisoner in the water. Of tremendous size, taller than either ship, she ascended until her elbows brushed against the *Passat*. She flicked the pirate ship with a finger, and it rocked violently. One of the sharks, larger than the rest, cavorted in front of her, and she smiled indulgently.

"Holy Mother..." Angelo prayed on his knees from the bottom of the raft but still peered over the border of casks.

"Hail, our Queen!"

The top of her head exceeded the pirate ship's tallest mast as she gazed from side to side, a true queen of the sea. In a procession of leaping fish, another seahorse emerged from the sea, dragging something white entwined in ropes of seaweed. As the seahorse circled the area between the mermaids and dolphins, the object twisted and turned, bouncing high in the waves.

"It is that man! The one who killed—" Angelo gasped.

I nudged Browne. "It's Morse!" Or Greely.

Like an attraction from a chariot race in Roman times, he was towed in a wide circle that threaded in and out of the teaming sea life. Unbidden, Caparilli's words about Greely came back, "He cannot die." Damned to eternity in the sea, Greely would never die.

Jessica looked beyond the ships to the raft. In her eyes, I saw peace and sorrow. With a noble lift to her chin, she smiled, and I understood. The weeks of waiting, the undefinable sadness that we'd felt. She had held us here ... until now.

"Fuck this!"

On the deck of the pirate ship, Peech, having a fit, grabbed a rifle.

Jessica turned.

With a fingertip, she flipped the rifle from his arms and tumbled him backwards. The pirates spat off a round of shots over the rail of the *Passat,* and a cluster of tiny pinpricks dotted Jessica's face and shoulder. With ease, she swept scores of them from both ships into the sea. The sharks converged, teeth flashing, and the sea turned red under their screams of agony.

Peech backed up.

Our raft still moved away; I had forgotten, but Browne and Angelo hadn't. They rowed furiously.

Jessica plucked Peech from the deck and fed him to the largest shark hovering close by. The first bite was his right leg, and the second was his shoulder as the shark shook and tore Peech apart.

When nothing remained, the shark nuzzled her arm, and she patted him.

"Jessica!" I yelled and pointed to the young man.

CHAPTER 47

*The stroke of death is as a lover's pinch,
which hurts and is desired.*
-William Shakespeare

When Peech flung him over the side of the *Hussar*, Shaw descended into sudden coldness and a world of suffocating blueness. He relived the scene from a whole new viewpoint.

He surfaced again, threw his head back and drank air, gasping, and realized he'd almost died. Yet he was not afraid. For months he had been expecting this; death no longer frightened him. The last few weeks had inured him to gore and to suffering. Could anything be worse?

His vision cleared, and he coughed seawater. Then he ducked. A man with green skin and green hair took his arm. Shaw felt his other arm grasped and turned. A woman, just as green as the man, shyly held on to him. Together, they guided him away from the hull of the disabled ship. Shaw spied the flash of a fishtail and silvery scales molded into the woman's waist. Behind the man, a long tail propelled them through the water.

They held him above the surface, and his confusion grew with the excited shouts from the *Hussar*. From within the foaming waves, masses of golden hair broke the surface. A woman rose from the sea, growing to a gigantic size until she loomed between the two vessels. Beyond her, he spied a small raft and two men rowing. Shaw smiled grimly. They'd made it; Peech hadn't completed his tirade of death.

He looked at the perpendicular hull of the pirate ship. Some of the pirates leaned over the rail, and opposite that, scores of pirates swarmed over the disabled ship that sat much lower in the water. Shaw rubbed his eyes. Nothing changed. He glanced at the mermaid beside him, finding flat gold eyes that reminded him very much of a fish.

Suddenly, the water in front of him swelled. A shark, bigger than any he'd ever seen before, cut through the water from inches away. The merman and mermaid increased their grip on his arms as more sharks streaked by with soulless eyes. Shaw couldn't help a shudder, spying the myriad of shadows that swam just below the surface and under his feet. With effort, he brought his attention back to the massive, beautiful woman before him. Over everything, he heard music. Unbelievable! When the singing reached him, the last of his fear dissolved. If he died in this surreal place, so be it.

Music swelled, as sweet and natural as the sea, enveloping him as Shaw watched the sharks cavort. The colossal woman stroked the head of the largest shark with a fingertip.

That infuriated Peech, who leaned out of the pirate ship and yelled something as a volley of shots exploded over Shaw's head. The woman turned to the other ship and swept the nearest pirates into the sea. The sharks converged. Shaw panicked as bloody, foaming water rushed toward him. The mermen held on to him.

The woman faced the *Hussar*. Peech backed up.

She plucked him from the deck, squirming and squealing like she picked up a worm from the ground. The hateful bastard screamed like the men from the ships they destroyed. For weeks, Shaw had wished for revenge for all the innocent men Peech had murdered. He would enjoy the next few minutes.

She dunked him in the water, wiggling him like a piece of live meat to get the attention of the enormous shark that patrolled in front of her. The shark responded like a beloved pet. In that moment, Peech's scream embodied the images of the dead Albinos, the doomed sailors of the *Ascension,* all the other ships, and lastly, the pitiful woman they'd held in the hold.

Shaw blinked and shook his head. He'd heard a woman's voice. Then he saw her. A short woman with wild red hair stood in the raft and called to them. It sounded like she shouted, "Jessica!" The red-headed woman pointed at Shaw.

Jessica tilted her head in surprise and turned to him. She began to shrink, swimming toward him, until she floated inches away, of normal size and wondrous beauty.

"I must go back," she said with infinite sadness.

Shaw stared into her eyes. She appealed to him without asking anything.

"Why?"

"I cannot stay. My world is below." Beside her, the merman and mermaids hovered in attendance. She gestured to the raft. "You may return with them." Her words spoke of sacrifice and unshed tears.

"What...?" he asked.

Like a prick of a needle, she entered his thoughts. The sensation tickled his mind, the stimulation sexual, touching every nerve, memory, and desire. She moved inside him, exploring, unafraid and uninhibited. At the same time, he understood her sadness. Shaw felt the invasion of his past, of anything he thought he knew, and of dark places unfulfilled; she could cleanse his soul.

When he didn't respond, her eyes dropped, and she began drifting away from him.

Death no longer frightened him.

"Would you take me with you?"

"Would you go?" Jessica stopped and drifted lower until her chin rested upon the sea's surface.

Shaw nodded, feeling nothing as much as a release like an open void had been filled. He had found peace. Most of all, he had found what he wanted. Shaw opened his arms.

Jessica floated into his embrace. The mystery of the surreal touched him as their lips met, and the strange music soared.

As his world turned blue and fathomless, the sea rushed over him in welcome.

CHAPTER 48

Jessica began to shrink, her long hair trailing through the waves as she swam in the iridescent water. By the time she reached the prisoner, she looked normal size. I couldn't hear what she said, but the young man nodded and smiled. Jessica moved closer to him, and they kissed deeply. She waved to us as they sank beneath the glittering surface. My, what would Jessica's chaperones have said? And I could just hear myself explaining Jessica's premonitions to Browne.

In seconds, the assorted guards, consorts, and sea life followed her, descending under the surface. The water appeared glassy and calm as if nothing had happened.

Immediately, the wind picked up, and our raft began skimming the waves. At last, moving away.

She'd let us go.

While I adjusted the sail, Angelo and Browne rowed furiously. We were all conscious of a need to get away from our ship, not only from the rifle range.

Jessica had released us.

A thundering rumble came from the bowels of the *Passat*. Then she exploded into a ball of fire that rained over the pirate ship, setting it afire from bow to stern. Screams mingled with more explosions, but my eyes were only on the *Passat*.

Through my tears, she began to sink.

CHAPTER 49

"**S**ir!"

"I see them, Lieutenant." Admiral Villiers studied the raft through his glass. "Bring her to, Lieutenant. We don't want to run them over."

Villiers continued to watch the small raft, buoyed by a border of casks and under a small sail, heading toward them. He had fulfilled his mission. *Tarnation!* There were three men—no. Two men and a tiny woman. Why he could see her bosoms from here without the glass. A fine figure, and that hair as red as a flame. Quite pleased, Villiers exited the bridge shouting more orders, including that his dress uniform be made ready.

CHAPTER 50

Angelo yelped and pointed.

"What?" Browne came alive, scrambling to his knees.

I felt the cold immediately without his arms. In the distance, the pirate ship still burned. A light breeze had freshened, and we'd gone several leagues under the makeshift sail.

"Yes!" Browne shouted, pulling me to my feet and squeezing the stuffing out of me. I had to pull his nose to get loose from him and see what it was. After I did, I grabbed Browne and held on.

An enormous warship bore down upon them with her bells clanging and the American flag flying proudly from her mast. Through a flood of tears, I saluted it. I'd never seen anything finer.

They kept coming. "Err ... Browne, maybe you should fire off a warning shot or something. I don't think they see us."

God knows I didn't want the newspaper headlines to read that among the survivors of the *Passat*, the defiler of the President's son died in a raft looking like hell with a sunburned nose.

No.

The headline would read: "The defiler of the President's son weds Mr. Jack Browne. A handsome, sweetly arrogant, and honest man who loves Miss Cass Coulter. And loves the sea."

And I will be wearing a clean, dry dress, thank you.

Book Club
Questions

1. After you finished reading, did you find the significance of the title meaningful?

2. What were the main themes of the book? What do you think the author's goal was in writing this book?

3. How important was the time period or the setting to the story? Did you think it was accurately portrayed?

4. Were there any quotes before the chapters that stood out to you? Did they set you up for what happened in the chapter? Too much or too little?

5. Have you read any other books by this author? How would you compare them to this selection?

6. Were you entertained?

7. How would you summarize the story if you were to recommend it?

8. If you could talk to the author, what burning question would you want to ask?

9. Which character did you most relate to and why?

10. Did you feel like you were in Cass's shoes during the last half of the book?
11. Were the characters clearly drawn and depicted?
12. What scene resonated with you most on a personal level? (Why? How did it make you feel?)
13. How did you feel about the ending? Did you want Villiers to arrive there?

Author Bio

Lou's early work was horror and suspense. Later, her work morphed into a combination of magical realism, mystery, and adventure, painted with horrific elements as needed.

Lou is one of those writers who doesn't plan a plot—no outlines, no clue, and she sometimes writes herself into a corner. Atmospheric music in the background helps, especially "Black" by Pearl Jam.

More information is available at LouKemp.com. She'd love to hear from you and what you think of Celwyn, Bartholomew, and Professor Xiau Kang.

Milestones:

2009 The anthology story Sherlock's Opera appears in Seattle Noir, edited by Curt Colbert, Akashic Books. Available through Amazon or Barnes and Noble online. Booklist publishes a favorable review of my contribution to the anthology.

2010 The story, *In Memory of the Sibylline*, is accepted into the best-selling MWA anthology Crimes by Moonlight, edited by Charlaine Harris. The immortal magician Celwyn makes his first appearance in print.

2018 The story, *The Violins Played before Junstan*, is published in the MWA anthology Odd Partners, edited by Anne Perry. The Celwyn series begins.

2022 The partnership with 4 Horsemen Publications begins. Book 1, *The Violins Played before Junstan* is published.

2023 Book 2 of the Celwyn series, *Music Shall Untune the Sky* is published.

Book 3, *The Raven and the Pig* will be available in early spring.

The companion books *Farm Hall,* and *Sea of the Vanities,* follow in late spring.

More books from 4 Horsemen Publications

Fantasy

D. Lambert
To Walk into the Sands
Rydan
Celebrant
Northlander
Esparan
King
Traitor
His Last Name

Danielle Orsino
Locked Out of Heaven
Thine Eyes of Mercy
From the Ashes
Kingdom Come
Fire, Ice, Acid, & Heart
A Fae is Done

J.M. Paquette
Klauden's Ring
Solyn's Body
The Inbetween
Hannah's Heart

Lou Kemp
The Violins Played Before Junstan
Music Shall Untune the Sky

R.J. Young
Challenges of Tawa

Valerie Willis
Cedric: The Demonic Knight
Romasanta: Father of Werewolves
The Oracle: Keeper of the
Gaea's Gate
Artemis: Eye of Gaea
King Incubus: A New Reign

Kyle Sorrell
Munderworld

Discover more at
4HorsemenPublications.com

www.ingramcontent.com/pod-product-compliance
Lightning Source LLC
Chambersburg PA
CBHW050022120726
47903CB00006B/1877